BALLAD OF THE WAYWARD CHILD

A novel in stories by

KEVEN RENKEN

"Lightning Ranger" was originally published in The Scribe Magazine in 2019
"Come Over Here" was originally published in The Scribe Magazine in 2020

Published by St. Petersburg Press
St. Petersburg, FL
www.stpetersburgpress.com

Design and composition by St. Petersburg Press and Isa Crosta
Author's photo by Bruce Hardin
Cover design by St. Petersburg Press and Isa Crosta

Paperback ISBN: 978-1-964239-37-8
eBook ISBN: 978-1-964239-38-5

First Edition

BALLAD OF THE WAYWARD CHILD

••• A novel in stories by •••

KEVEN RENKEN

For Bill

COME OVER HERE

YOU ARE SITTING ON your grandma's porch with your grandma. She has her arm around you and the sun is shining on you and it feels good. It is warm so your grandma's arms are bare, so where her arm wraps around you the skin that you always thought looked funny touches your bare arm. But it doesn't feel funny, it just looks funny, all wrinkly like her face. She has on a green dress with little white checks all over it, and every time she moves she makes a rustling sound, like she's wearing a shower curtain underneath. You ask her about it, and she throws back her head and laughs, a high-pitched laugh that sounds like a singer trying over and over to hit the high note of a song. She takes the hankie that she has tucked in the band of her wrist watch and dabs her eyes with it. Putting it back, she shakes her head and tells you no, it's not a shower curtain, it's a slip, but people use shower curtains and slips for the same reason, to cover up with. You ask her why she wears a hankie with a wrist watch. She laughs again and you watch the lines around her eyes which are there all the time anyway get deeper. She tells you she has no pockets in her dress, and the hankie is the easiest to get to at her wrist. She hugs you and says you ask so many questions and for the umpteenth time you notice your grandma smells like she uses too much soap. Or rubs flowers all over herself every morning. One of the two.

She is babysitting you while your mommy is shopping, so after the morning cartoons and before lunch and way before naptime, the two of you are sitting on her porch in the sunshine watching the little white fluffy things float through the air and the little old ladies walk by. Several of them have hats on, and a few of them have hankies stuffed up their sleeves or at their wrist watches like Grandma. All of them have purses, resting in the bends of their arms with their forearms bent upright, stiff as can be, as if they can't stand to touch their purses with their hands but have to carry it somehow.

Grandma has been admiring your new blue jumpsuit with the elephant on the front, which you inform her is an early birthday present. Yes, your birthday is next Thursday isn't it? she says, and you nod your head, happy that she knows. How old is my little man gonna be? she asks, and you hold up all the fingers of one hand and one finger from the other hand. What number is that? she asks, and you shout it out loud. Six. I'm going to be six. That's right, she laughs. Six. You're going to be six. And what else do you want for your birthday? she asks, and immediately you blurt out that you want Batman comic books and Superman comic books, and licorice to eat. Again she laughs, and this time you notice that her red lipstick has somehow gotten a bit on her shiny white teeth, and makes her mouth look a little messy. It reminds you of when you eat Oreo cookies and then smile in the mirror. Only that was chocolate and looked neater.

Grandma waves to someone she knows and then asks you if you want lemonade. You say yes please, and do you have any Oreo cookies? She smiles, you see the red again, and she says she might have some. She gets up then, and goes inside the house, letting the screen door slam behind her, and you have the porch swing to yourself. You pump your legs hard to make it swing, and the swing goes back and forth, slowly at first, and then faster and faster. And just when you're trying to figure out how to make it go higher and faster and still not get caught by Grandma who will make you stop, you spot an old lady being pushed in a wheelchair.

It's Mrs. Strube.

You have seen her many times before and don't like her because she never smiles and never talks to anyone except to yell at them for some reason or another. And you saw her hit a dog once with a cane when it ran in her way and almost knocked her out of her chair. All the other kids who know her said she kidnaps little children and makes them disappear, and all the adults who knew her said she had lost her own little children when she was younger. Grandma just said that she was unhappy. And here she was today, her face all tight and unsmiling, her eyes tiny behind big glasses, her cane in one hand and a blanket across her knees. She is being pushed in a wheelchair by a young woman who is too big for her nurse's uniform, has a tiny black mustache you could see if you looked real hard, and wears her hair plastered back in a shiny black ponytail. You wait until they've passed the house before you yell into Grandma to ask her why Mrs. Strube has a blanket over her legs when it's so warm outside. She doesn't hear at first, but after you repeat it she says it's because Mrs. Strube lost a leg a long time ago and probably covers it up now because some people wouldn't like to see what it looks like. And would you please come in here and help me carry something?

You are off the porch, across the lawn, and down to the sidewalk in a second. Pictures of pulling off the blanket and seeing what it looks like to not have a leg are in your mind. They've turned the corner already by the time you get to the sidewalk, but you know you can catch up to them in no time. You have your super-speedy kid tennis shoes on. So you run as fast as you can, trying to imagine what the end looked like after they took the leg away, and hoping it would be more neat than gross.

You turn the corner and stop running for three reasons. One reason is because you're out of breath. Another reason is that the picture of Mrs. Strube whacking you with her cane is replacing the pictures of you pulling the blanket off her knees (or knee). And the third reason is because Mrs. Strube and her nurse with the mustache are nowhere to be seen. You stand for a moment, shifting your weight from one foot to the other, not sure what to do. Fear of being whacked is fast taking the place of your curiosity. You could always ask your grandma - she's old, maybe she's seen a person without a leg. Maybe she's even seen Mrs. Strube without a leg. You wonder for a little while where Mrs. Strube and her nurse went to so fast. This time pictures of Mrs. Strube being pushed 60 miles per hour down the sidewalk by her fast-running nurse are in your mind and you giggle as you turn to go back. But a patch of flowers just beyond the sidewalk catches your eye. Some tulips are purple and some are yellow and some are a mixture of the two. You run to them and bend down to smell them - they smell a little bit like Grandma. You bend down farther and let the tops of the flowers touch your face. It tickles a little. A breeze is blowing, moving the flowers back and forth on your cheeks. Deep in the leaves, near to the ground, the breeze sounds like whispering. Like voices.

Come over here.

You lift your head suddenly, listening. Did you hear something?

Maybe Grandma was calling you. You listen hard, but all you hear is the wind blowing. You look down, and deep in the flowers, down at the ground, you can see a big black wooly worm, the kind that makes your older sister run screaming from the room every time you dangle it in her face. You wade through the thick leaves and bend down to pick up the wooly worm. You stand up in the middle of the flowers and pet him as he scurries across your skin, and you keep turning your hand over and over to keep him from dropping off. His many legs on your bare skin tickles a lot and you switch him from one hand to the other. You get out of the flowers and walk down the sidewalk with your wooly worm. You keep moving him from hand to hand, and he keeps walking as if he's getting somewhere.

Come over here.

You stop, and the wooly worm, having come to the end of your hand, stops, turns, and starts up your arm. You listen very hard. The wind seems to be blowing stronger now as you can hear the rustling of the leaves in the trees. It still sounds like whispering, but you can't make out any more words. The sun is still shining, but a few clouds are in the sky now, big fluffy things that rear up at the top like dark ugly monsters. You shield your eyes to look closer at the clouds and then something touches your neck. You jump and whirl around, swiping at it wildly. It was just the wooly worm. He hits the ground and instantly curls up into a ball right beside a big pile of ants. They're swarming over the remains of what looks to you like a hamburger, and a single-file line of ants with pieces of bun goes off down the sidewalk. You want to look at the hamburger closer but there are too many ants. You wonder whether it's a McDonald's Big Mac or a Burger King Whopper that these ants have devoted their day's work to, and vow that you'll never eat either one again. You also wonder how it got there, all mashed and messed up, on the sidewalk. On your hands and knees, you follow the long line of ants down the sidewalk to see where they are heading. It amazes you how much some of them are carrying. Some are carrying breadcrumbs almost as big as their bodies. A few seem to stagger under their loads. One has obviously bitten off more than he can chew. A long stringy piece of half-raw beef is dragging between his legs, occasionally tripping him up and making him drop it, so that he has to go back and get it. You lay your head on the ground to watch him closer. He seems to raise his head to look at you.

Come over here.

Your head shoots up and the ant with the big piece of meat goes about his business. You look about yourself wildly. Who said that? You're sure you heard something this time. But you see nobody or nothing. The wind is blowing even stronger now, and your fine blonde hair is whipping about your face. You are thinking that perhaps you had better go back to Grandma and you look around you to see where the corner is where you turn and go to Grandma's. But you see something shining on the sidewalk. You run over to it, your small hands outstretched. It's a shiny, brand-new penny.

See a penny, pick it up, And all day long, you'll have good luck.

You pick it up and put it in your pocket, happy at your discovery. And then you scc another penny. You take the two steps required to get to it, pick it up also, and put it in your pocket, amazed at how lucky you are.
No more whispering, no more voices.

And then you see the third penny.

You go over to pick it up also, but it slips between your fingers and rolls off the curb onto the street between two cars. You step off the curb to get it, but this time it's dirty, so you wipe it off on your jumpsuit and then wipe off your hand after you put the penny in your pocket. Then you get down on your hands and knees to look under the car for more. You look under the car in back of you and then the car in front of you. And that's when you see it. The remains of a dead cat crushed under the wheels of the car. The cat's mouth is still open and one eyeball is hanging out of the socket.
A noise escapes your throat then, as you try to get up, stagger backwards, and fall over the curb. Your elbows are scraped but you don't care, you just have to get up. And you do, you're up, and there is blood running down your arms and you back away from the car.

Come over here.

And then you see your reflection in the car. Your eyes are wide, your hair is messed up, and your jumpsuit and knees are dirty. Your chest is heaving up and down. Everything is tinted red, bright red. And it all looks wrong, like too many colors together on the same page of the coloring book. The wind has stopped blowing and everything is completely still. No more whispering, no more voices. You're having trouble catching your breath. You stare at the reflection in the car door, wanting to go, run before it's too late, and knowing that it is already much, much too late.

Come over here.

And then the door opens and a hand reaches out for you.

JACK AND THE BEANSTALK

THE BOOK IS FULL of pictures where words are supposed to be. So even if you don't know what all the words are, you know what the pictures are and you feel like you can read. You feel smart. And it's something that you and Mom (not Mommy anymore) can do together. She reads the words and you shout out what the pictures are.

Once upon a time there was a. . .

Boy!

. . .that's right, a boy named Ike. . .

Jack! His name is Jack! The story is Jack and the Beanstalk not Ike and the Beanstalk!

Are you sure? It looks like Ike to me.

It's not Ike! It's Jack!

Okay then. Say the letters out loud to me.

J. . .(You point at each letter as you go)A. . .C. . .K. . .Jack!

Well! I guess you're right then. It must be Jack. So anyway, where were we?

At the beginning! Mom! How could you forget already?

It's Ike? Not Jack?

Jack, not Ike! (Heavy sigh, because adults have got to be taught) Mommy. . .I mean Mom, you're so silly.

And so it would go. She would read the words, even though you recognized some of them already – after all, you are seven now, and you know words – and when it came to the pictures she would point at the picture and you would shout out what the picture was. Boy. Mother. Food. Milk. Beanstalk. Giant. Goose. Golden Egg. Every time she asked what book you wanted to read, this is the one you picked. You knew it by heart, but that didn't matter. The boy who was Jack but really Ike needed to do something brave and heroic. It was easy to be brave and heroic when you sat in your Mom's lap, even though she would tell you time and again that you were getting too big to sit in her lap anymore. She would tell you that when it was too late, when you were already settling in there and your white legs with bony knees dangled almost to where they touched the floor. She would tell you that but then one of her arms would settle on either side of your body and the book would be a gate in front of you that no one could get past and she leaned over one of your shoulders, her chin almost resting there, her cheek brushing against yours, her breath like sugar because she drank pop every day all day. And her bigger hands would hold the book at the ends of the pages and your smaller hands would hold it close to the spine and no fingers would cover up words. And you would read.

This week you were sitting in the back of the room. At the beginning of the school year the teacher sat the students in alphabetical order, so you always sat behind Veronica, whose hair smelled like shampoo. Behind you was Larry, who always pulled on the collar of your shirt, which you put up with for a long time because Mom told you that Larry was probably special and couldn't help himself. But he never stopped either, and when you couldn't help yourself anymore you turned around and yelled his name. Which caught the attention of the teacher. Once it was in the middle of her giving instructions about a test, and she didn't like that you interrupted her. She didn't care that Larry was special but that he wouldn't stop pulling at your shirt and you couldn't help yourself and had to yell at him. She moved you and your desk into a corner facing the wall and made you take your test there. And then, to make it worse, she let the other students get a drink of water, one row at a time. The water fountain was right next to your desk in its new position of shame in the corner. Some of the girls whispered things to you before they bent over and put their mouth to the fountain. . .

Larry is such a butt.

Sorry Ike.

. . .and some of the boys would snicker. Larry bent over to take a drink and said a word you were told you should never say. Larry said it right into the fountain, but you knew he was saying it to you.

That's what the back of the room meant to you. But this week you were in the back of the room because every week after the first week the teacher rotated the students so one row always had a chance to sit in the front. And for this one week Larry was in the front and you were in the back and no one was behind you pulling at your shirt. The teacher, Mrs. Montgomery, made an announcement that before class started George had asked to do something with the class. You liked George. He didn't sit with you at lunch. He didn't run to catch up with you in the hallway. He didn't play with you at recess. You and Elizabeth and Veronica would draw the pattern of squares on the sidewalk with chalk and play hopscotch. Hopscotch you could do. You could hop on one foot for three hops in a row and then switch to both feet for one hop and then switch back to one foot, hop, switch back to two feet, hop, and then end on one foot again. George would draw four big squares on the sidewalk and play foursquare with the other boys. He threw the ball very hard and, more often than not, got the other boys out first. He was usually the last person standing in a square. When it wasn't your turn to hop, you would turn and watch George as he threw the ball hard at the other boys. When he was finished, he would rest with one arm holding the ball against his hip. His hand dangled off the edge of the ball without even touching it. He would wipe his forehead with his other arm and see you looking at him. He would smile and wave with the arm that he had just used to wipe the sweat off his forehead. Then he would bounce the ball and call to the other boys to play again. Today George was standing in the front of the class next to Mrs. Montgomery. His left hand was full of square white envelopes and he tapped the stack with a finger on his right hand. Mrs. Montgomery tells the class that George has something for just the boys and he is going to stop by the desks and give them something special. George starts up the row closest to the door and puts an envelope on the desk of each boy. The girls are straining their necks and turning around in their seats to see what it is. George goes down the second row and up the third, working his way closer and closer to you. The stack of envelopes in his hand is getting smaller and smaller. You are already making up stories in your head just in case he gets to the last seat in the last row and the envelopes are all gone. Finally he starts up your row. He puts one on Larry's desk and there is still one in his hand. You don't hear yourself breathe anymore, but you do hear the blood pounding in your ears. He reaches out to you with the envelope in his hand and it's all you can do not to grab it away from him. You wait and he puts it on your desk. You look up at his face and he smiles and waves at you, like when you're on the playground.

George turns and walks back to his desk. Mrs. Montgomery announces that everyone can open their envelope now. The girls are turned in their seats or straining to look over their shoulders. The boys tear into the envelopes, little pieces of white paper floating to the floor. There are cheers and shouts but you don't hear what they're saying. You hold the single square of thick paper up and stare hard at each word as you read it. An invitation. George's birthday. And a date. You know your numbers so you count the days. Fourteen days from Saturday. A party. And you have been invited. You are not friends with George. He didn't sit with you at lunch. He didn't run to catch up with you in the hallway. He didn't play with you during recess. But he invited you to his birthday party. Mrs. Montgomery is telling the class that they will do something special for the girls but you aren't hearing any of the words. George invited all of the boys to his birthday party. And he invited you.

Mommy/Mom gets to the part in the story where Jack takes the Goose
Who lays the
Golden egg
And climbs down the
Beanstalk
And you ask why, when you plant beans in the garden, don't the plants make stalks that go all the way up to the sky to some magic land where a giant lives? Mom has a quick answer for you.
Well, really, it's just a story, isn't it?
Oh, okay.
And really, you wouldn't want to make it so that a giant can come down here to our house would you? I don't think you'd like that very much would you?
No. No, I wouldn't.
No. I don't think you would either.
But I would be just like Jack in the book. I would get an axe from Dad's shed. And I would chop down the beanstalk. And the giant couldn't come and get us.
You would do that? Just like Jack does in the book? You would do that for us?
Yes I would. I would do that. I would be very brave, just like Jack. I

would be very brave.

Yes you would. You would be very brave. If you would do that, you would be very brave indeed.

Mom takes you shopping. First, you must have a new shirt and new pants to wear to the party. You find a green shirt and a green pair of pants and a blue shirt and a blue pair of pants. Mom asks you which shirt and pair of pants you like better and you can't decide. Mom takes you to the dressing room and you ask why it's called a dressing room. You expect to see dresses in the dressing room. She says no silly (you like it when she calls you silly), dressing doesn't mean just dresses. Dressing also means putting on clothes.

You know how I say, Ike go get dressed?

Yes.

Well, that means go put clothes on, right?

Right.

And you don't go and put on a dress when I ask you to go get dressed do I?

No I don't, you say, even though you have put on a dress sometimes, when Mom isn't looking. You say the answer that is expected.

So there you go. Dressing means to put on clothes. So you're going to go into the dressing room and get dressed in these clothes and come out of the little room and show Mom how you look. Okay? When she says "dressing room," she does this thing with both hands where she holds up the pointer finger and the middle finger and bends them down several times. She also puts extra emphasis on the words "dressing room." She hands you the blue shirt and the green shirt and the blue pants and the green pants and you hold them close to your body. You nod your head and smile. Mom has asked you to do something and it is something you can do for her. You go into the little room and stand in front of the mirror that goes from the floor almost to the ceiling along the back wall. There is a hook on the wall to your right and it's up a little higher than you can reach without standing on your tiptoes. You watch yourself as you undress in front of the mirror. You undo the buttons on your shirt first. You are very good at doing and undoing buttons and you count them as you start from the top and work your way down. One, the top button is never buttoned unless you wear a tie like Dad does when he goes to church. Two three four five and then you're done. Your chest and stomach are so white and you are so skinny that you can see your ribs. Mom says that people will think I don't feed you. Dad says that you should go outside and play more often. Get some sun. You would very much like to do what Dad asks you to do, but it is so hard when there are books to read stretched out on the couch and lying on your stomach on your bed with your stocking feet on your pillow. Jack and the Beanstalk. Baby Jesus in the manger with his mommy and daddy and all their surprise guests. Even The Cat in the Hat, even though Mommy always tells you never to answer the door when she's not at home, even if it's a cat with a hat on - but these two children do, and all kinds of things happen that their parents don't know about.

You unbutton your shorts and step out of them and drop them to the floor. Your legs are so white and your knees are bumps in the middle. You stare at your white underwear with the place in the front where you pulled out your thing and peed. No matter how hard you tried, no matter how many times you shook after you were done, there were always a few drops left over once you put your thing back in. So no matter how much Mom tried, the front of your underwear was a little bit yellow. She said you needed to drink more water, but who wanted water when you could have juice, or some of Mom's pop? You put on the blue shirt and went out to show Mom how it looked. She threw up her hands and made a sound and said you're supposed to put the pants on too so you go back into the dressing room and put on the blue pants and go back out to show her. And she throws up her hands again, but this time she smiles. That's much better she says and she hugs you before holding you at arm's length away from her so she can look at you better. That's much better. And you are so handsome. You smile back, your tongue running along your teeth and finding the places where baby teeth have come out and big boy teeth are waiting to come in. She says it again and she hugs you. You are so handsome.

She takes you into a store to buy George a birthday present. The store is called Woolworths and it has anything a seven-year-old boy could possibly want. You walk slowly through the section that has clothes for boys, but Mom says that clothes are not a good present if you don't know the boy very well and you don't know his size. Besides, you add, who wants clothes for their seventh birthday? She laughs and takes you by the shoulder to turn you towards the toys. Here there are so many choices. Board games like Monopoly and Ouija (when you pick up the Ouija box, with the spooky person draped in blue so that you couldn't see the face, Mom takes it from you and puts it down very quickly. That's not really a very good game, she says). There are jump ropes for girls and bats made of wood and balls with stitches going around either side for boys. Tiny cars of all different colors and shapes and little suitcases with handles to store all the cars in. Cowboy hats and guns in holsters. Green soldier helmets and long green guns made out of plastic. Your eye goes from one shelf to the next, taking it all in. Mom stands off to the side, holding her purse in front of her. See anything that he might like, she asks. You don't know because you weren't really friends. He didn't sit with you at lunch. He didn't run to catch up with you in the hallway. He didn't play with you during recess. He was simply another boy in your class who you wanted to like and he had invited you to his birthday party. He had invited all the boys to his birthday party.

You were about to ask Mom to pick a present for you when you saw it. A section to the right of where the games were. A section of books. You hurried over to the books and reached out to touch every cover. They were shiny and reflected your face like a mirror. You could see your fingerprints after you touched them. There were a lot of books you had read. Hop on Pop. One Fish Two Fish Red Fish Blue Fish. Bible Stories for Children. Abraham Lincoln. And there were a lot of books you hadn't read yet but instantly wanted to. You would reach out with both hands and lift them from the rack like they were the most valuable thing in the world, moving slowly and touching them like they might break if they were handled too roughly. You would open the front cover and gaze at the first page and then the second and then the third.

Hey. We're not shopping for you remember, Mom would say and you would look up at her, the book still in your hand. She would gesture with her hand towards the racks of books and you would shuffle back, still clutching the book so that you could see the cover. You would gently put it back with other copies of the same and then you would reach up and wipe the cover off so that some other child wouldn't also buy your prints when they bought the book. Your eyes moved from cover to cover. Which should you pick up next? You were reaching up for a book you hadn't seen before when you saw Jack and the Beanstalk. You froze, instantly so full of happiness that you couldn't speak. You lifted it out of the rack and the book made a sound like a whine when you opened it. You turned the pages to make sure it was the same one you had at home. There were the pictures instead of words. Boy. Mother. Food. Milk. Beanstalk. You didn't even have to look at the actual words because you knew the whole thing by heart. Once upon a time there was a boy named Ike. You turn and hold the book out to Mom, whose eyebrows are raised as if she's asking a question without actually speaking. You run to her, holding the book out in front of you with both hands. This is it. This is the best present in the whole wide world. George would like your present the best of all. And he would be your friend and he would sit next to you at lunch.

That evening you sit down in front of the television set, but not too close because if you sit too close it could sterilize you (whatever that means) or give you cancer. You're not sure what cancer is either, but every time Mom says the word she looks like she's about to cry, so you know it's very bad. You sit on your butt with your legs criss cross applesauce in front of you. Your older brother and sister are upstairs in their rooms studying. At least that's what they told Mom. Your younger sister is five, so she's all over the place. Sometimes she comes up to you where you're sitting and hugs you from behind, accidentally hitting you in the face when she does it. Then she flies into the kitchen to get in the way of Mom, who is putting food on the table for supper. Dad is sitting in his chair that goes back all the way and puts his feet up and his head back. The newspaper is open on his lap, but Dad's arms are crossed over his chest and his eyes are closed. Mom comes into the living room with a roll of wrapping paper, your little boy scissors, scotch tape, and the Jack in the Beanstalk book. She puts it on the floor in front of you as your little sister comes screaming into the room after her and you look over at Dad, whose eyes fly open as if someone's poked him in the ribs. It is your job to wrap the present. The wrapping paper has cowboys and horses on it. You pull the paper away from the roll and lay the book down on the paper like you've seen Mom do many times before. Folding the paper on the ends to make the corners is not the best , but you use extra tape to tape it down so it doesn't look half bad. Besides, it will take George longer to get it open, and that will be good. Dad is awake now, and folds the paper on his lap so that he can watch the television. The news is on and on the news a man who looks like Dad but has a moustache is talking about a place called Vee-Et Nom. Then the man is gone and they show a place that looks like a very green forest. There are men walking through the green very slowly, their bodies bent over. The men have green helmets on and have long guns in their hands. They remind you of the toys you saw in Woolworths this morning. There are loud sounds coming from the very green forest and there is dark smoke in the sky. The man with the moustache comes back on and says something about a death toll. You don't know what a death toll is, but when they put a number on the television screen, you know the number is very high, higher than you have learned yet in school.

Saturday is a long time coming, but finally it's here. It's the day of George's party. You are just now learning how to tell time in school, so Mom tells you that the big hand has to be on the twelve and the little hand has to be on the two before you can go to the party. You eat three bites of the grilled cheese sandwich Mom makes you to eat before you go - she says we can't have you only eating birthday cake. What kind of diet would that be for a growing boy like you, she says - and then your older brother reaches over and takes it and shoves the whole thing into his mouth. Mom doesn't have to tell you to go get dressed for a change, like she often does when it's time to go to church. After your brother eats your sandwich, you ask to be excused to go to your room to get ready for the party. You put on a new shirt and a new pair of pants and then spend a long time concentrating on tying your shoelaces. Captain Kangaroo on television tried to teach you how to tie your shoes, but the whole idea of a bunny with one ear trying to find its other ear bothered you with too many questions. How did the bunny lose the one ear? Did it hurt when he lost it? Why can't he find it? How will he put it back on? So you taught yourself without the idea of a bunny. Sometimes the results weren't the best, and today, because of the excitement of the party, they are probably the worst. After the shoes, you sit for a long time on the edge of the bed clutching George's present against your beating heart and listening to the sounds of your family around the dinner table. Finally, when you hear dishes being picked up and put in the sink, you go downstairs and stand in the doorway. Is the big hand on the twelve and the little hand on the two yet, you ask. Mom turns to answer you and stops, her mouth opening and closing and opening again. She is holding a plate in one hand and a glass in the other. You are supposed to wear the blue shirt with the blue pants and the green shirt with the green pants. Not one green thing with one blue thing. You look down at yourself. You have on the green shirt with the blue pants. You shrug your shoulders like it's no big deal and go back upstairs to change your shirt. It is a very big deal however, and you can't wait until the little hand is on the two. You come back downstairs with a blue shirt and blue pants on and pause in the doorway again, still holding the present. Mom looks you up and down. Did you remember to put on underpants this time, she asks. Sometimes you forget. You let go of the present with one hand and hold out the waistband of the blue pants. Then you turn and go back upstairs and take off the blue pants. You go into the dresser drawer where the clean underpants are kept and put a pair on before putting the blue pants back on. This time, you move slowly as you go downstairs. Lots of going up and down the stairs has made you tired. Now you're not sure you're going to even make it to the little hand being on the two. The dinner table is empty by the time you step into the kitchen this time, and everyone has gone their own ways besides Mom and your little sister, who has wrapped herself around Mom's leg as if she might fall if she lets go. Mom's hands are on her hips and she stands for a long time looking at you before saying Very Handsome. She turns to pry the little girl away from her leg before going to get her purse. Your sister waddles over to stand in front of you and looks at the present in your hands. She puts a hand on either side of the present and tries to pull it away from you and you shout NO! so loudly that she looks up at you, her eyes wide, her mouth quivering. She turns away from you and begins to cry, her one hand balled up into a fist and rubbing at her eyes. You look around, sure that the crying will bring Mom back into the kitchen - which it does, with scarf on her head and purse in her hand. She stops for a moment to look at the two of you before shaking her head and walking over to scoop your little sister up onto her hip. Come on, she says as she walks away. It's almost two.

You get to sit in the front seat with Mom on the way to the party, which is fun because it doesn't happen very often. Usually Dad drives the car and Mom sits where you are and you sit in the back sandwiched in between your older brother and older sister, who each claim a window and make you and the little sister sit in the middle where the hump makes you scooch your legs off to the side. Sitting in the front would be even more special today if it weren't for the fact that the little sister had to sit up there with you and Mommy. She has already forgotten the shouted NO! from a few minutes ago and is reaching over to try and take the present from you again. You wedge it on the seat between you and the passenger side door and turn away from her to gaze out the open window and feel the breeze as Mommy drives. In a few seconds you hear the little sister singing about the Itsy Bitsy Spider going up the waterspout and can hear the effort in her voice as she tries to do the hand movements that go along with the song. She puts extra emphasis on the spider being washed out and the sun coming out to dry up all the rain. You want to tell her to shut up, but Mom doesn't like shut up, she says it's just like cussing, so you sit and look out the window at the houses and the trees and the fences as they go by. You open the door before the car has even come to a complete stop in front of George's house and you barely hear Mom shout after you that she will be back to pick you up at four. You pause for a second and make sure you stand nice and straight before you ring the doorbell. Your house doesn't have a doorbell, so you are more than willing to do the polite thing. You like the pretty notes it makes as it echoes through the house. You hear the laughing and talking of children deep into the house as you wait, and over that the slow steady voices of adult women like Mom. You stand for a few moments listening to the sounds through the door. Maybe they didn't hear you? With the present under one arm, you reach up with the other to push the doorbell again when the door opens. It is George. His cheeks are flushed, and he barely makes eye contact with you, as if he's still really back where play is happening. Come on, he waves you towards the back of the house and then runs away towards the party sounds. He has left you standing in the hallway with the front door still open. Quietly, as if your actions might disturb the party, you reach over and push the door closed. To the left is a table piled high with every size and shape of wrapped gift. Many have bows on them and all are covered in brightly colored paper. Almost gently, you wedge your present between a big box and a smaller one, before heading into the house. You don't exactly know where the party is happening - you've never been here before - but you can certainly follow the sound.

You head down the hall slowly, touching the wall as you go. It opens into a kitchen, which is big and full of light. Other mommies are sitting around a table with drinks in their hands. Two of the mommies are smoking and dipping the hand with the cigarette towards the table to an ashtray when their cigarettes have burned too long. A mommy with a pearl necklace who must be George's mommy is standing and putting candles into the top of a birthday cake, a chocolate lump in the center of the table. Beyond the mommies is a wall of glass. Sunshine comes through the glass to fill the kitchen. Part of the glass wall is open, and out in the yard a group of boys are playing tag. They are shouting and laughing, and George laughs and shouts the loudest of all. It is his birthday after all. You step past the mommies - one of the smoking mommies waves her hand holding the cigarette at you as you go by - and through the doorway. It is like you stepped into another world, a world of grass and sunshine and sweat and boys.

Tag! You're it!

No I'm not! You are!

No, I tagged you! You're it!

You cheated!

I didn't cheat! It's my birthday!

As if that explained everything. You stand on the top step watching your classmates play. There are only two more steps and then you are down into the yard and into the play. But you don't know how to insert yourself into a game that has already started. So you sit on the top step and rest your chin on your hands on your knees and silently watch the game. You especially watch George, who never stops moving. His head and then his whole body whips around as he runs. He wipes his face with the bottom of his shirt, and for a second you get a glimpse of his white belly. Then he leans forward and puts his hands on his knees as he leans forward, tight and ready to start running again. Unlike on the playground at school, he doesn't look in your direction and wave. There is so much going on around him and he is looking here and then here and then here, his mouth open and taking in huge gulps of air. None of the rest of the boys wave hello or gesture for you to come join in the game. So you continue to sit. You tilt your face up and feel the sun on your face. Behind you there is a low and steady hum of the mommies talking in the kitchen.

You lose track of how long you sit on the step. The shouting and laughing and low steady hum of adult voices and the sunshine become like a blanket and wrap around you. It is almost as if you have fallen asleep and you are dreaming. You don't hear the steps so when the mommy's voice speaks directly behind you, you jump. Sorry Ike. An adult hand comes down and rests on your shoulder for a second and you turn to look at the owner of the hand. It is the mommy with the pearl necklace, so it is George's mommy, announcing that it is time to come in and eat cake before the opening of presents. Because you are on the steps you are up and into the house before the others rush in, a mass of bodies and sound. The table is right there and the mommies are on the other side of it. You count the candles on the cake as George's mommy lights them. One two three four five six seven of them. George stands in front of the cake with his hands on the table. He is leaning forward because he knows what comes next. His mommy blows out the match and waves her hands back and forth in the air as she starts to sing Happy Birthday to you. . . The other mommies join in though they sound sleepy as they sing. The other boys, however, are almost screaming it and they clap loudly when the song is done and George leans over the cake and blows on the candles. Little drops of spit fly out of his mouth and disappear over the cake. You wait patiently in line for a piece, thick with chocolate icing smeared onto a plate, to be handed to you. You use a fork to cut even smaller pieces off the piece you were given, putting it far into your mouth and closing your mouth to chew. All around you boys are eating as if they've never seen cake before. Some are putting at least half the piece into their mouth at one time. They smile at each other as thcy chew, chocolate icing covering their lips and teeth.

There is a rush of handing plates and forks back to waiting mommies because opening presents is next. You and the other boys are ushered into another room, where the presents have been moved and are sitting on a table. Mommies situate themselves onto chairs and couches or stand in the doorway hugging their drinks to their bodies.

The boys sit, some of them criss-cross applesauce, in a circle around the table of presents. George stands and hovers over the presents, his fingers moving even though they're not touching anything, and he looks at his mommy with his eyebrows raised. She nestles into the one chair next to George that is still empty with a notebook and a pen. She nods to George and writes down the names of guests and what presents they gave as he opens them.

He snatches a big gift from the center of the pile and lifts it out. He cradles the gift with one hand as he tears at the wrapping paper with the other. He flings the paper to one side - another mommy scoops it up almost before it hits the ground - and sets the uncovered box back down on top of the other presents. The box is held closed with strips of tape on the sides, and George reaches under the tape and pops it up so quickly that it seems as if he's done this before. The lid of the box is open and he reaches in and lifts out what is inside.

It's a dark green helmet.

As George puts the helmet on his head, you stare at it. You have seen that kind of helmet before, but you can't remember where. You're still thinking about when George, still wearing the helmet, grabs another long present off the table and tears off the wrapping paper.

It's a gun, with a long, narrow barrel and two handles, one in front of the other. It is a dark green, like the helmet, and it is attached to a piece of cardboard with the words MACHINE GUN on it. George picks at what holds the gun to the cardboard. Once it is free, he holds onto the gun with both hands and points it at his friends. He makes the same sound over and over again TATATATATATATATATATATATATAT ATATATATATATATATATATATATATATATATATATATATAT as he swings the gun in a large circle, pointing it at all of the boys and the mommies sitting on the chairs and standing in the doorway. The boys act out a big dramatic version of what death by machine gun would look like, grabbing their chest and grimacing before sinking to the ground. The mommies look at each other and laugh, small quiet laughs that sound as if they were still inside the mommies' mouths and not out in the air. Some of them open their mouths as if to speak but put a hand up to cover their mouths instead. You look around at the other boys - some of them are still moving around on the ground. You quickly drop to the ground to join them but don't act out the getting hit by bullets part. You look up to see George toss the gun to the side and reach for another present while some of his friends were still acting out the end of their best death scene.

And that, for a while, was how it went. Colored paper flying into the air and snatched out of the air. Boxes being ripped into. All manner of green plastic in George's hands. Trucks and toy soldiers. Guns and grenades. Helmets and shirts with stripes on the shoulder, all in George's size. All of it the same color green. At one point, Ike's package was in George's hands. He looked down at it and then put it to one side before continuing to reach for the other packages.

Until there was nothing left. Except for the present with the horses and cowboys on it. George held it at arm's length and frowned. He reaches out with one hand and tears the wrapping paper away. He continues to look at it once the wrapping paper was discarded. His face has no expression that you could read. All you want to do is walk up to George and pull it away from him. It wasn't like the other presents. It wasn't made out of plastic. It wasn't green.

It was a book.

But you don't need to. George smiles, a smile that only moves one side of his face. His hand drops to his side and the book clunks to the floor. He turns to the pile of green toys behind him and puts his hands onto the biggest plastic gun. He swings it in a wide circle, covering every person in the room.

TATATATATATATATATATATATATATATATATATATAT

He rushes past other boys in the room and heads towards the back yard. As if released, the others followed after him in a volley of sound almost too enormous to be contained. The mothers in the room follow them with their eyes, and then look at each other. Almost as one, they sigh. A few follow George's mommy into the other room, where the cake had been consumed just a few minutes before. Others wander into the backyard, where the boys are screaming and stomping up a storm.

In a minute, you are in the room by yourself. You look around. It looked like a war zone of boxes and paper and toys abandoned on the floor. The book lay on the floor a couple of feet away. You sink to your knees and crawl over to pick up the book. You open it to the first page and begin to read, though you barely have to look down to see the words. And that's where your mom finds you when she comes to pick you up two hours later.

Once upon a time there was a. . .
Boy!
. . .that's right, a boy named Jack . . .
Ike. His name is Ike, not Jack.
Are you sure? It looks like Jack to me. You told me his name was Jack. That the story was called Jack and the Beanstalk, not Ike and the Beanstalk. Once upon a time there was a. . .
Boy!
. . .that's right, a boy named Jack . . .
Ike. His name is Ike, not Jack.
Are you sure? It looks like Jack to me. You told me his name was Jack. That the story was called Jack and the Beanstalk, not Ike and the Beanstalk.
It's Ike Not Jack. Please Mommy. Let it be Ike.
Okay then. Say the letters out loud to me.
I. . .(You point at each letter as you go, even though they're not

there) K. . .E. . .Ike.

Well! I guess you're right then. It must be Ike. So anyway, where were we?

At the beginning! Mommy! How could you forget already?

At the beginning? Oh yes, there we are. Once upon a time there was a. . .

Boy!

. . .named. . .

IKE. (At this point you're exasperated and you throw up your hands) I told you already! His name is Ike. Not Jack.

It is?

Yes!

It's Ike? Not Jack?

Ike. Not Jack. (Heavy sigh, because adults have got to be taught) Mommy, you're so silly.

And that was how it went..

LILAC DAY

HE IS LYING IN the green grass so long that when he gets up it lays matted down underneath him. He lies back down and allows the grass to surround him and brush along his skin where it tickles as it moves. He likes the feeling of the grass on his skin, though he wonders if some of the tickling could be an insect, or insects, that have moved from the blades of grass onto the uncharted territory that is his pale white skin.

He considers the possibilities. A honey bee or bumble bee was not likely - they flew from place to place. So did wasps. So the most frightening possibilities were automatically crossed off the list, leaving him to now consider bugs that crawled. A ladybug would be very nice. He would let a ladybug with its pretty red back crawl on his skin anytime. One time he fell asleep in the grass and when he woke up there was a ladybug on his leg. He watched it crawl up his leg towards him, but just before it went into the leg of his shorts, where it would get into his underpants and then be very difficult to retrieve, he put his hand down and put his pointer finger in the ladybug's path. The ladybug paused for a second and turned away from the finger, but he moved it in her path again. Ever adapting, the ladybug mounted the finger and crawled up his hand and past his wrist to his arm. He is eight and has no hair on his arms or legs or crotch, and the ladybug made an easy journey up his arm to his shirt sleeve. He was debating about whether he should let the ladybug crawl into his shirt, though that would surely tickle too much and then he would have to take his shirt off and he never took his shirt off because his skin was very white and he could get a bad sunburn. That's what Mom said, and she always said true things to him and he didn't want to get burned by the sun. But that day he didn't have to take his shirt off because the ladybug got to the sleeve and paused again before its red back became short stubby little wings and flew away. He watched it as long as he could see it.

So a ladybug would be nice. He liked ladybugs. An ant not so much. A worm would be the best. All of those legs moving up his arm at the same time. And worms were pretty/ugly all at the same time. Another true thing Mom told him was that he used to put worms in his mouth, and how she knew he was no longer a baby when he knew not to do that anymore. An inch worm would do his inch worm thing, like chin-ups across his body, and he would be in awe of how magnificent and marvelous and indescribable the world was that one of its creatures could do something like that and he would find it so amazing. Not a wooly worm though. Never a wooly worm. A butterfly, the most amazing thing of all, would be much better. He changed his mind. The butterfly not the worm would be the best thing of all today. They flew like the bees and wasps, but they landed like they picked you - not to hurt you but to give you something like grace and beauty before going on to give it to someone or something else.

He closed his eyes as tight as he could and wished with all of his heart for a butterfly, right now, in this moment. With his eyes closed it wasn't quite ever dark. There were still spots of light that traveled across his eyes. Plus, the sound of the day, the sound of the breeze blowing through the grass and the branches of the trees, the sound of a bird somewhere making a call out to another bird or just to anyone who might be listening that he or she is there, filled up his ear more. And his nose would catch so many smells. Air had a smell, and so did grass, and so did he, a boy smell Mom said, the smell of laundry soap fighting with sweat. Running through it all was the smell of lilacs. There was a lilac bush right across the yard, and they were in full bloom right now. He didn't know flowers. He would ask Mom the names of pretty flowers, and she would tell him that he was only eight and he would hear words and then forget them because he needed to hear them more. But he knew lilacs, the purple flower with lots of little blooms altogether, because Mom said it was her favorite. He would go to the bush and pick lilacs for her and he would bring them into the house and hold them out to her and she would say that he should have let it just grow outside. But then she would smell it and smile and get a mason jar and put water in it and put the lilacs in the water and put them on the kitchen table in the center. And that was good because Mom smiled.

He opened his eyes. There was no butterfly. He could feel his blonde hair hanging down and brushing against his forehead as it moved in the breeze. He looked up at the sky. There were a number of trees where he was lying, and they framed a section of sky so light blue that it was almost white. A cloud drifted into the frame of the sky. Sometimes the clouds looked like people or animals or things. Today this cloud looked like the cotton that was in the bottles of pills when you first opened them after you got them at the store. The leaves moved around the edges. He had never seen a plane before, and he wanted to with all of his heart. He wondered what it would be like up there, and how far up there it went and whether it stopped or went on and on and on as far as anyone could go and then even farther than that. He couldn't even imagine how far that far was.

A bird flew across his field of vision and disappeared. He sat up to see where the bird went. He tilted his head back and felt the breeze on his face. Out of the corner of his eyes he saw the lilac bush at the far end of the yard and he reminded himself to pick another bunch of flowers to take inside to Mom. He stood up slowly and dusted off his legs and shorts and striped short sleeve shirt. It would not do to be dirty, even if you're outside. He stepped across the grass, measuring how far he reached with his legs as he stepped and the weight of himself as he put his foot down. He had just gotten a new pair of dress shoes and he didn't want to get them dirty, so he was barefoot today. With each step he would bring his feet together and then stand and look down at his toes as he wiggled them. He imagined that he was stepping across a big pit of snakes and they were moving their heads to try and bite him and he took bigger steps to avoid where he imagined the snake to be.

Finally he made it to the chain link fence and touched the pole running along the top as if he were playing tag and had just touched the fence to make it "IT." He sighed and looked all around him. The grass did not grow up close to the fence so there were no snakes there. However, there was a branch just about as long as he was tall. He picked up the branch. It was really just a stick but in his mind it was a mighty and powerful weapon. He held it up into the air and wished he had something mighty and powerful to say that would create magic that would transform it into a mighty and powerful weapon. And so he just roared, a mighty and powerful sound that scared birds out of the trees. And that was a good thing.

He hit the fence with the stick and it made a great clattering metallic sound. He took off running, but leaves the stick connecting with the fence. He ran along beside the fence, and the fence makes a rhythmic Da-da-da-da-da as he ran. It is the walls of a giant's castle and he is smiting it with his magical sword. He heard the word smite in church. Someone in the Bible smited someone else with their mighty sword, and at the time it sounded like a very good thing. He asked his older brother what smite meant. "It means to hit something," his brother said with a sigh. "Like I'm going to smite you if you don't stop being such a doofus." But today he wasn't a doofus. He was a powerful being, and he was smiting the walls of the evil giant's castle to knock it down. Or maybe the giant wasn't evil, just really angry that he was so big and couldn't find clothes that fit - like Mom, who seemed to be angry every time she took him shopping for clothes. You're getting so big, nothing fits you anymore, she would say. He didn't feel big. He actually felt pretty little, especially compared to the brother who called him a doofus or Dad, who was so big that he could block out the sun.

He may be small but he was powerful and he had a mighty sword that was capable of smiting. So he smited as he ran along the fence. Smiting deserved a noise to go with it, so he opened his mouth wide and let out a long cry. His chest rose up and down as he took in large gulps of air and he threw back his head to send the sound out to the giant who, no doubt, was lurking behind these walls. He got to the corner and turned, smacking the fence again and running, his bare feet tearing up little pieces of grass as he went. Halfway down he came to a gate. The way into the giant's stronghold. He smote or smited the gate three times and waited. The gate remained fastened and closed. He shrugged his shoulders and reached out to the clasp and lifted it. If magic doesn't work then you try other ways to get in.

The gate swung open and he stepped through, his arms stretched out triumphantly. The giant's fortress was full of trees, apples and cherries and apricots, because really it was an orchard and every tree was either the evil giant or one of his evil family - didn't they have even one member of their family who was good and kind like in the Bible? - and they had baskets of precious gems, red and yellow and orange, ripe for the taking. He just had to be brave and get them. He roared at the giant family, veins in his neck standing out as he thrust his head forward. He waited a second, listening for any of the giant family to roar back.

Nothing. Maybe they were afraid of him. He roared again and waited. Again, nothing but the sound of the breeze rustling through their branch leaf hair. From a distance a bird called to him with chirping. He walked in the direction of the bird sound, turning left to face one of the smaller giants. This monstrous creature was not as imposing as some of his relatives, but he was adorned from head to toe with gorgeous orange jewels. He stood before the orange giant and gave him another mighty roar. The giant quivered in the breeze and dropped one of his jewels on the ground at the boy's feet. He bent over to pick it up and held it up to the sun to examine it. He closed one eye because the giant was trying to use the sun to blind him and get his precious jewel back. But it was beautiful, round and soft with a seam running from top to bottom on one side, and he was not going to give it up without a fight.

He took hold of it with both hands and stuck his thumbs into the seam and pulled it apart in one move. The inside was a little browner than the outside and not quite as smooth. On one side rested another jewel, brown and shaped like a seed. He took out the seed and cradled it in his palm as he tore the two halves apart. He lifted one half to his mouth and bit down. The taste was so sweet, and juice ran out of his lips and down his chin. He tilted his head back to chew and swallow the whole thing.

As he lifted his hand to his mouth to do the same thing with the second half, the breeze picked up. A branch also adorned with orange jewels brushed past his face. He had let his guard down in the presence of his magnificent treasure, and the ogre had used his poison-tipped talons to kill him. He howled, the poison coursing through his veins, and dropped to the ground. The uneaten half of the apricot rolled out of his hand. He lay there for a few seconds, waiting for the poison to do its business and kill him. Even though his eyes were closed as he waited for death to close in, he could feel the sun on his face. The rest of his body was covered in the shadow of the giant who hovered over him waiting to strike again. He had to get away and maybe, just maybe, save himself.

He turned over onto his stomach and opened one eye to see if he could find the beautiful jewel that just seconds ago was in his possession. A short reach away it lay in the grass. Already one of the monster's workers, an ant, was crawling over it and reclaiming it for its master. He didn't like ants. He began to push his body across the ground, feeling the second brown jewel still nestled in his palm. He must live to fight another day, though a small part of him wasn't sure how much longer he would live once he got back into the house and had to explain to Mom how he managed to get grass stains all over his clothes.

But he couldn't worry about that now. He had to get to sanctuary. Using all of the strength he had in his skinny arms, he pulled the weight of his body out from under the shade of the giant and toward a bush that spread out in front of him several feet ahead. He reached out with both arms and dug his fingers into the ground and then pulled his whole body, dead weight because of the poison, up to that point. He was panting with the effort. He closed his eyes again. He couldn't look at the bush ahead of him anymore because it didn't look as if it was getting any closer.

Finally, he reached out, both hands shaking from the effort, and felt leaves instead of dirt. He laughed with relief. He opened his eyes then. Sweat ran like water into his eyes, but he could still see his fingers running along the length of stems to the edges of leaves sharp without cutting. Still on his stomach, heavy on the grass, he lifted his head up as far as his spine would allow. Above him, just out of reach, was the ultimate prize. The crown jewels. A fat cluster of lilac blossoms rested among the green, calling out his name.

He brought his arms down to the ground and made fists with his hands. He pushed with his whole weight against the ground, and as he did so he felt the giant's poison leave his body. Slowly he regained the use of his limbs. He tucked his legs underneath him and even more slowly stood until he came face to face with the lilac cluster. He bent his face, streaked with sweat and dirt, into the blossoms and inhaled deeply. It smelled like Mom. It was her favorite flower. She also had a small bottle of spray on her dresser. One time he was in her bedroom and sprayed himself with that bottle and it smelled exactly like this did. When he held Mom's hand, this smell came off her. When he sat in her lap, which was happening less and less these days because he was getting too big, this smell of her surrounded him. He would cry and she would ask him why he was crying because he wasn't hurt, and he would shake his head because he had no words for it. And he would put his thumb in his mouth (which, he was told, he was also getting too big for) and curl himself deeper into her where there was nothing but the warmth of her body and this smell.

He stayed with his face in the lilacs for a long time. No giants in the castle came to get him because he was safe now. He stood up straight but kept his hand on the blossoms. Finally he smiled and with one movement snapped the stem of the flowers off into his hand. He looked down into the other hand where he still clutched the apricot pit. Then he turned to this enormous lilac bounty. He must give this to her right away. It would make her smile, and that was a very good thing. Maybe it would be such a good thing that she wouldn't even get mad about the grass stains all over his shirt and shorts and legs and arms.

Maybe.

Just maybe.

He headed back in the direction of the gate in the fence, holding on tight to both of his treasures. He had lived a lifetime in one day. He would live to fight another day.

But right now, his queen deserved her bounty.

WHISPERS IN THE DARK

I'LL TELL YOU A story. And it will scare you so much that you won't ever be able to sleep again.

A soft chuckle came from the other side of the room. Ike's eyes hadn't adjusted to the dark yet, so he couldn't see what his brother was doing. Whether or not he was sitting up and looking in Ike's direction, smiling because he enjoyed this so much. Or maybe he was just lying on his back and talking to the ceiling, knowing it would bounce off and come back over to his side of the room and nestle into the sheets next to Ike's body. Fear was like having an over-attentive pet. It was always around and needed constant attention.

It's a story by Edgar Allan Poe. It will scare the crap out of you.

I'm telling Mom. You said crap. She said not to swear.

Crap is not a swear word.

Yes it is.

No it's not. Damn is a swear word. Hell is a swear word.

Ike opened his mouth but couldn't get any air to come out for a second.

Aaaaahhhhh. . .You said damn. You said hell. Mom said not to swear.

You said them too.

You said them first. I'm telling Mom. She said not to swear.

You tell her and I'll tell you the scariest story you've ever heard. A story so scary that you'll never be able to sleep again. Ever. In your whole life.

Ike heard bed sheets rustle. He knew that Pete was now sitting up in bed. Probably looking in his direction.

You wouldn't dare.

Oh I wouldn't would I.

No. . .

Just watch me.

No. . .

The scariest story you've ever heard. Ever.

Another chuckle. This one sounds deeper, almost like he's doing it into the pillow. It's. Called. He draws the words out, each one its own sentence. The. Black. Cat. By. Edgar. Allan. Poe. Then he makes another sound. This one sounds like he's copying the evil laugh he's heard in any number of scary movies he's watched after their parents have gone to bed and Ike crouched in the shadows just on the other side of the doorway and stared at the screen.

WUH-HAHAHAHAHAHA

Ike turns over and faces the wall. I'll bet it's just a stupid story anyway, he mumbles to the wall. Pete says nothing except to keep making the sound, low in his throat, almost whispering it, like it's a hum throughout the room.

Wuhhahahahahaha. . .

I'll bet it's not even that scary, Ike says to the wall. As he says it he feels the monster under his bed begin to grow. It is a small thing at first, no bigger than a bug on the floor. But the longer he lies in bed not being able to fall asleep, the larger it grows. He feels its back as it grows, pushing against his mattress, the ridges of its scaly spine clawing into the stuffing and lifting it off the frame. He clutches the edge of his sheet and, even though it's a moist summer night, pulls it over his head. The monster is now bigger than the bed on its back. Soon it will be bigger than the room. Soon the floor will be unable to hold onto it. Ike, the bed and the monster will go crashing down into the living room below.

Wuhhahahahahahaha. . .

Pete continues the sound, low and quiet like a whisper. Then Ike hears him turn over on his side. The room is quiet. Ike is holding his breath. Listening. Waiting.

The next day during study time, Ike asks if he can go to the library. Which means, in his small fourth grade classroom, walking over to the rows of bookshelves over by the windows. They are in some kind of order, so it doesn't take Ike very long to find a book with the name Edgar Allan Poe on the spine. It was heavier than he thought it would be, because Pete told him it was a story. But it is many stories. Ike scans the table of contents while carrying the book back to his desk. Sure enough, there it was, The Black Cat, about a third of the way down. He turns to the first page of the story with shaking fingers. The words are right in front of him, and if he read them then he would take away their power. He looks at his math book and notebook, open to the most recent assignment, on the desk. Math is not his strong suit, and he has been struggling with the work. He knows he should spend study time to finish the assignment. But he looks back at the story. Before he knows it, he has finished it. I had walled the monster up within the tomb. He read those words again and again. He was going to say those words back to Pete.

That night is just as warm and humid as the night before. Ike has on a blue pajama top and blue pajama shorts. He has only in the last year switched from pajamas with kitties on them to plain ones. The sheets cling to his legs. Pete is fifteen and wears only a t-shirt and underwear. Pajamas were for sissies, he said. He turns slowly towards the smaller boy, who is holding his breath again. Okay, Pete says. The Black Cat. By Edgar Allan Poe.

Ike whips around in bed. It is dark and he can't see, but he thinks he's facing his older brother. I already read The Black Cat! Today at school! It's about a guy who kills a cat or he thinks he did, and then he kills his wife and he thinks he got away with it. But then the cat makes a horrible sound from behind the wall and the police hear it and he gets caught! The end! So there! Ha! Ike turns away and stares at the ceiling. He tries his best scary voice, like Pete did yesterday. He drops it as low as he can and draws out each word, giving it added weight. I had walled the monster up within the tomb. Then he laughs, but so quickly that he forgets to keep it in his lower register and it comes out like a giggle.

There is silence from the darkness on the other side of the room. He hears Pete sigh. It is the sigh of someone who has run out of patience for a child. Okay, he said finally. Well then, I'll just have to tell you another one. And this one is even scarier than The Black Cat. Ike hears Pete sigh before the teenager rolls over in bed. So you better do a lot of reading tomorrow. The room is silent. Ike pulls the sheet up to his chin, but keeps his face out. He reminds himself to breathe, and when he does it sounds shaky. He makes a mental note to check out the book of stories tomorrow and read as many of them as he can.

And underneath the bed, he feels the monster begin to grow again.

It is a half hour before supper and Mom has said he can watch one television program before they eat. He only has three choices, but right away he knows which one he is going to pick. A handsome, well-dressed man with dark hair is talking to the audience in a low voice, steady and calm. It was lower and scarier than either Ike or Pete could hope for. The man is saying that the people watching are in the Twilight Zone, and then he tells the story about a man on a plane. The man is sitting by the window, and every time he looks out the window he sees something on the wing of the plane. He pulls the shade on the window, but can't help thinking about it and keeps looking. And every time he looks, Ike gets scared and moves farther away from the television. He starts right in front of it, even though Mom says it's bad for your eyes - but he's already wearing glasses, so how much worse could they get? - to his dad's chair across the room. By the time the man in the story opens the shade and the creature's face is pressed right up against the window, Ike has squealed and is standing right outside the door to the room, holding onto the wall and peeking in. He thinks the farther away from the scary he is the safer he must be.

Just then Pete comes up behind him. He has been working with dad and smells like sweat and soap. Ike knows Pete is there a split second before Pete whispers in his ear, but it makes him jump and turn in his direction anyway.

If you're so scared, why are you watching it anyway?

Ike is embarrassed that he caught and scared him and turns away to look back at the screen, afraid he might miss something.

Because I want to see what happens!

Pete brushes past him and smacks him in the back of the head as he does so. You're such a doofus, he says as he crosses directly in front of the TV, deliberately blocking Ike's view. And when he's past, the man on the plane is being taken away on a stretcher. And neither he nor the man ever find out what's on the wing of the plane.

It is hot again and he is lying on his back in bed. His pajama top sticks to his back but he doesn't turn over on his side to let the air in. He cannot sleep and he listens to the old house make sounds. It's like it's a living thing. Pete has his back to him in the other bed. The long breathing tells Ike that he is asleep. Ike lies very still. Even though the air is almost stifling, he has the sheet up to his neck. His fingers grip the edge of the sheet so that it doesn't move. He has tried putting his whole head under the sheet, but he can't breathe and has to stick his head out again.

So he grips the sheet under his chin and listens.

He has no idea what the crazed killer will sound like but he is sure the house will let him know. And he knows also that the crazed killer will be carrying an ax and will chop off any body parts he sees. So his whole body is safe up to his neck. He can live without fingers though maybe not all ten. He tucks six fingers under the blanket and continues to grip the edge of the sheet with only four fingers. Four missing fingers seem surviveable. His head? He'll deal with that when the time comes. Which could be any night now. He has been waiting days, weeks, months.

He calculates how the crazed killer will get into the house. The most logical conclusion to Ike is the front door. Everyone who comes to visit use the front door - and even though he has never known a crazed killer, he can only assume that they would most likely follow suit. And once he thinks that he begins to relax. Surely such a polite and thoughtful crazed killer would also be very methodical in his approach and kill people in the order that he finds them. Which means he would kill Ike's parents in their bedroom downstairs first. Then he would come upstairs and kill both of his sisters in their bedroom before coming to the bedroom at the end of the hall where Ike and Pete slept. Surely he would hear the crazed killer by that time and would be able to make his escape. Ike knew he couldn't count on Pete to save him, so he had his exit all planned out. His window opened up onto a one floor drop onto the roof of his dad's study. From there he could jump to the ground and run to the neighbors. Who, granted, were a ways away. He continued to listen. The wood settling in the old house sounded like the weight of feet, indeed a whole body, on the floor. It happened but then it happened again somewhere else. There were killers all everywhere in the house. Or nowhere.

Suddenly he had to pee. He tried to ignore it, but soon he didn't even hear the sounds of the house because his full bladder was all he could think about. He had heard the boys at school talk about other boys and call them bedwetters and laugh behind their hands. He didn't want to be called a bedwetter. He already had enough names sent in his direction. The only problem was that the house only had one bathroom, and it was downstairs next to his parents' bedroom. That was a long way to walk in the dark. And it messed with the game plan of the crazed killer. If he was in the bathroom it would put him first in the killing order once the very polite crazed killer walked through the front door. He would kill Ike as he stood in the front of the toilet with his weenie in his hand.

For a few feverish seconds he struggled with murder versus name calling. Name calling won out. He swung his feet over to the side of the bed and for a few seconds felt around in the dark for his bunny slippers. He couldn't find them right away which briefly put him into a panic. Maybe the crazed killer liked bunny slippers as much as he liked murder and he took them? Also, his feet were on the area rug on the side of the bed, groping around. The area rug was solely the domain of the thing under the bed - anything on the rug was fair game and could be pulled under the bed and into. . .well, who knows where. But then one of his toes grazed the fuzziness of one slipper and he almost gasped with relief. He stepped into them and stepped away from the rug and the bed.

He stared out into the darkness, letting his eyes adjust. He moved slowly, his hand touching the wall as he went down the hall and the stairs. One brief collision with the ottoman in front of his dad's favorite chair was the only thing he encountered before making his way through the kitchen and into the bathroom. As he stood in front of the toilet and peed he listened very closely to any change in the rhythms of the house. Someone in his parents' room snored pretty loudly.

Otherwise nothing.

He went over to the sink to wash his hands and turned on the faucet. No water came out. He moved both handles, hot and cold, back and forth with no results. He bent over to look at the faucet, his head almost in the sink. One single drop dripped onto his cheek.

Suddenly something wrapped around his throat and tightened. He reached up to try and loosen it. It felt like a vine, covered with hundreds of prickly thorns, digging into the tender skin of his throat and pulling him towards the drain. He opened his mouth to call for help but no sound came out. It was just too tight. He felt his body being pulled into the sink. He reached out and put his hands on the porcelain, trying to hold on. He was losing his grip. . .

And then he woke up. He was sitting up, his hands making tight fists on either side of his body. The air was still full of the sound that did indeed escape from his throat. For a second he remained frozen and then he heard the sheets on Pete's bed move. He slowly turned his head and saw Pete also sitting up in bed looking at him.

Way to go, doofus. Ike really couldn't see Pete's face but he could hear the smirk in his voice. That's gonna get Mom up for sure. And she is NOT gonna be happy. He turned away from Ike and settled back into his bed. His back to Ike was a solid presence of disapproval. Ike remained sitting up in bed, listening to his parents downstairs and the steps of one as they headed up the stairs going up to check what the sound was all about. From the other bed, Pete chuckled. And then, so quietly it was almost a whisper.

Wuhahahahaha. . .

Ike couldn't take his hands off the box Pete got for his birthday. Usually his older brother put together models of cars, but this one was very different. The picture on the front was maybe of a man, though it didn't look like any man Ike had ever seen before. The eyes were wide and white. They looked like they were about to pop out of his head. The skin was gray and lined, and the mouth showed jagged teeth that looked frozen in a growl. The head had wisps of hair on it but was mostly bald. Surprisingly, the figure had a nice black and white suit on it (Pete called it a tuxedo), and a cape that hung almost all the way down his back to his feet. The face was bad enough – it was just human enough but just enough not that it put Ike on edge, expecting and wanting one thing but getting something else pretty different. Imagine his crazed killer looked like that and you woke up to see that looking down at you!

But what really bothered Ike was that the figure held his right arm up over his head and in the hand was part of a face, the fingers through a hole where an eye used to be. Pete told him that it was just a mask, but Ike knew it was the skin of a face. He could see where the eyes were supposed to be, and the nose. The box had the words "The Phantom of the Opera" on it. He asked Pete what a phantom was, and Pete told him it was a ghost. And that was that – from that point on, this was his Crazed Killer. But this one hardly looked polite. This one looked frozen in a position of bloodthirsty zeal, having just ripped the face off some unsuspecting innocent. To further convince Ike, the base of the figure had what looked like a small prison window rising out of the floor. There were bars across the window, and clutching the bars was a person who had obviously been trapped inside. The Phantom had just ripped his face off and left him, in pain, to slowly die.

Pete labored over the model for more than a week. Anytime the kitchen table wasn't being used for meals, he spread newspapers and put out all the pieces of the model. He glued the pieces together with great care, his face so close to the model that he was breathing on it. Ike stood in the kitchen to the doorway, horrified. Where are you going to put this when it's done? he asked, his voice quavering. In my room, stupid, Pete said back, almost holding his breath with concentration. Why? Ike couldn't stand the thought of that thing in his room, looking at him all night as he slept. Once Pete opened the bottles of paint and started adding color - Ike was right, the figure's skin color was gray - Ike thought he was going to throw up. The paint smelled, and Ike thought it smelled like blood. Not that he knew what blood smelled like, but he knew that this was it. Pete stuck his tongue out the side of his mouth as he drew the brush along the edges of the figure. At dinner, the smell of the blood paint hung in the air and Ike couldn't lift a fork of food to his mouth to eat.

Finally it was done. The figure stood in the center of the kitchen table, triumphantly holding the ripped-off face aloft for all to see. The dying man's pained face looked out from between the bars at the base. When the paint finally dried, Pete carried it carefully, slowly, almost with reverence up the stairs to the bedroom at the end of the hall. That night, when the news came on and it was time for bed, Ike lingered in the bathroom, brushing his teeth one at a time and sitting on the toilet for so long that his dad finally had to knock on the door to make sure he was okay. He walked out of the bathroom slowly, his head hanging, not meeting his dad's eyes. The crazed killer would not get him last now. He would start out in Ike's bedroom, the bedroom at the end of the hall upstairs. And he would rip his face off, the one part of his body he couldn't hide under the sheet, by now made of iron in his mind to keep away the weapons of crazed killers.

He took the fifteen steps upstairs one at a time, resting both feet on each step before moving up to the next one. He pushed open the bedroom door and for the first time he noticed that it creaked on its hinges. Pete sat on his bed, smiling at Ike. The Phantom of the Opera figure was on the dresser closer to Ike's bed, turned in his direction. Pete was finally getting his wish - Ike would never be able to sleep again. He looked at his older brother. It hurt to even see out of his eyes or breathe out of his nose. His pained expression only made Pete smile even wider. Without a word he swung his legs into the bed and turned his back to his terrified sibling. Ike changed into his pajama top and shorts as if he was walking in mud. After he finished he lay on top of his bed on his back. He stared at the ceiling.

Turn off the light doofus. I can't sleep with the light on, Pete said to the wall but also to his younger brother. Ike still lay there. If he didn't breathe or didn't move, maybe his older brother would forget he was there. Or maybe, just maybe, not forget and fall asleep anyway.

LIGHT. Much louder this time. Ike slowly got up and walked over to the wall by the door. He had to walk past the dresser and the figure but he kept his eyes stuck to the light switch. His arm rose as if on its own and pushed down the light switch. He stood in the dark before slowly turning around to walk back to the bed. This time, however, he couldn' help but notice the Phantom on the dresser.

It glowed in the dark.

A sound escaped his throat as he ran past the dresser. He dived into bed and threw the sheet over his whole body. He curled up into a ball, closing his eyes as tightly as he could. If he couldn't see it then it must not exist. But he could still smell the blood paint. He pinched his nostrils shut and shuddered. He could hear his brother chuckle from across the room. With his leftover hand he covered up the ear not buried into the pillow. Muffled, he could still hear the laughter as it got louder. Following the laughter, he could tell his brother got up from bed and moved across the room to the dresser where the figure was. The laughter paused there for a second but then moved in his direction. As it got closer, the laughter changed to the sound he hated so much. Finally it was right over him. Right outside the protection of the sheet.

WUHAHAHAHA. . .

Ike threw his whole body in the direction of the sound. At the same time, he swung his arm out in the direction of the sound, making a noise that could not shape itself into something coherent but needed to escape from his throat anyway. Before the swinging of his arm threw the sheet off his body, he felt his arm connect with something that was both sharp and soft at the same time. Something made of plastic made a clattering sound as it hit the floor.

And then he was sitting up and looking at his brother. The look on Pete's face was one that Ike could not read – it was all open and had not yet shifted into meaning. The older brother looked down to the floor and Ike followed his gaze. There was something dark on the ground, but he couldn't make out what it was. Pete sprang into movement, quick and with very definite meaning. As he stomped over to the wall switch and flipped on the light and as the words poured out of his mouth onto his younger brother, Ike stared at what he had done. The Phantom of the Opera lay on the floor on its side. The hideous face was glaring and growling at the floor. The figure had broken off from its base, so the only thing still connected was the man with the pained face still gripping the bars of his little prison. The arm the figure held aloft had broken off. The hand with the ripped off face had scooted across the floor and was resting on the rug by Ike's bed.

Pete was doing his chores and Ike was tagging along. Because Dad said to. Pete hadn't spoken one word to his younger brother since the incident with the Phantom weeks before, and to Ike it felt like a win. He was choosing to ignore the tension surrounding his older brother whenever Ike was around, and instead filled the silence with sound. His own voice going on and on about whatever topic was of interest to him at the moment. Of special interest were subjects that got an eye roll, or a sigh, or an attempt to move away and get out of the room whenever the younger boy showed up. This felt like weapons to Ike. For once he was armed against whatever this was with Pete.

Today he also wanted to show off his new toy. He had recently bought a holster with a gun with his own allowance money. It was just like the kind of gun that Little Joe had in "Bonanza," his favorite show, and he felt strong and powerful like Little Joe was in the show. As Pete carried buckets of feed, Ike straggled behind him and pulled the gun out of its holster and then put it back in as quickly as he could. Then he would point the gun at something and make the sounds with his mouth of guns going off like they sounded in the show. Sometimes he pointed it at his brother's back. The holster was tied to his legs so it wouldn't swing when he walked, and after he pretend shot something, he would holster it and then hurry to catch up to his brother's retreating back.

Pete stopped at an iron tank used to water livestock. It hadn't rained and the water was low. There was a hose attached to a spigot next to the tank - Pete unwrapped the hose and dropped the end into the water with a plunk. He turned to lift the handle on the spigot and Ike picked that moment to unholster his gun and point it at his older brother's back. He started to make the Pew! Pew! sounds that are his version of what a firing gun sounds like. But he doesn't quite have his technique down yet and the gun catches on the edge of the holster, flips out of his hand and plops down into the water just like the hose did a minute before.

Ike stood frozen, not daring to look in the direction of the gun - instead his eyes are locked on Pete's face, who obviously saw the blunder. And his older brother is smiling at him, but with one side of his face lifted higher than the other. Like a smirk. Ike felt the blood rush to his face. He briefly thought about pretending it didn't happen and leaving it there and walking away. Pete leaned into him, his face large in all that Ike could see.

Oops.

The single syllable was like spitting into Ike's face. The smirk barely moved. Ike took a step back, his hands up in front of his face like he was trying to erase the image of his brother leaning into him. Instead he walked over to the tank and looked down into the water. The gun lay on the bottom, silver like treasure. The water moved above it, making the object ripple. It was like he was dreaming what he was seeing. He was at the sink again and looking down into something dark and unknowing. He slowly stuck his arm into the water and looked at the gun as he reached for it.

The push from behind sent his face into the water. His mouth was open and water rushed in, making him swallow and then sputter as he spit the water out. He stood and turned around, water dripping from his face onto his shoulders and arms and chest. Pete stood inches from him, the hand that shoved Ike's head into the water still lifted, cocked and ready. His smirk was opening up into a laugh. Ike ran his drier arm across his face. What did you do that for? His voice, higher than it needed to be, sent droplets of water out into the air from his lips. The older boy didn't answer. He simply put his arm down to his side and shrugged his shoulders. Ike screamed out the next words. I dare you to do that again!

And he turned around to the tank and bent over to retrieve the gun.

The second shove was decidedly stronger. Ike's face slammed into the rim of the steel tank. His mouth, which seconds before was opened to utter a dare that no older brother could possibly ignore, struck the metal with a jolt that sent a shock through his entire head. He staggered away from the tank and sat on the ground. His ears were ringing. He held his hand open in front of him and blood dripped down onto his palm. He looked up at his brother, his hand still open. Blood edged along his gums and onto his lips. And then a pain, dark and intense, went into his mouth and filled up his whole head. It forced everything else out that it encountered, so Ike's nose filled with snot and his eyes ran.

And the sound. The sound started low and went high as it escaped his throat until it was like something that only dogs could hear. The hand with drops of blood joining together in his palm went up to his throat and covered his mouth. He staggered to his feet, his skinny legs getting tangled around each other before finally he stood upright. His eyes broke away from his brother's face and turned in the direction of the house before he ran off, his hand still up to his mouth. The sound followed after him, carried on the wind and fading away as his figure made it up the hill and into the house. His older brother looked after him. The expression on his face could not be read.

The dentist took x-rays of Ike's mouth and determined that the roots of the two front teeth, permanent unfortunately and not baby teeth, were not damaged. But broken was still broken. There was nothing they could do except let the area heal. If they wanted, they could do something cosmetic at some point in the future once he was done growing and his gums stopped receding. Ike's mom, appropriately distraught, let Ike pick where he wanted to stop on the way home and he picked McDonald's for a chocolate milkshake - which he could then not eat because it was too cold and his teeth were too sensitive. Even with a straw. He couldn't eat supper either. Everything hurt too much. Which was fine because he had no appetite. Tonight he would go to bed with nothing but ice to eat, which he himself put on his tongue to melt without touching his teeth. And by the time he went upstairs to his bedroom, Pete was already in his bed, his back to his younger brother and the rest of the room. The light was still on and there was no admonishment from his brother to turn it off.

Nothing except silence.

So Ike stood in front of the dresser, where previously had rested the figure of a Phantom, and looked at his reflection in the mirror. In his mind he did not look the same. His gums were red and swollen. The two front teeth were broken off almost at the gum but at a jagged angle. The ice hadn't washed away the taste of blood in his mouth. He could still taste and smell it. He opened his mouth wider and tried to smile. It hurt and he grimaced. But he held the smile as long as he could and looked at the reflection of his mouth in the mirror.

It looked like he was growling.

LIGHTNING RANGER

YOUR FINGERS ARE STRETCHED out wide, stiff as popsicle sticks, and not just from trying to reach from a middle C to an F with your ten year old hand. You have been going to lessons once a week and practicing as much as your mother makes you. You knew this was coming. There were eight people in front of you, but they have all, miraculously, taken their turn. You must now walk to the piano.

Before your turn, you were sitting at the end of the pew, pale wood with a red cushioned seat, and your feet were swinging. Your shoes are shiny black and they stand out against the red carpet in the choir loft. Everyone must notice them. Nothing else about you would draw people's attention. Your short-sleeved shirt is white, and your junior choir fake bow tie is crammed in at the collar. Despite your mother, who said it was too hot in May, you have on your sweater of three shades of purple, material soft and furry like the stuff older girls wrap around their rings after they get them from their boyfriends. Your pants are also black. Your hair is cut close to your head, except for little bangs in the front. So people would not look at you. Except for the shiny black shoes, which seem to glow against the carpet. And as you walk, one of them squeaks. Now everyone will notice for sure.

Every step takes you further out of the safety of the choir loft. Each step allows you to see more and more people sitting in the sanctuary of the church. All their faces are looking up, white and round. The carpet is red all over. And you have the feeling of looking down into a sea of reflected moons. You are afraid that if you see your parents you will surely stop where you are, or turn around and run back to your seat. So you stop looking, and instead focus on the old worn cushion on the piano bench. Surely it was red like everything else at one time. But now the edges are frayed and have no color.

You scoot up onto the bench. It doesn't matter that your feet don't touch the ground here, because you haven't learned to use the pedals yet. You look down at the keys. They are brown and worn and cracked on the ends, like your permanent front teeth that your brother accidentally broke against a hog trough last summer. You reach up, and then you notice that your hands are already stretched out to reach across part of an octave on each hand. But your knuckles are white, so you've been doing it for a while.

You bring your left thumb down to touch middle C, and the sound of the note almost surprises you. The song you're playing is called "Lightning Ranger." It was the last song in your beginning piano book, so it was the best choice to memorize. Eight measures. Middle C to F, back and forth for four counts, then up one note to D and G, back and forth for four counts, then back to middle C to F for four counts before ending with a D for one count and then G for three. The right hand does nothing until the fourth measure, when it plays the D and the G an octave lower.

The second four measures are the same except the end. Instead of holding the G in each octave for three beats, you're supposed to hold it for one. This is not that hard for you - the concept of holding a note for three counts was actually harder to grasp. But suddenly you're to the eighth measure, and it's not clear to you how you got there. Did you play the rest of the song? It seemed so fast, maybe you skipped some parts. Maybe you're actually at the fourth measure instead. And then your hand is shaking because you don't know what to play. Your mind changes lanes in mid-thought, and the hands do something else, responding to a signal that is so basic you don't even realize you had it. The right hand plays the right notes, but the left, the oh-so-trusty left, that is used to playing these notes because that's all it plays, plays the A instead of the G. The sound, at least to you, is jarring. And what's worse, it makes it sound like the song is supposed to go on, so it takes the audience a moment to clap. When they do, it sounds the same as it did for the rest of the piano students. But you feel warm, very warm, and your eyes are suddenly tired, too heavy to stay in your skull, weighing your head down until you face the floor. All your heavy eyes see is the red carpet, and this time, you are sure, it is reflecting your face.

Fast forward three months. Her face is down into yours, and it reminds you of one of those scary-looking dried-apple faces you see at roadside stands and county fairs. But she is not scary like the apple people, because her eyes disappear into the wrinkles of her smiling face, and that interests you. Still, you don't really know her. She is a distant relative of your father, and you aren't sure whether or not you want to take her hand. She is looking at you but talking to your mother. Your brother, determined to scar you, either physically or mentally, is smirking over your mother's shoulder.

"I understand he plays the pie-an-o. Is that right? Does he play the pie-an-o?" She turns to look at your mother just long enough to see she's there, and then her shrunken-apple face with the disappearing eyes is back in front of your face. Over your mother's shoulder you see your brother has moved closer. The smirk, riding halfway up the side of his face on one side, makes him positively stupid with glee. Evidently this woman is a cheek-pinching bundle of family love from way back. Your eyes dart to her hands. If they make any sudden movements towards your face, you're in for some trouble. For now, they're hovering at her sides.

"Yes, Auntie, he does. He plays the piano." It's hard to tell what your mother's thinking as she responds. A touch of pride, tempered with a sigh maybe.

"And I'll bet he's real good at it too, ain't he?" The head whips around again to look at your mother, a trail of long gray hair following that almost brushes your face. "You're real good at it, ain't ya?" And then the face is looking at you again, but closer this time, close enough to feel the breath on your face, and to notice she has hair on her chin. "You're such a good-lookin' boy." And she obviously has you off guard, because the hand is up before you realize it, and your cheek is in a death grip from which it may never recover. "You're sure to play the pie-an-o real good." And then she releases the cheek, and surprise of all surprises, your face feels like it's sliding back to its original shape. And then she's out of your face and standing up straight. Not that there's much difference, because even at full height, she almost looks you straight in the eye.

"Well," she says with a loud breath. She claps her hands, which felt like the interior of your father's car when they had hold of your cheek, for emphasis. "Will ya play for me?"

It takes you a moment to realize she's talking to you. Or maybe you're stunned at such a notion. This is an outdoor family picnic. You're supposed to be playing in the grass, or lying on a blanket and eating fried chicken. But playing the piano?

"Will ya? Will ya play for me?" She looks like she's about to bend into your face again, and the hands have started their hovering. You certainly don't want to be in the death grip again, but you don't have your music with you. The only song you know by heart is "Lightning Ranger," and it's been three months since you played that. And then, in your opinion, not very well. You look over at your mother. She is wearing a dress that looks like a tablecloth, red and white gingham, and her arms are crossed in front of her, and she looks like she's actually considering it. Somewhere in the outskirts of your vision is your brother, his smile now so wide it's threatening to take over his face.

"Wa. . .wa. . ." is the only sound you can make, even though your mouth keeps moving like a gasping fish, and your paralyzed stare is supposed to convey some message to your mother that she obviously isn't getting. "I'm sure he'd love to," she says, and her face breaks out in a grin. "Wa. . .wa. . ." you manage to sputter again, louder this time, surprised at this sudden betrayal. Your brother's grin is now relaxed and goofy. Somehow, he seems pleased, a co-conspirator in this venture.

"Well good. Glad to hear it." She smiles again, this distant relative with the dried-apple face, and suddenly the hand is there again, pinching your cheek so that you want to scream and push her hand away. But you see your mother's face over her shoulder, her smile softened by the perpetual worry you always see on her face, and you grimace.

"Actually, it's not me." The dried-apple woman lets go of you and stands straight again, laughing when she misinterprets the look of hope on your face. "Oh, I"ll be there a-listenin' to it, you can bet on that. But there's someone else who wants to hear you play. Someone'd really get a kick outa it. It'd mean a lot to 'im. Ya don't mind, do ya? Ya don't mind if someone else listens?"

This was turning into a regular concert event. Once again, you turn to your mother, but she is walking away, no doubt to go sell tickets. Her arm is around your brother's shoulders, and she is coaxing him along, though he's straining his neck to see every last expression on your face. So you're left alone with the dried-apple woman, who is looking straight at you, expectantly. For the first time, you realize she has blue eyes, and you wish she would smile again so they would disappear. If not, you may drown in them.

"No," you say, too quiet for anyone to hear, even the dried-apple woman. But she does, somehow, and she breaks into a big grin. Her eyes do disappear, but you don't feel safe, because you feel her arm on the back of your head, and you realize she's leading you to your doom. Or a piano, whichever turns out to be more terrifying. At least she smells good as you walk together towards the house. It's lilacs, like the bush in your backyard at home. Your mother's favorite flowers. You close your eyes, breathing in deep her lilac smell, thinking of your mother. The dried-apple woman holds you close against her side as you go, and your feet seem to be walking on their own.

"Well, alrighty, you just sit down right here and I'll go get things ready." She speaks before you stop moving. Her hands are on your shoulders, guiding you down, and you open your eyes. You are facing her ample bosoms. She sits you on the front step, and as she scurries into the house, she turns her head long enough to say "I'll be right back." All that jerking around of her head, you notice, whips her long gray hair through the air in dangerous arcs. And then she is gone.

She is not gone long enough to suit you. You lean your head back and soak up the sunshine, and somehow you know there won't be any more if you ever come back out. Behind you, through the screen door, it's dark, darker than underneath the covers at home in bed when you're hiding from the night time monsters. You can't see anything, and you can't hear anything. You wonder what she meant by "get things ready." Maybe she had sheet music, or is getting you a higher chair to play from. That would be nice. You look down at your legs, pale white and stretching down the two steps towards the ground. The toes in your shiny black shoes, which you must wear even out here since you have no arch supports in your feet, don't make it to the ground. Maybe you won't be able to touch the keys and won't have to play.

But then you hear her coming from inside the house. She starts talking before she even opens the door. "Okey-dokey, everything's all set." You have to get up so she can open the screen, and it briefly occurs to you that if you don't move, maybe she won't be able to get out. But you do, and the screen swings open, practically banging against the doorframe as it does, and she holds out her arm to catch it. The other arm, wrinkly like her face, is held out to you. Your fingers are slightly curved, and it reminds you of the hands in pictures of the Virgin Mary.

"You can come in now." The arm reaches out to you. "Come on. I can't wait to hear your song." You take her hand after looking around for any crowds that might be attending. Her hands are rough. The screen slams as she leads you into the house, which gets darker the farther you go. You have to blink your eyes, but you were just too used to the bright sunshine. You lean against her and shade your eyes with one hand.

She turns you left off the porch and into what you guess is the living room. It smells, like the clothes in the chest at home where your mother keeps her wedding dress. And there's another smell, one you can't identify right away. You strain to see. The shades are all pulled, which makes it even harder. As your eyes grow accustomed to the dark, you begin to pick out pieces of furniture. The first one you see, of course, is the piano, big and tall and straight, like it was meant to be against a wall but is instead in the middle of the room. Maybe she had moved it for you. Or maybe the wall space was all taken, because everywhere you can see, there are dark shapes of chairs and tables pushed against it. Some of the tables, surprisingly, have plants on them, plants which look none the worse for wear for having grown in the dark.

A couch is to the left of the piano facing it. And that's when you notice that there's someone else in the room. He does not move, his body is the length of the couch, and his skin is splotchy, purple and yellow. But it's his labored breathing that you notice first. Since he almost blends into the couch, it's as if the couch itself is breathing, gasping as it inhales and rattling as it exhales. The only thing that moves are his eyes, which search the ceiling as each breath leaves his body and disappears into the air.

In here, the dried-apple woman seems different. Her eyes don't disappear when she smiles, she moves slower and quieter, and she whispers to you when she speaks. "Here ya go," she says, gesturing towards the piano. "Oh, I can't wait. It's gonna be sooo beautiful." And she squeals, but it's a quiet squeal. And she doesn't pinch your cheek this time. She watches you sit at the piano, and moves around to behind the head of the couch, where the man is staring into the ceiling, and puts both her hands on the back, holding on, waiting. You stare down at the keys, cleaner than the ones on the piano at church. The man gasps and stares at the ceiling.

And you play for them. Middle C to F for four beats, then D to G for four beats, then back to middle C to F for four then both hands for the fourth measure. Repeat measures five through seven. Your fingers are in all the right places, the keys are underneath where they should be, and "Lightning Ranger" sounds just as it should. And then you come to the eighth measure. You pause, your hands above the keys. You look at the dried-apple woman, who simply raises her eyebrows. The man does not move. You look down at the keys. Your hands are frozen.

And slowly you lower your hands to the piano bench. The fingers curl around the edges of the bench. You look over at the dried-apple woman, and as you do, one hand reaches up and wipes at your eye. The fingers come away wet. You open your mouth. You want to speak, or at least you know you are expected to say something.

And then you are running. Through the living room, onto the porch and out the door, down the steps in one jump, hitting the ground so hard with your feet that it jars your whole body. But you don't stop there, only stumble for a second, and then you're off again, crying and gasping for breath as if you're never going to breathe again and swiping at your face with the back of your hands. Nothing comes into focus, like you're riding on the Ferris wheel on the playground. And you feel the same too. Something is stuck in the pit of your stomach, and it's moving up, and you have to get somewhere safe before you throw up.

Finally you come to the family car, a blue Galaxy 500 with a white roof. The door is heavy to pull open, and even harder to pull closed once you climb inside, but you have to be where no one can see you, and you have enough little boy strength to swing it shut. You sit in the hot car, full of sunshine, your head thrown back on the seat, for a long time. You can't seem to catch your breath, and you feel the sweat running down your neck and into the back of your shirt. Your chest is heaving and your heart is pounding so hard your chest hurts.

You don't throw up, and finally you can breathe again. You lift your face out of the beam of hot sun coming through the back window. No one has come looking for you yet, which is fine. You just want to be left alone. As you sit there listening to your breathing, you realize how much it sounds like the man who listened to "Lightning Ranger." And you notice before you look that your fingers are moving, fingering the notes to "Lightning Ranger," going over and over it time and time again, especially the last measure, the measure you couldn't play for the man dying inside the house.

STORY ABOUT A STORY

THIS IS A STORY about a story.

Actually, it's the story about the telling of a story.

At first glance, the story about a story appears to be about two young women. Really, they're two girls because they're both under 18. But for the sake of this story we'll call them two young women, so as not to appear to be culturally insensitive. Even though that doesn't become a thing for about 40 more years. So, young women.

And besides, they're both almost 18. Almost.

First there is Theresa. She is the teller of this tale within a tale, so she is the major player here. The protagonist, as it were. A little description of said protagonist might be in order. Just in case you need a picture. Just in case you want to not like her later, and you want to see in your mind's eye who you're not liking. She is 17 and three quarters years old. So just barely 17 at this point. In three months she will turn the big one eight and then, her mother and father say, her boyfriend can propose to her.

And she can say yes. If she wants.

So she already knows who she is going to marry. He is big and tall and has brown hair and smiles when he holds her hand. He has already taken to sitting with her family in their pew during church. He is already 18, so he is just waiting for her. His name? For the purposes of this story it isn't important. Until, of course, she takes his last one. About nine months from now, give or take.

Theresa has red hair, which is worn in the style of the day. There are bangs, some height at the top and some flip at the bottom. There is a headband involved. She likes her skirts a little tight and a little high. Makes her boy, her man, look but not touch. Okay, well, maybe touch just a little. Not a lot - for the "lot," he's gonna have to wait until there's a ring on her finger. And there are the boots. Almost up to the knee. Heel of three inches or more. Always matching the too-tight-too-short skirt. Or maybe the blouse. Or brown. Yeah, brown. If all else fails.

Then there is Eleanor. Yeah, Eleanor. She herself would roll her eyes and tell you that her parents loved former first lady Eleanor Roosevelt and. . .well, there you have it. Yes, it sounds like an old lady name. But with any luck, she would tell you, she would eventually be an old lady. And then, she would also tell you, she would be all caught up. Be right where she was supposed to be.

Eleanor, like Theresa, is about to become engaged. But first she will discover that she is pregnant. Which she hasn't yet, though she is. A slight case of the cart before the horse, as it were. A little became a lot - and now we're here. Or she's here, or will be as soon as she realizes that her period is weeks, not days, late. And she tells her boyfriend, who she's been dating since she was a freshman. And he, in a panic, gets down on both knees (odd, I know) and asks her to marry him. And she will be, by that time, already 18, so she can say yes if she wants to.

Without having to ask anyone's permission.

Eleanor dresses way more conservatively than Theresa. She's already nabbed her man, so there's no reason for anything else. Longer hair, down past the shoulders, down to the boobs. Bangs. Also a headband. Blouses with long sleeves and modest collars. Longer skirts, what the fashion of the day refers to as a "midi-skirt." Rarely a "maxi-skirt," though that particular choice was never out of the realm of possibility. A modest flat, though sometimes she also opted for a boot as well. Almost always brown in her case.

By the way, Eleanor is the listener of this story within a story. A passive observer as it were. But she's not the antagonist exactly. She may, actually, in fact, be the hero of this particular tale.

Before Theresa marries her beau and has a passel of kids, and long before Eleanor marries her beau (to legitimize the pregnancy), squeezes out a couple kids of her own, divorces her husband because he turned out NOT to be her soulmate but more mainly a provider of sperm, briefly lost her shit and then got her shit together, long before any of that - Theresa and Eleanor found themselves the teachers of the same Sunday school class. Ordinarily they would have older women do it, wives and mothers and such. But what with Ladies Aid and various other duties in the church, this particular gig has fallen on the shoulders of two teenagers almost (but not quite) out of high school. This particular class was eleven year olds, so the teachers were only six years older than the students.

Which created quite the interesting dynamic in the classroom. Or, to be more specific, the Sunday school room. They would spend ten minutes talking about how Cain killed Abel, or how Lot's wife turned into a pillar of salt because she turned around to see all the same-sex fornicators burning to death in Sodom or Gomorrah. The rest of the time, about 40 minutes or so, they would talk about boys at school. Or girls at school. Or boys and girls at school. Every once in a while they talked about how much their parents drove them crazy. And how they (the students, not the 17 year old teachers) couldn't wait to drive themselves. Though one boy, a smaller boy named Ike, whispered that he was secretly a little afraid to drive, a secret he begged the others to promise they wouldn't tell (a secret that didn't hold). Or sometimes they just talked, to and over and on top of each other.

Because they liked how it sounded.

On the day in question, the day in which the story within a story took place, there was a lot of that. A lot. It might have been a full moon or something. Because god knows a full moon can get folks all riled up in about a half a second. So lots of talking. Over each other. Which leads to shouting. And sometimes screaming. Which isn't, let's face it, ideal under the best of circumstances. But when your classroom is really just a corner of a large basement partitioned off by wheeled things covered with posters of Jesus and sheep - and right on the other side of the partition are other children, younger children, who are using crayons to color in pictures of Christ on the cross - then it's a potential recipe for disaster.

So it's time for a field trip. Out of the basement and up the stairs to the outside, where the sky is gray and could possibly maybe produce some rain later. It's Theresa's idea, because she is, after all, the protagonist of this story, to take the walk up to the cemetery. Short walk really. The church is just down the hill from where all the gravestones were, and the hope was - once again, Theresa - that the uphill climb would wear their little undeveloped lungs out and they would shut the hell up.

Not Theresa's words. And definitely not Eleanor's. Eleanor, for her part, was already wondering why she felt nauseous all the time and whether or not she would even make it all the way up the hill and back down to the church again. Quite a lot of huffing and puffing for someone who's not quite 18. And of course there's the ever-present danger of throwing up. Barfing chunks as it were. Or chunk, since she could barely choke down a single piece of toast this morning. But she is not the protagonist, nor the antagonist – she is just (it seems) the dutiful sidekick, destined to follow Theresa's lead. At least in this regard. So she will grit her teeth and bite her tongue and take lots of deep breaths – whatever it takes to make it all the way.

So they trudge up the hill. Eleanor hurries a little bit to catch up to Theresa – which leaves a gaggle of eleven year olds dragging their feet behind them, acting as if the very act of walking is causing them actual physical pain, and grumbling about it because grumbling about it might actually make it – the pain – real. And therefore justify the grumbling. The effect before the cause perhaps. The complaining gives fuel to the trudging and eventually the trudging becomes something akin to stomping. And all the while the complaining gets louder and louder, until it rolls off the surrounding hills and back into Theresa's face and neck and ears, and Eleanor's stomach, which already has movement and is somehow triggered by all of this sound.

Suddenly Theresa stops and turns so suddenly that the young people stumble and stare at her, startled. Jan is carrying a sweater and he drops it. He bends to pick it up, but then freezes. His eyes dart up to Theresa's face.

"No!" Theresa's voice is sharper and louder than perhaps it needs to be, but it has the desired effect. The children stiffen even further. Jan, his knees bent, his one arm reaching halfway to the ground, looks at the others. For assistance, perhaps.

"NO!" Again, but amped up this time. If she weren't so irritated, she would be delighted by the reaction. Their faces are all turned in her direction, their mouths and eyes open round circles. Except for Jan, who is creeping upwards towards full standing height as if he's in slow motion. He's now looking back and forth between Theresa and the other children.

"You.

Need.

To.

Stop!"

And Jan does, though his knees are still bent – just a little, but still enough that he winces with the effort to hold it. But she is not necessarily talking to him anyway, because she has raised an arm and is now pointing at the others. At this particular moment in time, Jan doesn't see himself as one of the "others." At this moment in time, he sees himself as someone who didn't do particularly well in physical education class and faked doing knee bends every chance the coach wasn't looking. He snapped his knees into a locked position and was finally standing upright, his breath coming in deep inhales and exhales, his sweater clutched to his chest. Theresa turns in his direction just long enough to make him want to pee himself, but then scans across the whole group.

"Too. Loud."

Her sentences are coming out short and choppy. One. Word. At. A. Time. Out of the corner of her eye, she sees Eleanor's puzzled face. She, Eleanor, opens her mouth then closes it then opens it again. Still, no words come out. Theresa turns to point at her, even though she, Eleanor, is surely the quietest one of the whole lot.

"Too loud."

Theresa says it again. This time there are two whole words in one sentence. So progress has been made. She looks down at herself pointing. She lowers her arm slowly before turning back to the huddled mass of young'uns. Their faces dart back and forth between Eleanor and Theresa, who takes a deep breath. She needs not only a word, or even a whole sentence. For this story, she needs a whole story.

"Way too loud. Way, way too loud."

As she says this, she points at a small grove of trees lining the graveyard that stretched out to her left. She leans down into her students' faces, her arm stretched out away from her to point at the trees. She wags her finger.

"If you're not careful, you're going to catch the attention of Crazy Hazel. Crazy Hazel. Have you ever heard of her?" She looks from face to face, her eyes wide and questioning. Almost as one, they takes a step away from her and looks at each other. Jan mouths the name - "Crazy Hazel?" - his face scrunched up as if someone else in the group had passed something unpleasant into the air around him. Theresa nods her head at him and said the name again.

"Yes. Crazy Hazel. She went to our church. And she had a little boy just. About. Your. Age." -

She points at each kid as she says this -

" - And he died. Yes.! Died! Suddenly and unexpectedly. Like children sometimes do. And that death. That loss of a young child -"

She waved her hands in the air as she continued -

" - Was more than she could handle. And she lost it. She went insane. And now-"

She stabs her arm in the direction of the grove of trees -

" - She waits, deep in the shadows of those trees, to find a child to take his place!"

She stands hunched over and breathing on the children, her arm wagging in the direction of the trees.

"So you need to be quiet. Right now. Or Crazy Hazel will come out of those woods and pick one of you to take with her!"

In this story within a story, this was the moment where there was absolute silence. Not even the birds in the aforementioned trees. Because it's just the right moment for it. The calm before some kind of storm. And everyone is frozen in place.

Until Theresa saw movement out of the corner of her eye. She turns to see Eleanor, newly-pregnant-but-doesn't-know-it-yet Eleanor, who is neither the protagonist nor the antagonist of this story but merely the faithful sidekick. And now is her moment. And she is waving her hand at Theresa.

Once she has Theresa's full attention, she points to her left.

Theresa turns.

A little boy has his head down. He is the smallest child in the group, smaller even than the girls. His body is curled in on itself and his shoulders are shaking.

"Ike," Eleanor whispers as she leans forward.

"What?" Theresa looks back and forth between Eleanor and the boy, who is by now making soft sobbing sounds.

"What?" she asks again.

Eleanor continues pointing. "Ike," she says again. "You know. He was the one who. . ." She pauses, perhaps for effect. "You know. . ."

Something akin to a lightbulb goes off in Theresa's brain - followed in very short order by something darker and indescribable. She stares at Eleanor and then turns her head towards the boy, who has lifted his hands to cover his face. By this time his whole body is shaking and he continues to look at the ground.

"Oh. Okay. Right. I. . ." Theresa sighs, a heavy deep thing that settles itself inside of her. At least it was still quiet. Though the birds were back.

The story within a story was done, if not necessarily finished.

She sighs again. The other children were now looking at Ike, who was now sniffling and wiping his nose. Eleanor looks at her expectantly.

Theresa hesitates before speaking again.

"Well. . .maybe we should go back to the church. . .if she is out there, maybe the church is the safest place for us to be." She shrugs. "Though who knows? Maybe she's not out there today. I mean, even Crazy Hazel needs a day off." She gestures for Eleanor to follow her. "Shall we?"

And with that, she heads off back down the hill towards the church. The students look at each other before following slowly after her. Eleanor walks over and puts her arms around Ike. She hugs him and whispers in his ear before holding him next to her and guiding him down the hill after the others.

And what did Eleanor whisper to Ike before they went back to the church? Of course, one can only speculate since it was whispered into his ear alone, and some things aren't necessarily meant to be shared. Perhaps she said "I think you deserve some ice cream later." Maybe she whispered "Don't you let Theresa fool you. She's really the Crazy Hazel around here." And maybe, just maybe, she said to the trembling little boy "I know you are the protagonist here. I know this is your story. I know you are very brave. You must continue to be brave. I know you have it in you." Though perhaps that was beyond the abilities of a 17 year old girl, pregnant or not.

But for now, she was holding him.

And that was warm.

And warm was good.

He felt safe.

And for now, that was enough.

TOWEL HAIR

HE HAD EATEN MACARONI and bologna on a piece of white buttered bread and then folded over, and he was full and sitting on the front step of his house. The taste of cheese, the sweetest taste that wasn't sugar, was still in his mouth. He ran his tongue over his teeth in the hopes of finding more cheese. His blonde hair was short all over his head. His daddy, now dad, told him he could grow it long as long as he took care of it, and he didn't take care of it. So daddy now dad buzzed it off with an electric razor every two weeks.

He wore glasses with black frames that looked too big for his face. He had only worn glasses for one year and he was proud of them. He thought they made him look smart and he thought that smart was one of the best things to be in the whole wide world. He also wore a short-sleeved collared shirt and dark green shorts with brown socks that went almost all the way to his knees. The skin that he saw between the socks and the shorts was very white - he never played outside - and marked with scabs. He was not sure how that happened because he never played outside. But he fell a lot, even when he was inside, so maybe that's how.

He picked at one of the scabs. His hands needed to be busy. Usually he would pick until the scab bled and then he would cry and go in to see his mommy, now mom, and claim he didn't know how that happened, I know you told me to leave it alone. She would put a Band-Aid on it and pat it and try to make her eyes look mean even though her mouth was smiling. You are twelve now, she would say. You are a big boy. Big boys don't cry, do they? And he would sniffle and nod his head and run the back of his hand across his nose. She would pat the BandAid again and stand up and tell him to run along and he would go back and sit on the front step. And that would have made today even more fun than it already was.

It was good to be twelve, he thought, even though it didn't feel any different than it did to be eleven. Still, Daddy now Dad said it meant a lot to be twelve. He agreed with Mommy now Mom that it means he's a big boy now and that he should start acting like a big boy. On the morning of his birthday he walked downstairs with his stuffed lion and gave it to Mommy now Mom and told her he didn't need it anymore. The lion's name was Snagglepuss, after a cartoon he watched on TV. It wasn't true that he didn't need Snagglepuss anymore, but that was what big boys did. Plus, he figured a way to cheat – he wadded up the top of the blanket when he first got into bed and held onto it like he was holding onto the lion. Yes, that was cheating, but maybe that was also something that big boys did now.

Another thing he was expected to do now that he was twelve was to call his Daddy Dad and his Mommy Mom. They had asked that of him before, but it didn't stick. No one who was a big boy used the words Daddy and Mommy anymore. He liked Mommy and Daddy, but he didn't want to be called a baby – especially by his older brother, who was eighteen and could drive a car and said he was almost a man – so he used Mom and Dad instead. Except when he forgot, which was a lot. And then his eyes would dart around to see if anyone heard before he changed the word in his mouth and said it again.

He only wanted one thing for his birthday, even though he still got a cake with twelve candles that he had to blow in one try and presents to unwrap. Mostly clothes, because Mom said he grew out of his old ones so quickly, and books because he liked to read. The one thing he wanted was for his best friend Jan to come over and play. Jan was exactly eleven days older than him, and so Jan naturally did everything first. He lost his first tooth first, he got his glasses first. He turned twelve first. Jan was almost a head taller than him already, so he had to look up to see Jan's face. Jan never wore shorts, only long pants, and he laughed at everything and seemed so grown up already. Like he was a teenager. To spend the day with Jan, who he had known since he was five, was all he wanted for his birthday. And finally, because things got in the way, like tonsillitis – Jan, of course, had his taken out already – today was finally that day.

He ate his lunch and now he sat on the front step waiting for Jan to arrive. He stopped picking at his scab – there was no blood today – and looked up at the sky. Mommy. . .uh, Mom. . . told him not to look into the sun, that it would make him go blind. She also told him that if he sat too close to the TV he wouldn't be able to make babies, and that he shouldn't go swimming for an hour after he ate. But he was a boy so he couldn't make babies anyway. And he hated to swim. Being blind sounded different and maybe more interesting than being able to see. So why not see if it was true? He had to squint, so maybe that's what she meant, that you had to close your eyes so you couldn't see. And it made his eyes water, though he didn't want anyone to think he was crying. Still, he was not blind. He put one hand up to shield his eyes, and he noticed how the skin of his fingers looked pink and glowing in the sun. He left the shield hand up and brought his other hand up so that the sun was behind it. He spread his fingers wide and as he watched it was almost as if he could see through his skin and see the sky. Almost, but not quite. He turned the glowing hand sideways and cupped his palm and fingers and the hand became a fish that swam in and out of the water. Jumping out of the water the hand was lit by the sun and was like it was made of gold. Curving back down into his imaginary ocean there was no sun turning his hand into gold. He moved his hand up and down, wondering how long he would do this before his eyes would make so many tears that he didn't have any more water left in his body.

He heard tires on gravel and he dropped his hands. He turned to see a car pull up next to the wire fence that surrounded the yard. Dad had put up a fence a few years ago because, as he said, there were children and a dog, and it wouldn't do if any of them ended up in the road. The car was blue and white. Dad or his older brother, who both drove cars, would know what kind of car it was, but he only knew it as Jan's car. Jan's mother, a short woman with a round face and round body and round hair (literally, it was all curls) was driving, and his older brother – who Jan called fat, even though Mom always said that people weren't fat they were just big boned – was sitting beside her. The older brother did not look happy, but then he never did. Maybe Jan got all of the happy for both of them.

Before the car even came to a complete stop the back door on the driver's side flew open and Jan was out the door and away from his mother and brother, his mother saying well wait now and shouting after him what time she would come pick him up. Jan didn't even turn to look at her, just waved his hand in her direction. He unlatched the gate and was into the yard before the family dog, who looked to everyone like the dog who always saved kids from wells on TV, came around from the front yard barking and jumping at the idea of a new human who might do some petting. Jan stood in front of him and looked down. He was in every way the opposite of his best friend - dark where the other boy was fair, tall where he was short, big where the other was little. Their dark-framed glasses looked the same however. Jan's just looked like they fit his face. I'm here, he said, looking down into his friend's face. He looked like he was sweating a little bit. There was something coming off of them that they could both feel, an energy that ran into itself and bounced off. It reminded the blonde boy of what it was like when Mom did the laundry and he helped her sort the socks after they had been in the dryer. They clung together and when he held them up and pulled them apart the socks made a sound like bacon frying all in one second.

Jan put his arm around the shorter boy. Whadya wanna do today? They both shrugged and laughed. Jan opened the screen door and Ike walked through. The door made a nice slamming sound as they entered the house giggling. Ike's mom was sitting at the kitchen table, a big bowl of peas on the table in front of her and another bowl cradled in her lap. Her right hand went to the bowl on the table and brought a pod back to her lap where both hands popped the peas out into the bowl in her lap before discarding the shell in a basket on the floor. They stood and watched her, the movement repeating itself in their brains so quickly that they couldn't look away.

He came back before Jan did, took Jan's hand, said come on and led him through the kitchen into the living room. Their shoes - his were dress shoes made especially for his flat feet - hit the stairs hard as they ran up the steps to the second floor of the house. The laughter and chatter continued as they clomped down the hallway to the bedroom at the end, and it was only after they went into his room and he closed the door that they paused and took a deep breath. He had his own room, at least for a while. His eighteen-year-old brother had moved into his own room at the top of the stairs, and until his baby brother moved from his crib into a regular bed, he had this room all to himself. When he was not quite such a big boy, he would lie in his bed with his eyes closed but still could not block out the idea of something under the bed that would come out and grab him while he was asleep. Which led to the question of how that something got under the bed in the first place which then led to imagining someone breaking into the house to come kill his whole family. The thinking that eventually let him fall asleep where he dreamt about death and woke up crying until he was almost a big boy was that someone would come through the front door like every other person and politely kill as he found people. The fact that his parents would be killed first because they slept downstairs didn't bother him as much as the comforting thought that he would be found last, way at the end of the hall upstairs. And he had his escape route, by jumping out the window, already planned out. So he liked his room. He felt safe there.

Jan sat down on the edge of his bed and leaned back on one elbow. Jan was always doing that - leaning against stuff. Lying down in places, stretching out across things. Like he was at home wherever he was. He smiled the biggest and whitest smile ever.

Did you watch Dark Shadows?

Dark Shadows was their show. It was on from 2:30 until 3:00 every weekday afternoon. During the school year he would rush through the door after school only to catch the last five or ten minutes. But in the summer he would make sure his chores were done by 2:30 so that he could spend the next half hour in Collinsport, Maine, where vampires and werewolves lived like normal people. Barnabas Collins was scary but Quentin Collins was scary and pretty (his mom told him he meant handsome, but he liked pretty better). It looked like it hurt every time he changed from a person to a wolf and back again. Jan said that when he grew up he wanted to move to Maine because that's where all the vampires and werewolves lived. What if a vampire bites you, he asked. Jan shrugged. Then I will live forever. But what if a werewolf eats you? Or tears you apart? Jan shrugged again. Then I'm dead. Jan had it all figured out.

He and Jan liked all the monster people, but what they loved the most were the human women who always seemed to get attached to the family somehow but had no clue what was going on until it was usually too late. The last thing you would see of them they were screaming in the dark as death came at them. They always looked very pretty, even when dying. Their hair was up at the top and curled at the bottom and held into place with a hair band of some kind. They wore mini-skirts and tight sweaters that made their chest look very, very there, and tall boots with high heels that they could never somehow run in, falling down at the last possible second, turning to the camera, opening their mouth and putting one hand up, palm out, to cover it.

Then the TV went to black and he could only imagine what happened next, though he had a feeling it was something very much like what happened when the murderer in his mind politely came through the front door and killed his family. It gave him chills.

He and Jan wanted to be those screaming women. He sat at his desk (Jan always took the bed), so he turned around and got his sketch pad and two sharpened pencils. Next to drawing, he liked sharpening pencils more than almost anything else in the whole wide world. He liked watching the pieces of pencil come out of the top of the sharpener and curl away from the pencil and drop to the floor. He liked how the lead on the pencil was so sharp when you got done that you could almost hurt yourself with it. Sometimes he would turn the pencil long after pieces of it stopped coming out the top because he just wanted it to be as sharp as he could make it. And it meant you got to draw a long time before stopping because the pencil wasn't sharp anymore. He gave a piece of paper and a pencil to Jan and handed him a book to draw on. He kept the pad for himself and drew on the next available blank page.

They talked for a long time about the stories of their screaming ladies. They covered every detail. Jan's women were usually based on some older girl he knew from church or school that he thought was pretty, and he was imagining how their lives would turn out if they didn't get eaten. Today her name was Theresa Klempke, and she had all the right things – big hair curled at the bottom, tight sweater, very there chest, short skirt, high heeled boots that she would fall in while running away from the monster in their story. She married her high school sweetheart right after they both graduated. Her husband's family had money, though Jan wasn't sure why. And the husband had recently died after only about a year of marriage, in some kind of horrible accident (or was it? With Jan there was always some kind of mystery), so that she was a widow at nineteen. And she was a friend of the family and trying to get away from it all – which is how she ended up in the place where the vampires and werewolves lived. Ike's screaming women were always based on some famous woman he had read about in the encyclopedia that week. This week he had just read about Eleanor Roosevelt, so he named his woman Eleanor. Only she was prettier than the real Eleanor, much prettier. And today, like usual, Eleanor had a long dress and a longer dress or skirt than Theresa. She was the less brave one. She was about to be married, but she was only nineteen and in no real hurry. The man she was about to marry was away a lot (doing what? He never decided. Work maybe, though then he had to decide what the work was) and so she decided to travel with her friend. She had the time. She was lonely. She loved Theresa like he loved Jan.

And then, once they were in Collinsport, something happened to them, though they never described anything bloody. Usually it was something that left the actual ending open, like discovering a secret door with something important in it, but then the door closes once they're inside the room and then they can't get out and there's no one to save them. Sometimes it was a place where people were buried, so they were stuck with dead bodies. As with the scabs on his knees, the idea of blood was better than the actual blood itself. And as they talked, they drew the women, a figure of a woman floating in the middle of a blank white piece of paper. The second picture - he handed a second page to Jan - was of the actual tragic event itself, Theresa and Eleanor trapped and turning in horror at some scary thing coming at them. It was a non-specific scary thing today, something that looked like a large animal, a space alien and a ghost had a baby. Regardless, it was obvious that the women were doomed.

It was Jan's idea. Let's play the scene. Which would involve dressing up. This made him pause. This, the wearing of women's clothes, was something that he agreed would no longer happen now that he was twelve and a big boy. Dressing up in his sister's and mother's clothes was brought up specifically when the talk about being a big boy took place before his birthday. But Jan was in front of him now, smiling, and Jan's smile was like looking into the sun. It was so strong you had to squint to look at it. He turned away from Jan and went to the top of the stairs and listened. He heard nothing happening downstairs. He thought about where people were.

Daddy Dad was working.

Older sister and younger sister were both visiting friends at their houses.

Older brother took the car and drove who knows where.

It was baby brother's nap time.

Only Mommy was in the house, around somewhere.

He went up onto his toes and stepped onto the stairs. He winced every time the wood made a sound, a tiny shriek like he'd stepped on a baby animal. He counted the steps, fifteen in all, before he made it to the bottom. Jan was right behind him. The steps spilled into a little hallway which had open doorways to four separate rooms - his daddy dad's office, a room with a piano in it and therefore called a piano room, the living room and his parent's bedroom. He took a tiny step towards the living room and looked in. The TV was over to his right and all the chairs and couch were facing in that direction. Below the floor he could hear his mother's voice. She was humming a song that he knew from church. Now she was down in the basement doing the laundry, but who knew how long she'd be down there.

He skipped across the living room in five steps and into the kitchen, turning to Jan and putting his finger to his lips as he did so. Once in the kitchen he went right to the drawers between the sin and the stove. The top one was the silverware, but the one below that was for the dish towels. He had one that was his favorite. He had no idea what color it used to be, but it was old and faded and looked yellow. When he put it on his head the ends touched his shoulders. He grabbed another black one that Jan liked. Just then he heard his mother's footsteps on the bottom step coming up from the basement, so he hurried out of the kitchen and through the living room to the stairs. He and Jan were giggling but also making Ssssshhh sounds to each other.

Once back upstairs, they went down the hall again, but instead of going all the way to the end to his room, they turned left into his sister's room. This was where the real treasure was. First they went into the closet to the left, which held his mommy mom's wedding dress wrapped in plastic. This closet was full of things she never wore anymore. He chose a pink bathrobe made out of thin material and patterned with dragons. Jan picked out another bathrobe, slightly heavier but longer. He said he liked the pink flowers on the blue background and he would not button it down all the way so that once he had high heels on he could stick his leg through like he saw movie stars do in magazines.

They helped each other on with their robes and fished through the old shoes on the floor - a white pair for him, a black pair for Jan. The heel was short enough that they could walk a straight line without falling down. Across the room was his sister's dresser. She was two years older than he was, she was a real big girl, almost a woman, and she had combs and pins and barrettes and hair ties on it, as well as lotions and bottles that sprayed good smells into the air and on your skin. He found a red hair band, and Jan helped him arrange the yellow dish towel on his head so that it hung down to his shoulders and still made him look like he had bangs. The head band held it in place. Jan did his own hair, wrapping the black towel around his head before using another red headband to hold it down. Jan called it his up-do, whatever that meant.

They looked at each other in the mirror before returning to the closet. They had been doing this ever since they became best friends, and yet they still couldn't look away when they saw what they had done. They were pretty. He grinned so wide, but kept his teeth closed like he saw women do in magazines. He stepped closer and leaned towards the mirror to get a closer look. He didn't know who the person was grinning back at him but he liked her. He looked at Jan's eyes in the reflection in the mirror. Hubba Hubba, both Jan and his reflection said at the same time. He didn't know what that meant, but he liked the sound of it. Hubba Hubba, both he and his reflection said back to Jan.

They stood side by side and continued looking at their reflections. The air in the room grew very still. In the world of the reflection it seemed to sparkle. He could not hear himself breathing. He felt himself in the room, in the moment, and yet didn't feel like he was there where the image was looking back at him. He reached out one hand to touch what he saw. His fingers encountered hard glass. The reflection did the same, and for a few seconds the two were touching fingers. He smiled at the reflection. The reflection smiled back. He looked at Jan standing next to him and their reflections did the same thing. Jan was smiling that smile. The air around him felt like it was sparkling like it was the mirror, like it felt when he drank too much soda.

And then Jan leaned over and kissed him on the cheek.

He closed his eyes. He could feel Jan's lips lift off his cheek but stay right there, so close that he could feel Jan's breath. Even with his eyes closed, the dark had little flashes of light in it. Sparkles. Fireworks in the dark. All the air in the room seemed to go to the air between his cheeks and Jan's lips. His cheek burned.

Then Jan laughed, a gust of air against his cheek. He opened his eyes and Jan pulled his face away. Jan took his hands and rocked back and forth, shifting his weight from one foot to the other as they held hands. He rocked with Jan. They were dancing. He giggled, throwing his head back and looking at the ceiling. There was light everywhere in the room. Let's go get the high heels, Jan said. Still holding hands they turned towards the closet.

His mommy mom was standing in the doorway to the room.

Her hand was on the doorknob. Her other hand balanced a laundry basket full of folded clothes on her hip. Her mouth was open and her lips were moving. No words were coming out. Suddenly she dropped the laundry basket and it fell onto its side and clean clothes rolled out onto the floor. She stepped into the room so fast that she was right in front of him before he even knew it.

What is this?

Her voice sounded harsh and sharp. What? Tell me!

He tried to answer but all of a sudden the inside of his mouth was so dry. He thought he knew the answer but he could think of no words to tell her. Dressing up was the easy answer but it wasn't the whole answer and he couldn't think of a way, or didn't have enough time, to tell her. Not now. Not here.

I thought we talked about this! She took his arm. Her fingers had a grip on him that almost hurt. Didn't we? Huh? Didn't we talk about this! You weren't going to do this anymore! You are a big boy now! Big boys don't need to play dress up! Do they? Huh? Do they? She shook his arm and he tried to pull the rest of his body away from her, wishing he could pull away from his arm and get away and leave her with just the arm. His eyes hurt. Her face got very close to him and studied his face. You do not do this anymore. You understand me?

No more.

You are too old for this.

She let go of his arm, which tingled. He rubbed the place where she had hold of him, his face down. His eyes were now wet and he was sniffling. She looked over at Jan, who had retreated to the corner of the room. Your mom is coming to pick you up after your show is over, she said. Take that off and put it away before you come downstairs. Her head shifted over to him. He couldn't look at her. You too, she said. Put this all away. And don't' get it out anymore. She walked back to the doorway, where the laundry basket lay on its side on the floor. She bent over and swept the clothes back into the basket with one hand. She started to walk out the door and then stopped and turned towards him. She was not looking at him. You and I will talk about this later. She turned away, reached for the door to close it, then stepped into the hallway, leaving the door open.

He and Jan stood where they were, listening to her footsteps going down the stairs. The room was quiet. It was like they were both holding their breath. Finally Jan sighed. As he snuck a sideways look at him,

Jan pulled the black towel and headband off his head with one hand. He lay it on the bed and slowly took off the blue robe and lay it on the bed next to the black towel and headband. Jan stood and looked at him for a long time. Jan sighed again, dropped his head to look at the floor and walked out the door. He reached out at the last second and closed the door on the way out.

He stood in the middle of the room listening to Jan's steps on the stairs. He counted all fifteen steps as Jan went down. He didn't move until he could hear the Dark Shadows theme song playing on the TV. That meant it was 2:30 and his favorite show was on. Today, however, he didn't want to see it. He lifted his head and looked around the room. Considering how much had happened in here today, it looked almost the same. The only thing that was different was the things Jan had put on his sister's bed. He had expected it to look worse, like it had been hit by a tornado.

He took a big breath, and the end of it sounded and felt like it hurt coming out of his throat. He reached and with the back of one hand wiped the wet away from his eyes. Then with both hands he very carefully lifted the headband and dish towel off his head. The headband he put on top of Jan's, and he lay the towel on the bed. It was not hair. It never was. It was, after all, just a towel.

He felt stupid. He folded it carefully in half, making sure the edges matched, and then folded it in half again. That was the way Mommy Mom did it - he had watched her, and helped do it, many times. He did the same with the black one. He put the yellow one on top of the black one in a neat pile by the blue bathrobe. He walked the bathrobe over to the closet and hung it on the first hanger he found. He looked down at himself. He still had on the pink bathrobe with the dragons. They were so quiet, these dragons. And it had been so loud in here just minutes before.

He slipped the robe off one shoulder and then the other and held it to his chest. He paused again, listening to himself breathe. Another deep breath hurt as it passed through him. She told him to hang it up. He reached into the closet for a hanger and then paused. He looked down and saw the pair of white shoes that his sister no longer wore but weren't in bad enough shape to throw away. The shoes had been the one thing he hadn't worn today.

His breath caught in his throat. He looked toward the closed door. He heard the muffled sound of the TV. He took a step forward and stuck out one leg. He slipped his foot into a shoe. With his brown sock on it fit exactly right. Like Cinderella and the Prince. He rested all of his weight onto his back foot and pointed the foot with the white shoe. He moved his ankle around so that he could see the shoes, and his leg, from all angles. Perfect fit. He put the foot down and slipped the other foot into the other shoe. He stood in them, and stepped away from the closet. He looked down at his feet in the shoes. He felt different somehow. Taller, even though the heel was short (it was for a fourteen year old girl, after all). He stood up with his chest out and his shoulder blades back. He felt taller and bigger all over. He looked down at the shoes again. He liked the look of them on his feet. Not since Dorothy clicked her ruby red slippers together in The Wizard of Oz did he like the way a pair of shoes looked on a pair of feet.

From downstairs he could hear the sound of his baby brother crying as he woke from his nap. And just like that he was back in the room, and he was only twelve, and he was doing something his Mom and Dad didn't want him to do. He stepped out of the shoes and sank back down to his twelve year old self. He picked up the shoes and started towards the closet but then stopped and turned back to the bed where the pink bathrobe lay. He picked up the robe and put it over his shoulder. With the shoes in one hand and the yellow towel and headband in the other, he slipped out of his sister's room and took the six steps to get back into his room. This is where it had all started. And he had plenty of hangers in his closet. He slipped the edges of a hanger into the shoulders of the robe. He put the yellow towel and headband around the shoulders and hung it up between his shirts and next to the one suit he owned and hardly ever wore. He put the white shoes behind his dress shoes. It was a deep, deep closet and they would be safe there. At least for a while.

He closed the closet door but kept his hand on the doorknob for a little bit. Downstairs he could hear his mother talking quietly to his baby brother. No doubt there was a bottle involved since he was quiet now. He could hear the actors saying dramatic lines on Dark Shadows. No one had called him to see where he was. Not even Jan. But that was okay. For now, he was okay. He let go of the door. There would be a talking to later. He knew that. But right now all he wanted to do was watch his favorite show. He would worry about the talking to after. He paused at the top of the stairs. So much going on there. So quiet up here. It almost made him want to stay. Almost. He put out his foot, no longer wearing a girl's white dress shoe. The step made a little shriek when he put his weight on it.

He counted the steps all the way down.

MONSTER

THE SOUND OF THEIR voices came from the back of the sanctuary. It skimmed off the red carpet that ran up the middle of the room to the altar, bounced off the cross above the alter, ricocheted off the stain glass windows of Jesus lining the walls on both sides, and exploded back onto the young boys who burst through the vestibule into the place of worship. They were thirteen years old and full of the joy of being alive, the pure unfettered pleasure of taking in oxygen, converting it into carbon dioxide and expelling it. There was no way to contain so much life brought together in one place, so that the energy spilled throughout the religious symbols and flowers on the altar and the Bibles and hymnals and fans shoved into the backs of pews and spilled out into the hallway from where they had just come. They flung it at each other and lobbed it back and they bent back their heads and cackled from deep in their lungs, which sounded like ancient lightning shot out of them and into the air. They stumbled between the rows of pews, a tangle of legs and arms.

There were four of them, and they were so different. Mark was the most athletic, and therefore, or at least it appeared to all who outwardly observed them, the natural leader. He had already had his growth spurt and his torso, previously a map of skin stretched across ribs, was beginning to muscle up a little bit. He moved unlike someone so young - all the parts clicked together into what would eventually become what was often referred to as a well-oiled machine. Close behind him was Jan, just a hair taller though possessing of the limbs of someone so elegant as to be almost feminine. Though talking like the others, almost on top of themselves, Jan had the watchful eye of someone much older, the expression of someone biding their time until their time would come. To his side but back a step was Isaac, but called Ike because of the president. Ike was the smallest of the four, all pale knobby knees and bony limbs. Everything was pulled in very tight, held close to his torso like he was hugging it so it wouldn't get away. He adored Jan and was constantly maneuvering to stay close to his side. Taking up the rear was Danny. He moved as if flailing in water, so it was good that he was behind the rest – with his arms and legs moving in seemingly opposite directions, he could have served as a propeller and pushed the energized air they created away from and behind them.

Their dialogue came out in jumbles of words and phrases and circles around them and out –

Who farted?

You did.

He who smelt it dealt it.

Aaahhh. . .

Lots of sounds that weren't words at all. They continued down the aisle. Mark, looking for someone to dominate, pushed Danny. Danny, as if caught by surprise, exaggerated the push and stumbled to the floor. Jan took a step back. Put a hand on his hip and watched the madness, shaking his head. Ike is caught by the stained glass window at the front of the church and stops and stares. This time of day the sun is at just the right angle and beams of light break through the colored glass. The face of Jesus, who in this window is cradling a lamb, seems to shine. Ike has seen this window since he was a baby, but every time he stops and looks at it. Jesus is so beautiful, like a woman with a beard.

Something hits his leg and he stops looking at the window and looks down. Mark pushing Danny has somehow been transformed into the two of them wrestling. Mark is on top of Danny, trying to pin his arms to the carpet. Danny is kicking and one of his legs has connected with Ike. Danny is laughing, his face aimed at the ceiling, but he isn't struggling very hard. Attention was attention, even if it painted him as a loser.

Suddenly he goes limp, as if he is dead. His legs are splayed out on the carpet. His arms are pinned to the carpet at the wrists by Mark, but Mark is not getting any resistance and he jerks forward a little bit, his teenage hurricane force slamming into nothing. Jan is off to one side, now leaning against a pew, his hip cocked out away from his body, his hand resting on his hip. He is rolling his eyes to the heavens. Mark rolls off of Danny and sits next to him. They are both breathing hard. I feel like I need a cigarette now Danny says, a surprisingly adult and dirty thing to say, but they all get it and laugh – even Jan, who must play his role and appear to be above all of this madness. Ike covers his mouth and his eyes are wide. He cannot believe this is happening in the house of the Lord. He looks to Jan, and takes his hand away from his mouth. It is okay to relax into the moment because Jan is obviously enjoying himself.

From somewhere up by the altar someone clears their throat. All four jump and turn in the direction of the stained glass Jesus. They have read about miracles in the Bible all the time, so it wouldn't be out of the realm of possibility to have a stained glass figure come to life right in front of them and express displeasure at their antics. But movement to the left, in the choir loft, catches their attention, and their heads, as if attached to one body, swivel in that direction. Reverend Scharke takes a step towards them but then sits in one of the pews in the loft. It was hard to tell how long he had been there. A smile is pulling at the edges of his mouth. One hand holds onto the pew in front of him. He is old enough to be their grandfather and is heavier than he should be, all round lines and curves, and limps when he walks. He takes a couple of deep breaths before he speaks. He nods his head.

Blessed morning to you.

They stutter as they respond. B-b-blessed morning to you Pastor Scharke.

I see we have brought a lot of energy to the study of God's word this morning. He allows the smile to win the tug of war with his face. I like to see it. Lots of energy in celebration of God's word. He claps his hands and reaches for the pew in front of him to pull himself into a standing position. The four boys stand as if frozen in place. They are having trouble looking him in the eye and instead look at the ground or at each other. The pastor scans the room as if he is taking in a view of something amazing like the Grand Canyon or a beautiful sunset. Where is LouAnn? I don't see LouAnn. Mark snickers under his breath. His eyebrows go up and he looks around him as if she's invisible and he just can't see her. Danny laughs out loud at that but then covers his mouth. He tries to make no sound and his eyes squint with the effort. Jan and Ike look over their shoulders at the back of the church, where they had entered mere minutes before. Ike shrugs his shoulders. I don't know Pastor, Jan said. She must be late. You know how she is.

As if on cue, LouAnn appeared in the lobby at the back of the sanctuary. Jan made shushing sounds and touched Mark's arm. They all turned to look at her. She stood in the lobby with her head down but her eyes up and looking back at them through round glasses that emphasized the size of her eyes. Her hair was very dark. There was a barrette holding it back from each temple, but the part was jagged like a lightning bolt and the ends looked uncombed. She shifted her weight from one chubby leg to the other as if the floor was hot. One hand was up at her mouth picking at the skin on her lip and the other played with the edge of her bibbed skirt.

Welcome LouAnn, Reverend Scharke said, holding his arms out to her. I was just asking where you were. He focused solely on the girl as she walked slowly down the red carpet, ignoring the boys on either side of him who looked at each other and smiled. I. . .sorry I'm late, she said. By this time she was in front of the pastor. Mark took a step away from her. But you're here now, the reverend said. That's all that matters now.

He turned and walked away from the group. Come children, he said. The good word of the Lord awaits. Mark hurried after him with Danny following close behind. Jan and Ike looked at each other again and turned their backs on LouAnn to follow the other three. LouAnn stood planted in the middle of the aisle by herself. It was several seconds before she went after them, stumbling on the steps to the altar before turning into the choir loft to leave the sanctuary.

Reverend Scharke always sat at the head of the table with the blackboard behind him. To his left sat LouAnn, slumped into her chair, her shoulders hunched over her work, her face down and her hair not pinned back dropping down and casting a shadow. Every so often during the lesson, particularly when he needed an answer to a question, the pastor would reach out and touch LouAnn on the arm. Two or three chairs separated LouAnn from Jan and Ike, with Mark and Danny sitting opposite them. They all sat with a green book open in front of them. The book was called "This is the Christian Faith" and they were slowly working their way through it, underlining sentences and talking about what the book said. When they were done, they would be confirmed in front of the whole church.

Today they were learning why God sacrificed his only son. Scharke would hand LouAnn the chalk and tell her to write something on the board. Her hand shook as she wrote and the words look like they were written by someone who was six. In the margins of page 142, Ike drew stick figures of a man pushing a woman off a cliff and a woman dropping a stone on a man's head. He spent the most time on a drawing of a cemetery. The centerpiece of the drawing was a dark scary tree with gnarled hands for branches. On either side of the tree were gravestones where he wrote birth and death dates. On one of them he wrote the name LouAnn. Later in the lesson, while they were underlining a passage, he discovered that the book had misspelled the word Bible. Instead of the letters BIBLE, the book had printed BBILE. He crossed it out and corrected it, all the while looking at the pictures already in the book of people suffering.

They took a break and Pastor Scharke disappeared into his office. The four boys bolted down the stairs into the basement, where the Sunday School classes met and the Ladies Aid had their lunches and chili suppers and ice cream socials. The room was divided into halves by a series of portable partitions. In each half there were three tables butted up against the wall and running parallel to each other. Each table was surrounded by chairs, like piglets looking for their mama's teat. Bibles and books and pencils and crayons were arranged neatly on each table just waiting to be messed up. One wall was lined with bookshelves filled to the brim with hymnals. The boys looked around. This was their recess and this was their playground. They just didn't like any of the toys at their disposal.

Look at this, a voice said behind them. The four turned to see that LouAnn had quietly entered the room. In one hand she held out a book of matches. Look at this, she said again. She opened the book and tore out a match. She closed the book and expertly drew the match across the front at the bottom. There was a spark and the head of the match lit up with a small orange flame. The head turned black as the flame crept down the stem of the match toward LouAnn's fingers. Look at this, she said a third time.

Then she moved the lit match to the hand holding the book of matches and touched it to the skin of her forearm. The book of matches fell to the ground. She looked back up at the boys and smiled. She held the still smoking black match in one hand and held out the arm with the red spot beginning to form out to the others. Look at that, she said.

Ike's mouth dropped open. He turned his head to look at the others. Jan had covered his mouth with his hand. Danny was frozen for a second, then began flailing his arms in wild patterns around his head. Mark's neck stuck forward. His eyes and mouth were large circles. No one spoke for a second. The silence sat heavy in the room. LouAnn bent over and picked up the book of matches off the floor. Her head still tilted towards the floor, she lifted her eyes up toward Mark. She held the book of matches out to him. Want to try, she said.

Mark flung himself away from her as if he had been shocked awake. And the litany began, the chant of words that they had developed ever since they had known her. Ewwwwwwww Loouuuuuuueeee! No! Grossssss! Danny danced away with him, throwing his head back as he joined the refrain. You're grosssss! So grossssssssss! Jan winked at Ike as he picked it up. Don't touuuuccchh meeeee! You're so grossssss! You pick boogers!

Ike stood in place blinking his eyes. LouAnn shifted the book of matches to her other hand and reached out for him, the only target that wasn't moving. Without thinking, he flinched as if he'd been slapped and jerked his shoulder out of her reach. Mark floated into view in the peripheral vision to her left. You're a Booger Monster! LouAnn turned and reached for him. He danced just out of range. EWW Lou! The Booger Monster! Danny was behind her. She turned to touch him and he skittered away. EWW!! Don't let her touch you! She's Lou the Booger Monster and she'll turn you into a monster too! Jan whispered in her right ear. She whirled around in the direction of his voice but Jan was already gone. EWW Lou! THE BOOGER MONSTER!

Ike had stepped right in front of her, so close that his vision of her briefly went blurry. He spat the words into her face. The drops of spittle landed on the lenses of her glasses. She stopped for a second and blinked. The breath was starting to come from her in ragged short bursts. She reached for Ike and he bent his torso away from her and curved his body towards the others. Without thinking he laughed. This was like playing tag. The others laughed with him and moved into him and then away as the hand not holding the matches reached towards their voices. She was no longer even grabbing for the person. It was more like she was instead reaching for the air where the sound had landed in order to capture the sound before it hit her in the face.

Finally she stopped moving altogether and stood absolutely still as the boys continued to circle her, darting close to her and then far away. The hand holding the matches dropped to her side and the book went to the floor again. She didn't bend over to pick them up this time. Instead, she stood very still, her head bent to the floor, her hair covering her face. Both arms were rigid at her sides. Slowly one arm reached up to her face. One finger went into her left nostril and stayed. It was still there, and the boys were still dancing around her, when Pastor Scharke found them a little while later.

The reverend sat in front of the blackboard. This week there were no words on it because there was no LouAnn to write the words. The boys sat in the same places they always sat, but with the books unopened in front of them. They looked at the older man, waiting for him to speak. Jan coughed into his hand once. Pastor Scharke sat for a long minute, looking down at his hands, held in a praying position on the table in front of him. The thumb on top, as if of its own accord, moved back and forth across the thumb underneath it. It was the next week, and everyone had already heard the news in this very small community, but he still felt that he should tell them. Announce it. Perhaps by doing so it would give the news even more weight than it already had.

He cleared his throat before he started. He didn't lift his head up as he spoke, instead watching one thumb moving across the other. There was a fire, he began. Of course you know this already, but. . .uh. . . He stopped and started again. You may have heard there was a fire. At LouAnn's house. Not sure how it started. He paused again. LouAnn was alone at home at the time. The fire people. . . they couldn't get to her right away. There were. . . significant burns. He looked up and at the boys one at a time. So our prayers are with her. Of course. The good Lord doesn't give us something we can't handle. I will visit her in the hospital. Of course. I will bring her all of your best wishes and prayers. And once she's out, I will be in contact with her parents about continuing her instruction. Your confirmation date is still a year away, so even if I need to do one on one with her at home. . .

He caught himself. Wherever they're living. . .I'm sure if she's up for it, and with the blessings of the Lord, I don't see any reason why she still can't be a part of your class. Do you? He looked at each boy in turn and asked the question again, waiting for a response before moving on to the next.

Do you?

Do you?

Do you?

Do you?

And each boy nodded his head so that the pastor would stop looking at him.

It is another Saturday. A year has come and gone, and there has been change in the boys, as is often the case when growth is still happening and dying hasn't yet begun. Mark has filled out even more and now looks like he's already in high school. Jan is taller now, and there is something about everything about him - his hair, his clothes, the way he carries himself - that is even more refined. Danny has calmed down, though at times it seems like he barely has a grip on it and there are moments when there are still explosions of energy and movement. Only Ike has grown very little. He is still the shortest one in the group and wears clothes from a year ago. His pant legs don't touch his shoes anymore though, so that's a good sign. His eyes are still wide and he is still looking everywhere with a sense of awe. They are sitting in the first pew and Pastor Scharke is standing in front of them instructing them about tomorrow, Easter Sunday, the Sunday of their confirmation, will go. He gestures with one hand and rests the other on his ample stomach straining the buttons of his black shirt. He looks up and smiles.

Oh there she is.

Welcome LouAnn.

He holds out both arms and goes around the pew to walk down the red carpet to the back of the church.

We missed you.

The boys turn. LouAnn is standing back there, but she is lit from behind by sunlight from a stained glass window so they can't really see her. None of them have seen her for a year. Come boys, Scharke says as he passes them. Let's welcome LouAnn back into the fold. They all walk slowly up the aisle. The reverend is in front of them and is blocking their view so that they still can't see LouAnn. And then he is hugging her and they all see it and stop.

The arms that wrap around the pastor's black shirt are covered in scarred skin. Not just pink but orange and red. The skin looks like bubble gum that's been chewed and stretched tight. The fingers don't appear to have joints to them anymore where the fingers could bend. Indeed, they don't look like fingers at all anymore. They are merely claw-like things that have grabbed the older man, pulling him in and away from them. But he does pull away and he is smiling. A bead of sweat has broken out on his forehead and a lock of hair, usually combed straight back off his face and held in place with shiny pomade, has come loose and dangles towards his glasses. See? I told you boys, he says. LouAnn made it back in time for her confirmation.

And he points toward the girl, but he doesn't really need to because they are all already looking at her. She wore a sleeveless blouse. All the way up to her shoulders was nothing but scar tissue. She held her arms away from her body as if she were about to reach out to them. But this time they could not escape. To a man, they felt as if their feet were planted to the floor. They could not take their eyes away from her. She reached up to her face and brushed a strand of hair away from the edge of her mouth. The arm didn't bend as it moved, like her joints didn't work anymore. The edges of her mouth struggled with a smile. And she held what used to be her arms out to them and took a step in their direction.

Look at this, she said.

Look at this.

Look at this.

HERE

AS SOON AS THEY turned the corner, he could see her.

For as long as he could remember, it was always the same. Mom (or Dad, so rarely he couldn't even remember) always went the same way, and as soon as she turned the corner he would look six houses down and to the left. And he would see her. If she knew he was coming, she was always there on the porch, waiting. Today was no different. There she was, as usual. But wait, something was different this time. And had been for a while. Usually she would be looking to her right, looking down the street for their car. But recently, and especially today, her head was rotating. He watches as they get closer. Her head is turned to the left, away from them. Her neck is stretching out away from her body, and she is making short little jerking movements. It reminded Ike of a bird he once saw in their backyard. The jerking would continue as she turned her head, but sometimes she would pause. It looked like she was scanning. As Ike and his mother got closer, he could see that she was squinting. By the time they were pulling into the driveway, the old woman on the porch had turned her head all the way to the right and was looking directly at them. But she only blinked once and then twice before starting to turn away again.

The car door is almost impossibly heavy, and Ike struggled with it until his mother took hold of the outside handle and yanked it open in one clean movement. Ike stumbled out onto the curb.

"Sorry. I didn't. . .Sorry." Mom doesn't look at Ike when she says this. She has already let go of the door and is heading up the sidewalk to the old woman on the porch. She was clearly in a mood. She was mumbling, but after a few seconds it was loud enough for the whole street to hear.

". . .said he was gonna be here. . ."

"Where is Calvin?"

"Calvin. Said. He. Was. Gonna. Be. Here."

"Where is he?"

This inner-now-outer monologue about the virtues (or lack of virtues) of Ike's uncle continued until she got to the porch. From Ike's vantage point by the car, picking himself up and dusting himself off, it looked as if she jumped right past the steps and landed squarely on the porch floor. She was at the old woman's side in an instant. She cradled her mother's arm in both of hers and leaned towards her. The old woman was looking out by now. Out past Ike, out past the Galaxie 500 Ike and his mother arrived in, out to the street beyond.

"Mama. . .Mama, it's me. Kathryn. Your daughter." She is whispering but not. Ike is fourteen now, and just became a freshman in high school. Besides math and science and social studies and history, he is taking drama as an elective - and in drama class he has already learned what a stage whisper is. It is loud enough for everyone to hear, but still said enough like a whisper to appear as if it was only meant for the person next to you to hear. Ike's mom is stage whispering now. Except that she's not on stage, she's on the porch of Ike's grandmother's home, and she's talking directly into the old woman's ear - though not so loudly, of course, as to startle her.

She's stage whispering in real life.

And she continues.

"Mama. . .Mama. . ." She reaches up and turns the old woman's face so that she can look directly into hers. She keeps her fingers lightly resting on her mother's chin. She's almost over-enunciating as she speaks.

Enunciation. Another thing Ike learned in drama class.

"I'm here. Today. Just like I said I would be. Just like I told you. Remember? Remember how I told you? How I told you that I would come and get you. How I. . ."

And here her voice started to break.

". . .how I would come and get you. And take you. . .take you. . .and your things. . .somewhere very nice. . .very nice and very special."

And here she let go of her mother's face so that she could run her arm across her own face. Grandma searched her daughter's face. She reached out and traced the path of a tear as it ran down Ike's mother's cheek.

"Who? Who are you?" The old woman's voice shook as she spoke. Her eyes darted back and forth in front of her daughter. "Who are you? Do I know you? Do I know you? Do I know you?" She repeated the sentence over and over again. The sound faded until it seemed to echo on the inside of her mouth.

Mom made one last angry swipe across her face with the back of her hand. And as if on cue, a green pickup pulled up in front of the house, coming so close to the Galaxie 500 that it looked as if it were kissing the bumper. Uncle Calvin tried to squeeze himself between the kissing and then hurried around the front of the Galaxie, keeping his head down. Ike's mom had turned in his direction. She was sending what Ike, who had by this time made his way up to the porch and was hovering in the general direction of his mother and grandmother, could only describe as a death glare. In Uncle Calvin's direction. He was bounding up the sidewalk, all sweaty and flushed. Uncle Calvin was usually all sweaty and flushed, because he was a farmer and worked outside all day. His face and neck were always red, though you could see a line, a strong line, right below his collar where the skin was white. Same thing with his upper arms. He wore a blue work shirt with the sleeves rolled up past his biceps, and you could also see the end of the red lines and the start of the white lines there. Uncle Calvin usually smoked, a cigarette dangling from his mouth and bouncing when he talked. But never around Ike's mother. Because she didn't like it.

So he would arrive. Late, like he was today. With the cigarette just barely holding onto his lips. And he would make it about halfway before he would reach up, grab the cigarette, and flick it away from himself as if it never existed.

So Ike waited. As his mother glared over his grandmother and sent rays straight from the bowels of hell towards his uncle, Ike leaned against the porch railing and watched Calvin.

And waited.

And waited.

And bling! There it was, his arm out, and the little flash of white spinning over and over in the air and into the grass. And then Uncle Calvin was on the porch, bounding up without using the steps (like his mom) and wheezing a little bit from the effort (unlike his mother - cigarette). And flushed and sweaty (not like his mother at all, even at her most angry).

"Sorry. Sorry. . .Sorry. . . Hi Ike. Howya doin'?" Uncle Calvin didn't look in Ike's direction when he said this. Rather, he waved a calloused palm and five fingers towards him and kept his eyes focused on his sister's face. His sister, who at that moment had her arm around their mother's shoulders. Mother's fingers tapping Grandmother's arm.

"Sorry." Uncle Calvin said again. He shrugged. "Sorry. . .uh. . .I, you know. I lost track of time."

"Oh I know." It was Ike's mom's turn to not look at someone when she talked. Maybe it ran in the family. She gazed at her mother, who by this time had cupped her hands to her cheeks as if checking for a fever. Mom held her gaze on her mother. "Believe me, I know."

She turned to her brother and sighed. "Well, I hope you're ready. To lift. A lot of sh. . ." She paused and looked at Ike before continuing. "To lift a lot of stuff. I went through it. There are piles. Keep. Donate. Toss. I've already done some tossing, but you're gonna do some too. Because I shouldn't have to do everything. The keep pile is the smallest one. Of course. Because. . .well. You know. . ."

As she talked, she released her hold on Grandma and turned towards the front door. The door was already propped open, so Mom leaned into the screen and screamed into the interior of the house.

"Marge! Are you in there? Or did you just leave the front door wide open so that my mother could go and get herself killed?"

From a distance that sounded not only from the backyard but from all the way across the street, came a voice high-pitched and crackling with age.

"Sorry Kathryn! Sorry! I got her out there on the porch so that she could wait for you. But then I. . .well Kathryn, I hadda go poo. You know how I am, how I get, once I got that tummy thing."

Ike, who had moved a little closer to the drama, could hear his mother sigh and see her look over her shoulder at her brother with a look on her face. He could also see over her shoulder through the screen door into the house. There were lots of shadows, but one of them separated itself from the rest and began a slow rocking movement in their direction.

Marge, no doubt.

Ike's mom leaned even closer to the metal mesh of the screen door. She was so close that it looked as if she were wiping her nose on it. "Too much information, Miss Margie. Too much information honey." She was shouting again. Still. She gave another look at Uncle Calvin, including Ike in the look, before swinging the screen open and stepping inside. She took one last look over her shoulder.

"Calvin. You come with me. Ike. . ." She said this as she shook her head at her mother. "You stay with Grandma. Talk to her. You know how to do that, right? And by all means, do not. . ." She said this while already deep into the house, but talking loudly enough that the whole block could hear. "Do not let her hurt herself. Think you could do that?"

And then Uncle Calvin let the screen door slam, and they were both gone. Ike heard mumbling and shuffling and grunting and lifting. He stood next to the door, and it almost hit him as it swung open again. Uncle Calvin huffed and puffed as he appeared carrying a box so big that it looked like he was hugging it. Face included. He staggered down the steps and across the sidewalk towards his truck. Ike looked over at his grandmother. She hadn't moved in a long time. She was staring at the steps down to the yard. She hesitated for a moment and then stepped forward, reaching for the railing with both hands. Ike hurried forward and took both of her hands in his.

"No Grandma. No." He found himself talking slowly and over-enunciating like his mom did. He turned her and led her back to a white porch swing. He put his hands on her shoulders and eased her into it. She looked at him, confused, but didn't resist.

As he sat next to her, he heard his mother's voice –

"Talk to her. You know how to do that, don't you?"

– and he opened his mouth to obey. And closed it again. He sat staring out at the street, where Uncle Calvin was attempting to lower the tailgate while still holding onto the heavy box. He followed the sidewalk with his eyes until the road curved and he could no longer see. He kept his eyes on the vanishing point.

He looked.

And he waited.

"Where's the boy?"

He blinked. Grandma spoke again.

"Where did the boy go? There's supposed to be a boy. Here. There's supposed to be a boy here."

Ike looked at the old woman. She was also looking at the sidewalk where it disappeared around the curve in the road. Ike looked back and forth between her and the sidewalk.

"What Grandma?" This time she blinked. "What did you say?"

Grandma continued to stare off into the distance. Her fingers fluttered up to her face and tapped on her cheeks. "A boy. There used to be a boy here. And then he was gone."

Calvin stomped his way out of the house again, holding another enormous cardboard box. From deep inside the house came the hum of Ike's mom and Marge talking.

"I tried to find him. I went out and I tried to find him. I did. There was a boy. The boy was here. And I was. . . I was supposed to. . . supposed to. . . to watch him. And. . . and he was gone. . ."

Ike reached up and took his grandmother's hand away from her face. He held it tightly in her lap, and patted their combined fists with his other hand. "Grandma," he began.

"So I wait. I wait here for him. Here. For him. I think. . . I think he's going to come back. I will close my eyes. . . and I will open them. And he will be right here. Beside me. Where he was. Before I closed my eyes. And he was gone. . ."

With her free hand she reached up and covered her eyes. "I don't know where he is. . . I don't know where he is. . . He was here but now he's gone. . . He's gone. . . so I wait. . . I wait for him. . . for him. . . I know he will come back. . . He will come back. . . Here. . . He will come back here. . . I know that. . . "

By this time her shoulders were shaking and she was sobbing quietly. "If I wait," she said softly and into her hand, "If I wait here, long enough, he will come back. . . here. . . here. . . he will come back here. . ."

Ike squeezed her hand tighter. If such a thing was possible. Already he had very little feeling in his fingers. "Grandma. . ." He leaned in as he spoke. "Listen to me Grandma. . ."

The shoulders continued to shake. "If I wait. . . If I wait right here. . . right here. . . he will. . . he will come. . . back here. . . he will come. . . back here. . ."

She repeated the same phrase over and over and over again, softly, into her hand. Ike shook the hand gripped in his fist.

"Grandma. That's me. That's me. I'm the boy. I'm the boy you're talking about."

Grandma shook her head, her free hand still in front of her eyes. Ike continued, his voice shaking. "Grandma. That's me. I'm the boy. The boy who disappeared. I disappeared for a while. I was gone. But now I'm back. They found me. And now I'm back. Here with you. I'm back. They got me and brought me back. I'm here now."

She looked up then. She sighed, a deep heavy sigh that shook her whole body. Ike could feel it through his fingers. She sighed again before speaking.

"A little boy. . . He was so little. Too little to be by himself. And he wasn't. He was with me. But then he was gone. He was here but then he was gone. . . I lost him. . ."

"Grandma. . ." Ike tried again, shaking her hand with his.

". . .so I will wait. Right here. . . right. . . here. Until he comes back. And he will come back. . . he will. . . I just know it. . . I just know it. . ." Her shoulders began to shake again.

"Grandma. . ." Ike lifted her hand with both of his and brought it up to his lips. Not knowing what else to do, he kissed it. "Grandma, that's me. That's me. I was gone, but now I'm back. I'm back and I'm here. I'm here."

As if on cue, the screen door swung open and Ike's mom stepped out onto the porch. She stood for a second and watched Calvin as he shoved the two boxes around the back of his truck. It looked to Ike as if he was moving furniture around a room and couldn't find the ideal arrangement. Two boxes in, and it was already a struggle. Mom sighed and shook her head before turning to her mother and son. She sighed again and shook her head a second time. She held her hands out to her mother. For the first time, Grandma looked up and made eye contact with her daughter.

"Mom. . . Hi Mom. Hi Honey." Ike's mom reached out and touched her own mother's trembling cheek. "I know. . . I know. Honey, I know. I know. It's a lot." She crouched down in front of both of them. Her hand slid down Grandma's face to touch her on the arm. She held her there. Grandma's face followed her.

"Listen," Mom continued. "We're gonna take a little walk, okay?" She looked up briefly as Uncle Calvin stomped past them on his way back into the house, letting the screen door slam as he went. "We're gonna go in, and get a few things for you. And then," she patted her arm as she spoke, "and then, I'm gonna take you on a ride. You like car rides, right? Don't you like car rides? I'm gonna take you on a nice car ride. And we're gonna take you to your new home. You wanna go to your new home, don't you?

It's a beautiful place, isn't it? You even said so. You said it was the most beautiful place you ever saw. Didn't you? Didn't you say that?"

Grandma looked from her daughter to her grandson and back again. She said nothing. Mom took her hands and helped her stand up. Ike watched the two women as if from a great distance.

"Come on Mom." Ike's mom put her arm around his grandma. "You come with me, okay?" They both moved with a slow shuffle towards the door. Grandma leaned into her daughter and began to mumble.

"Boy. . .Where's the boy. . .There was a boy. . ."

Mom reached up and cradled her mother's head against her chest. "I know Mama. I know. . . I know. . ."

The two women continued to talk over each other as they slowly made their way into the house. Ike listened as the voices blended together with Uncle Calvin's and, no doubt, Marge's into a background hum. Ike closed his eyes and listened to the hum as it continued. It was like there were bees inside his head. He listened for a while until he heard the screen door creak. He opened his eyes and turned to see his mother. The look she was giving him wasn't exactly the death glare she had directed at his uncle earlier. But it was at least capable of putting someone in a coma. Ike stood quickly and stepped towards his mother.

"Were you napping?" His mother stood with one hand on the open door and the other on her hip. "Really" Didn't you just get up like two hours ago? Two hours?" She held up two fingers. "But I would never bring that up." Her hand went back to her hip. "Well, you better wake up - and pronto, buster. Uncle Calvin needs your help." She snapped her fingers. "So get off your butt and get in here. There are boxes to be lifted and moved and whatnot."

And then she was gone, headed, no doubt, in the direction of the humming. Ike stood slowly and stepped towards the door, in no absolute hurry to move in the direction of anything even remotely resembling physical labor. The door creaked again as he opened it. This time it sounded downright spooky. Uncle Calvin rushed past - he was carrying a much smaller box this time, but he still almost knocked Ike over. The boy stood for a minute and watched his mother and Marge hover over piles of stuff, moving items from one pile to the other. He stood quietly for a minute, hoping that being silent also meant that he was invisible. It had worked sometimes before. That was not something he had learned in drama class.

But not, alas, this time. His mother picked up a package from one pile and, without even looking up, held it out to him. "Here," she said. She sounded very tired. "I found this. It's for you. It's from Grandma."

He looked over at Grandma, who was sitting stiffly on the edge of her own couch. She was staring at nothing. He stepped around landmines that used to be his grandmother's belongings as he moved towards his mother. She shook the arm holding out the package.

And then it was in his hand, even though he didn't remember taking it. He turned it over in his hand. It was a brown paper bag. On one side, in his Grandma's handwriting, it said "For Ike." He reached inside.

It was two comic books. The covers were colorful, as comic books were. Super-heroes with muscles were jumping or flying or lunging toward or with or away from each other. Words were everywhere. He looked over at Grandma again as he slipped them back into the bag. He would look at them later, much later, in the privacy of his bedroom, long after he stopped moving boxes with his Uncle Calvin. And he would remember that he felt some kind of way about one particular cell where one super-hero bear-hugged another super-hero from behind.

But what he really remembered was the piece of paper that drifted down to the floor as he put the comic-books back in the bag. He picked it up and looked at it. It was a receipt for the comic books.

It had a date on it.

The date was a month after his sixth birthday, when he'd stepped off the porch onto the sidewalk.

She bought them after.

After.

She had hoped the boy would come back.

DIARY OF A DESCENT INTO HELL

<u>**September 1**</u>

So Coach says we have to keep a journal. I guess so he can actually prove he does something in P.E. besides sitting in his office and. . .

Oh yea, I have to turn this in. So forget that last part. Even though I'm fooling no one. I'm gonna keep this version for myself. Write what I want and keep it somewhere, hidden away from prying eyes. Tuck it under a mattress, like Anne Frank. Though come to think about it, I'm not sure where she kept her diary.

Anyway, I'll keep this one to myself. And turn in some other fictional bullshit.

Bullshit.

Ha! I wasn't even going to write the word. Since I never say it out loud. I want to but I don't. But it's so much fun to even write it down. But it's so much fun to even write it down. I think I need to write it a bunch of times.

BullshitBullshitBullshitBullshitBullshitBullshitBullshitBullshitBullshitBullshitBullshitBullshit

That was fun.

And.

I just thought.

I will write this. And I will send it to the school board. And make Coach lose his job. Because they'll see what a bad teacher he is. No, not just a bad teacher, but a monster. No, not a monster, but the devil himself.

The devil.

Okay, well maybe I won't show this to the school board. Could you imagine? Regardless, Coach is still the devil. And I'm still going to write this. Because it makes me feel better. And because it's the truth. And that's what's important here, right?

So abandon hope all ye who enter here (yes, I'm fifteen - and yes, I know Dante. So suck it.). What follows is my experience in hell.

September 8
Jumping jacks.
Leg lifts.
Pushups.
Squats.
Side rotations.

I'm forgetting some, I know. Fifteen of each, though to be honest my soul leaves my body after three or four and goes to a sacred heavenly place with my patron saint Barbra Streisand until the pain is over. So I'm just guessing 15 repetitions of that. Whatever that was. And that was after the dreaded locker room experience. You change out of your clothes until all that is left is your white cotton undies and your equally white skinny body. And then, as if you're not embarrassed enough, you then put on a pair of shorts with leg holes so big that I could wear them (the leg holes) around my chest, and a T-shirt with arm holes so big I could wear them (the arm holes) around my waist. Skinny white arms and skinny white legs for all to see.

And while I'm trying to hide behind my locker door so that no one can see, I am surrounded by members of the basketball team and members of the softball team and members of the track team and members of the wrestling team, all swinging free and snapping towels like nobody's business.

Why do they even have towels already, since we don't do the shower thing until after.

More on that later.

No, actually, do you wanna hear about the showers? Do you? Because it's a topic. Because they actually expect you to take a shower after all of this. Whatever this is. Take off all of your clothes, even the white cotton undies, and walk into a large, tiled area where you turn on water and get all wet and risk that all of these bros might actually join you? In all their towel-snapping glory. Not that they'd actually have their towels in the shower.

But you know what I mean.

I don't wanna be naked in front of these people anywhere, but especially not in a shower. So maybe I won't take a shower. It's not like Coach is checking. Though the idea of taking P.E. fourth period. And then having to go through lunch. And fifth period. And sixth. And seventh. All sweaty and. . . All sweaty.

Maybe I'll wear my underwear.

Yeah, I'll wear my white cotton undies.

Because they don't need access to my privates. If even only to point. And laugh.

And joke about how theirs is so big. And mine is so small. Though most of them have failed Algebra I, so that handling a ruler even is like taking Trig.

But then there might be touching.

Or, actually, yanking.

Because none of these assholes. . .

Assholes. Another great word. I'll take it out when I give this to the school board.

None of these assholes have exactly a soft touch. If you know what I mean.

So my choices are smelling bad the rest of the day. Or shower in my drawers and have soggy drawers for the rest of the day.

Or. . .

I could go without my drawers.

I hear that's a thing.

September 15

Basketball.

We start with basketball.

Because that's coach's thing. He lives and dies by the basketball season.

Which I mainly know about because I play in the pep band. So on Tuesdays and Fridays I go back to school, because it's so much fun to begin with, and I sit in the bleachers until my back hurts and blow my French horn when the pep band plays "25 or 6 to 4." Again and again and again.

Unless we're losing.

I don't think we have a song for when we're losing.

Maybe "Bye Bye Miss American Pie."

Which is not the name of that song. But whatever.

So I'm also taking a drama class. Or rather I did. And who would have thought that one would have anything to do with the other. But your boy here has some skills. And your boy is gonna use those skills to help him pass P.E.

This is how it works. Coach picks jock one and jock two to be "captains" for the two "teams." And then he stands there and scratches himself while the two pick their players.

I don't even need to tell you who ends up being the last man standing. But I will.

It's me.

No one wants to play with me, because everyone knows I can't play. What, Ike run down the court? And catch a ball? And dribble the ball?

I don't even know how to spell dribble. Is that right?

So, granted, I don't want to play with any of them either. Still, it stings just a little bit, standing there all by myself until one of the jocks rolls their eyes and has to take me.

But back to the drama/P.E. hybrid thing.

Because, after the teams are chosen, Coach goes back into his office. And sixteen horny teenage boys are basically left to their own devices. And I will say, to their credit, most of them do make at least a decent effort at actually playing the game. Running up and down, yelling, throwing the ball to each other, making the occasional basket. Pulling at their junk the entire time. And I do mean, the entire time.

Jesus.

And I sit on the bleachers the entire time. Which I don't mind in the least. There are one or two other kids sitting out this glorious experience, gawky, skinny kids like me. And I should be friends with these kids, but I'm not for some reason. So I make a mental note to look into that at some future date.

But right now, I'm making myself eligible for an Oscar.

Because who should make their grand re-appearance into the proceedings but Coach.

"You been out to play yet, boy?" he yells.

At me.

Boy.

Huh.

Which is when my massive amount of acting training kicks in. I lean back and wipe my forehead. My mouth drops open and I start breathing so hard it's like I'm imitating porn sounds.

Not that I've ever watched porn. But from what I've heard. . . .

"Yeah Coach," I yell back. Breathing heavily of course. "Yeah. I was just out there. I just sat down."

More wiping of forehead. If I could sweat on cue, I would. Coach grunts and heads back into his office.

Babs would be so proud. And she has an Oscar.

September 22

Shit.

Coach figured it out.

Today, after the teams were picked, Coach stayed in the gym. "I want that boy to go in," he announces to everyone.

And he points.

At me.

I look around. Everyone's looking at me like I just farted. Coach snaps his fingers and waves me onto the court, where the most miserable jocks, and almost jocks are standing, looking like they wished they could fall through the floor. I stand slowly and move forward with weighted, heavy, Frankenstein feet. I'm the one who's praying for a vast hole to open up beneath me.

And the game begins.

And he stays to watch.

Shit.

So it's time to act again. Act like I can't get out from behind the al-most-jock supposedly "guarding" me. Act like I'm getting lost in the crowd of horny teenagers whose shorts are too short for their own good.

Though technically, I'm not acting. Because I am getting lost. I am ducking behind every human being I can. I don't want anyone to throw a basketball at me. I might break a finger. And even if, by some mira-cle I were able to catch said basketball, I would then have to dribble towards the basket.

Dribble.

Now there is a thing I can't do. Bounce a ball against the floor while running, a level of hand-eye coordination that I am just not capable of. I can barely walk. But I take the ball in both hands, when I some-how manage to catch it, and I run with it in what is, I think, the right direction. Which in theory is what you're supposed to do.

Except Coach has a whistle. And he blows the whistle. Because carrying the ball without dribbling it is something called "traveling." And I travel all the time, because I can't dribble. And that, as they say, is that. No one throws me the ball anymore. After a while, I don't have to hide behind anyone anymore. All I have to do is run around like an asshole.

September 29

Coach again.

He blows that whistle of his. And points at me. Of course. "You," he yells (because I have no first name). "You," he says again. Then he points to everyone else on the court. "Throw him the ball."

So now, it seems that not only must I run around like an asshole, but I must wave my arms and call out for someone to throw a ball at my head.

Heaven help me.

October 6

I caught a ball.

And I broke my finger.

Hmmmm. . .

See September 22.

I hate to say I told you so, but. . .

One plus though. No physical activity for six weeks. So no P.E. Doctor's orders.

What a pity.

November 17

Six weeks of fourth period in the library has been heaven on earth. But now I'm back in P.E. class, and I feel like I have entered the seventh circle of hell.

Wrestling.

I don't think I even realized that was a thing. Two guys throwing each other down onto a blue mat and hold each other in a variety of positions. Which in theory sounds positively delightful (sounds, in fact, a lot like that porn that I've heard so much about), but which in reality turns out to be pretty godawful. A lot of grunting and sweating and pulling and slipping away from each other, only to go at it, and each other, again.

For three periods of two minutes each.

Six minutes.

Which might as well be infinity.

Six minutes of this. All so that one guy ends up on his back for three seconds. While the other guy holds him there. And I suppose that I could in theory simply allow myself to be "pinned" for those three seconds. Believe me, it wouldn't be hard. Fall onto my back, let the jock fall on top of me, and that would be the end of it. Thank god.

But somehow, I can't seem to let that happen. Odd, but I can't. So I grunt and sweat and pull and slip away as best I can.

As best as I know how.

December 1

So I wrestle Joey because it's done by weight, and he's a skinny little twerp like me. But he is also a spazz - and when I say spazz, I mean he is wired for sound. Wrestling him is like riding in the drier and he is the clothes and he is all over you all the time.

I can hardly keep up.

And yet I try the best I can. And at the end of six minutes I am exhausted and sopping wet with sweat. And somehow, miraculously, the score is tied.

Tied.

Shit.

Which means that we go again, and the first one to get a point wins. So somehow he falls, and I fall on top of him. And I hope and I pray that I can hold all of those clothes in one place until the drier steps in.

Three. . .

Two. . .

One. . .

And someone smacks the mat. And it appears that I may finally, for once in my life, have actually won something.

But later that night, actually later that afternoon, my chest starts to hurt. I mean, really hurt. It's like I can't breathe. After three days, which is the deadline after which she will incur a medical bill, my mother finally takes me to the doctor. And the verdict. . .

I mean, the diagnosis? A cracked sternum. Which means no physical activity at all, for (once again) six weeks. I'm barely allowed to walk.

And just in time for the holidays too.

January 12

I must apologize.

WARLOCK

VOO LAY VOO KOO Shay
Ah Veck Mwah
Ses Swaw
Voo Lay Voo Koo Shay
Ah Veck Mwah. . .
They repeated the first part of the song over and over and over again, even after the lyrics were sung in English.
Hey Sista, Go Sista
Soul Sista, Flow Sista
Hey Sista, Go Sista
Soul Sista, Go Sista. . .
Jan laughed.
That's French, right?
I think so. It's certainly not Spanish. Spanish is all I know.
Well. . .Spanish. And English. Obviously.
Obviously.
I wish they taught French at school.
I know. I wish.
Then we could know what they're saying.
Yeah. We could know.
What do you think?
What they're saying?
Yeah.
I don't know.
I don't either. I heard. . .
Yeah?
I heard 'Do you wanna sleep with me.'
Something like that.
Something like that. Yeah. Do you wanna fuck me. Maybe?
You think? Maybe. . .Yeah, maybe. . .

Yeah. . .
You think though? This song is over the radio.
So? It doesn't count if it's in French.
Really?
Yeah. Really. French makes it classy.
Classy. Yeah right. Well how the hell do I know? They only teach fucking Spanish at our fucking high school.
Ha! Fucking Spanish. You're right. . .Fucking Spanish!
And they continued singing their favorite part of the song as they drove down the road.
Voo Lay Voo Koo Shay
Ah Veck Mwah
Ses Swaw
Voo Lay Voo Koo Shay
Ah Veck Mwah. . .

When they arrived, the sun had already disappeared behind trees, though the forest still glowed gold on green.
Spooky, Ike said.
Their counselor had already set up his group's tents, and was directing teenagers where to put their stuff. Where to sleep. Mark was there, off to one side, talking to girls from another group. Of course. He waved when he saw them and trotted over, looking over his shoulder as he came. There was a bounce in his step as he walked, as there often was after he talked to girls.
Lutheran women. The best. Am I right? He almost shouted at them as he approached. Jan and Ike looked at each other, and Jan shrugged his shoulders. If you say so, he said, sighing.
Just then Ike saw their counselor, up to his waist in tents and wading his way in their direction. He waved at them like he was drowning, and one of them was supposed to throw him a life jacket. They moved in his direction, sans life jacket, and stopped when they got directly in front of him. His arm was high in the air, but his finger was pointing down.
This is your tent, he said breathlessly. I put it up for you. You're welcome.
And then he was away, to parts unknown. Ike and Jan looked at each other and burst out laughing. You're welcome! You're welcome! You're welcome! They gasped over and over and over again as they threw back their heads and howled. Ike rolled to the ground, his eyes closed.

He was wheezing with the effort to catch his breath. Jan fell on top of him, and for a second Ike could feel Jan's breath in his ear before the boy rolled onto his back.

For a minute they both stared up into the sky. The golden glow was gone and little pinpricks of light were beginning to appear in the dark blue sky. The moon was full. Ike and Jan had talked many times about the image they saw on the moon, and what it looked like. Tonight, it looked like a buffalo, but a buffalo that was falling onto its back. The legs looked like they were kicking out and away. Maybe kicking moon men off of his home.

Jan's breath was warm in his ear.

Wanna go in?

Where?

The tent. Our tent.

They scurried up, little tufts of grass flying out from underneath their feet. The flap was open, and they bent down to crawl in. Their sleeping bags were open and laying side by side in the small space. They lay on top of their bags for a moment without speaking. Their bodies were barely touching.

So we're seeing a witch? Jan whispered.

Why are you whispering? Ike practically shouted back.

I don't know. Don't want him to hear me?

If he's a real witch, then he'll be able to hear you no matter where you are. . .

I never thought about that. . .

And he's not a witch. He's a warlock.

Warlock? What's a warlock?

A male witch, you dumb bunny.

And they laughed at that. Dumb bunny indeed.

They weave their way between the tents. It is so dark by now that they trip over the ropes attached to spikes in the ground. And also other tents. They trip, they fall, they giggle, they get up. They continue to weave. In the distance is a bonfire, a chunk of flame that seems to get farther away the closer they get. Finally there is fire fully in front of them. Teenagers surround the pile of burning wood. Mark has his arm around a girl they've never seen before. Scattered amongst the crowd is the occasional adult. From the expression on their faces, most look as if they're trying to pass a kidney stone. Jan stopped and sighed.

What?

All the best seats are taken.

Ike shook his head.

The seating is in a circle around the fire. Every seat is a good seat.

Jan nodded. The expression on his face was one Ike can't read.

Yeah, I suppose that's true. His eyes darted across the crowd of people. Though I do suppose it depends on where the Warlock is gonna stand.

Ike nodded in agreement just as Mark, with his free hand, waved to them. They trudged over, where Mark's other hand was floating in the general vicinity of the girll's left breast. Mark gestured to the log he and the girl were sitting on.

We got room. Sit next to us. He pointed next to the girl while his left hand inched closer to her breast.

Jan nodded again and scooted in next to the girl. Yeah, there's plenty of room here, he said, smirking. Especially since she's practically sitting in your lap.

The fingers on Mark's left hand twitched. That's me, just being a good friend. Giving you someplace to plant your ass. And with that, he pulled the girl closer to his side.

And his left hand came to rest in its final destination.

Ike slid into place on the log beside Jan, who leaned over and whispered in his ear.

Someone's hopin' to get lucky tonight.

And then he hummed. Quietly at first, so quietly that it felt like nothing more than a buzz on the inside of Ike's ear. But then it grew louder, until the buzz and the hum, and Jan's breath, filled Ike's ear and flowed out and seemed to touch the whole side of Ike's face. The humming had a melody to it, but Ike didn't recognize what it was until Jan started saying words.

Voo Lay Voo Koo Shay

Ah Vech Mwah

Ses Swaw

Voo Lay Voo Koo Shay

Ah Veck Mwah. . .

And the words got louder and louder until they filled up Ike's head and came out of his mouth and Ike was singing too, Jan and Ike singing together, the words pouring out and away from them like water, until it touched the next person and the next person and the person after that. Pretty soon, everyone sitting around the bonfire was singing. They all knew the words and they were singing.

Seemingly out of nowhere, a young man bounded into the center of the circle. Backlit by the fire, he looked like a shadow. When he stepped forward to talk and stabbed his hands into the air for emphasis, features could be seen. Glasses. Dark hair parted perfectly to one side and slicked across his scalp. Hands that were moving as if weaving a spell in the air.

Hey there, ladies and germs! Everyone having a good time?

Scattered cheering and applause.

Lotsa food, am I right? I ate so much, I think I'm gonna. . .

Held his stomach, opened his mouth and made a guttural sound as he bent over.

Am I right? Huh? Am I right?

Significantly less cheering and applause. Someone off to one side shouted Barf much?"and the polite cheering was replaced with loud raucous laughter. Chants of Barf much, barf much rose out into the air with the sparks from the fire. The counselor held out his hands and waited for it to die down.

Yeah, yeah. I hear you. Well, let's get to the main reason we're here. It is my supreme pleasure to introduce our guest speaker for the evening. Once a member of the Charles Manson cult, he is here now, about to be in front of you, a born-again Christian. He's here to talk to you about his life before Christ. Ladies and gentlemen, it is my supreme pleasure to introduce to you. . .

Just then, a figure walked into the glow of the fire. Ike remembered seeing pictures of Charles Manson in the newspaper when he was arrested. And from where Ike sat, this man looked like Charles Manson. Or Jesus. He also looked a lot like the images of Jesus Ike saw in Bibles and picture books and stained glass windows in church. Long brown hair, just uncombed enough to look like it had been blown in the wind. Full beard, but trimmed to within an inch of its life. Yes, either Charles Manson or Jesus. It was, Ike decided, a surprisingly fine line.

Jesus Manson strolled around the fire, his hands open, his palms out. He was smiling like he had a secret . But it wasn't a secret, it was a story. A story about a famous Hollywood director who made an equally famous movie about a woman whose baby belonged to the devil. The only problem was, it wasn't fiction. It was autobiographical. A year after the movie came out, the director and his Hollywood starlet wife were going to have a baby - a baby which was, according to Jesus Manson, promised to the devil. However, the couple changed their minds. At the time, JM belonged to a very powerful coven in Los Angeles, and members of the coven were asked to go claim what rightfully belonged to the antichrist.

And they tried. God knows they tried. They even cut into the starlet's stomach to try and retrieve the fetus. Which, of course, they couldn't do. It was dead. As was everyone else in the house at the moment.

All of this JM described in great detail. Silence wrapped around the fire as everyone listened, almost without breathing.

Just then Ike smelled something. It smelled like no one had taken out the garbage for more than a week and something - actually everything - had gone rotten. Ike looked over at Jan, who was waving his hand in front of his nose as if that would make it go away. He giggled when he caught Ike's eye.

That's not you, is it? He leaned in to whisper.

Ike recoiled as if he'd been slapped. No. He frowned. I thought it was you. He looked over at other people listening to JM. Looking over shoulders. Wincing. Holding noses. It was there and it was sliding into and in between and around JM's story. And it was getting stronger. It was as if the smell had grown legs and was heading in their direction.

Jan was still leaning into Ike. He giggled again.

It's a monster. And it's coming to get us, he said. By that time he was holding his nose. Ike bent over and gagged. The smell was everywhere. There was no smell of fire, no smell of sweat, no smell of fresh air. There was no smell of anything except this rotten trash monster who, if the smell was any indication, was almost right on top of them.

And then it wasn't.

As JM went on about the blood and gore that took place with the director and his wife. As Ike and Jan looked at each other with wide eyes. Holding their breath. . .

The smell that was so strong it threatened to eat them alive. The trash monster smell. It started to lessen. Ike, pinching his nostrils closed, opened his mouth. He could almost taste it. Almost. He let go of his nose and took a small breath. And then a larger one. And an even larger one.

It was almost there. Like something that lingered even after it was gone. Like a memory. He looked over at Jan, whose hand was covering his mouth. His eyebrows were raised expectantly.

It's gone, Ike said, breathing deeply.

Jan moved his hand, almost in slow motion. His whole body heaved up and down as he took huge breaths. He was almost gasping for air.

What was that? He inhaled and exhaled. It was like a monster was coming to get us and then left without. . .

Ike looked around at the other people around the fire and shrugged. They were still listening to JM's story. But chests were moving up and down. Heads were tilted up to the sky. Mouths were open and taking in large gulps of air. JM himself didn't seem in the least bit phased by any of it. He was deep into his story. So deep, in fact, that he was almost finished. He was wrapping it up.

With this one sentence.

And that, ladies and gentlemen, was the devil at work.

Back in the tent. The time for witches and warlocks and trash monsters is done. Perhaps. Ike and Jan were both on their backs looking up at the ceiling of the tent, which they cannot see. Jan laughed.

That was intense, wasn't it.

Yeah. Intense. That's a good word for it.

And spooky.

Yeah. Spooky is an even better word.

The laughter died down. Silence floated through and filled the tent. They still can't see the ceiling, though if Ike squinted really hard, he thought he could see a brightness that was the moon shining through. Ike can't see Jan either. But he can hear him. And feel him.

More silence. And then Jan rolled over on top of him. Ike can feel his breath on his face. Ike blinked. Blinked again. Jan's face slowly comes into focus. He is so close. And so heavy.

Hello there.

Hello.

Intense. . .So intense. . .

And spooky. Spooky too. Don't forget spooky.

Pause.

Speaking of intense. . .

Yes?

Speaking of intense. . .You wanna?

Wanna what?

You know. . .

His face filled Ike's entire field of vision.

You know.

His mouth was on Ike's mouth. His breath warm and filling Ike's with warm. And then there was tongue. So much tongue. And it was everywhere and touching everything. Teeth and tonsils and that little thing that dangles from the back of your throat. It fit. Somehow.

Jan pulled away. He was taking short little gasping breaths. He was maintaining some crazy eye contact.

So you wanna?

It was so quiet inside the tent. No sounds from outside. Jan had stopped. Ike himself felt like he couldn't breathe. He swallowed hard.

Maybe. I don't know. I don't know. Maybe. Maybe not. Probably not. I mean, isn't he right outside?

Who? The Warlock?

No. Who knows where he is anymore. Our counselor.

Our counselor? You mean Mr. Barfman?

Yeah. Isn't his tent like right next to ours?

I don't know. Is it?

Yeah. I think so. I think so.

Jan sighed so hard that Ike could feel it in his own rib cage. Jan rolled onto his back.

Yeah. Okay. Maybe you're right.

Silence once again filled the tent. Quiet quiet more quiet. Quiet so thick it was like soup.

And then Jan started singing. Softly at first, like he was whispering in Ike's ear. And then louder and louder until it was all that Ike could hear. Until long after Jan went quiet and slept with a light snore. Until long after the concentration of light that was the moon spread across the sky and became daylight. He heard it all night. Until he sang it quietly. To himself.

Voo Lay Voo Koo Shay
Ah Vek Mwah
Ses Swaw
Voo Lay Voo Koo Shay
Ah Veck Mwah
Hey Sista, Go Sista
Soul, Flow Sista
Hey Sista, Go Sista. . .

AKIRA

HE HAD BEGGED HIS parents about this for months. Because raising five children wasn't enough and anyway Pete and Beth were both out of the house now anyway and he had his bedroom to himself now anyway so if it's a boy he could share his bedroom with him. Right?

Right?

And the begging went on and on and on, like only the begging of a seventeen year old can. Begging that rang out and bounced off the hills and came back and came back and assaulted his parents' ears. Begging that no doubt would have carried much more weight except that the hills of rural Illinois were barely hills. Nonetheless, in the confines of a two-story farmhouse with lots of small rooms, it was bad enough, and often sent one or the other of them scurrying to the basement (okay, technically a three-story house) to see how the furnace was working or whether or not there was another jar of canned green beans to bring upstairs for dinner. Not far enough, however, and the begging eventually took its toll.

And a foreign-exchange student would be coming to live with them for Ike's senior year.

Which is why months later, Ike is standing with his parents and his fifteen year old sister and his seven year old brother outside gate eleven of the closest (almost two hours away) international airport.

And he comes bounding out and into view of the waiting family.

Well, "bounding" might not be the right word for how he moves, though what he does is certainly very fast. As a matter of fact, what first strikes Ike about Akira was how his body moved when he walked, how much his hips shifted so far from side to side, how one leg would step wholly in front of his body, and then the other one. It was as if he was walking a single line on the floor.

And then he is among them. And Ike's family are not big huggers, being somewhat stoic by nature and more than somewhat German by nature. But Akira is hugging, hard, first Mom, and then Dad, and then Little Sister. He pauses and takes Little Brother's hand as if it's a delicate thing that might break. He bows to Little Brother, slowly and reverently, while the others are trying to catch their breath. And then he was all over Ike, hugging so, so hard. And in that moment Ike, immediately, didn't know what to do with all of this.

That night they sat in the dark in Ike's bedroom and talked. Or rather, tried to talk. First, Ike turned off the light before he changed into his pajamas. Then Akira asked if he could turn the light back on to finish unpacking. So Ike waved in the direction of the light switch. In the dark, Ike hears him moving in that direction, clop-clopping as he goes. Ike has only known him for twelve hours and already he's noticed that he makes clop-clop sounds wherever he goes. It's the shoes he wears, but also the short steps he takes. Walking on a single line on the floor. He still has his shoes on now, and Ike flinches as Akira heads back towards his own bed against the wall on the other side of the room. Ike turns his head, still blinking, and watches him unpack. Every single thing he takes out of his suitcase is folded into an almost perfect square. Even the socks and underwear. He lifts every single thing with both hands and handles it like it's a raw egg as he carries it over to the chest of drawers that he and Ike will share. Ike had shoved all of his things into the bottom drawers so that Akira could have the top. Ike watches him as he goes back and forth between the bed and the chest of drawers, again and again and again and again. More trips than he can count.

And he feels like he should say something.

Wants to say something, in fact. He really does.

But he can't think of a single thing.

The next day is Akira's first day of school and Ike has to take him to the office. Molly, the principal's secretary, is a hefty woman whose ample breasts move like two restless children under her blouse every time she shifts her weight from foot to foot. And she does it constantly. Ike looks away, but Akira stares, his mouth slightly open. Molly clicks her brown (yes, brown) nails against the counter between them as they wait for the guidance counselor to print out Akira's class schedule. She tries to make small talk. She tells the boys how she ate in a Chinese restaurant once (which is totally beside the point, since Akira is Japanese) and she tried to use the chopsticks and she just couldn't do it. So she had to ask for a knife and fork. And is that how they eat in China all the time? Akira nods and keeps staring. Ike swallows hard and starts to count tiles on the floor.

Finally, piece of paper in hand, they make their way to Akira's first class - which, as it turns out, is also Ike's first class. English Four, which is taught by one Mr. Grey. The name couldn't be any more appropriate. He smiles like it's giving him cancer. One time, years ago, they read "A Christmas Carol" in class (because who hasn't already read that Dickens classic) and from that point on, year after year, his students have called him Ebenezer Scrooge. Behind his back.

Today, Ebenezer. . .er, Mr. Grey looks as if he can't quite pass a bowel movement. He holds the paper at arm's length and reads Akira's name out loud, rolling each syllable around in his mouth, trying, it seems, to find spaces between his teeth for each one. Finding none, he floats the paper in the general direction of his desk and in the specific direction of his trash can. Then he turns to the class and barks.

"Class!"

"Yes, Mr. Grey!"

"We know what's next, don't we?"

"Yes, Mr. Grey!"

"Alphabetical! Order!"

There is a slight pause as students look at one another.

"The last name starts with a K!"

More pause. And then students with the last names starting with L through Z shift up or down or over one seat. Mr. Grey gestures grandly towards the seat vacated by all the seismic movement and Akira, whose last name starts with a K, clop-clops towards it. Ike remains standing in front of the room letting this wash over him. Until he notices all movement, and indeed all sound, has stopped. He looks over and sees Mr. Grey looking at him. Grey's eyebrows are raised and his arm is out in another grand gesture.

"Seat," he says simply.

The next weekend is like every other weekend. No matter whatever else Ike wanted to do, certain things were a given.

Putting his work clothes on and following his dad around the farm all day was a given. Except that this time there was Akira. And he seemed to be everywhere these days. For instance, the tractor. Dad drove the tractor and Ike sat on the sideboard, the turning and vibrating of the tractor wheels underneath him like a comfort. But not today. Today Dad crawls up into his seat, and Akira is already up there, on the sideboard, his back to Ike. Dad barely looks at Ike.

"Thought Akira would like sitting there for a change. Since he's new here and all." He gestured behind. "You can hang on back there."

And off they go, Ike hanging on behind, Akira looking all around him as if he's never seen sky and ground and clouds and trees before. The tractor chugs up the hill and Akira is smiling out at the world. Ike's dad is staring straight ahead, like he's the only one on the tractor. Ike is holding onto the back of his dad's seat for dear life. Riding atop the wheel was one thing, all vibration and hum. Hanging off the back of the machine was something else altogether different, all violence and rattle. He barely stays on. Once they get up the hill he's more than happy to jump off.

Except that means the ride is over and he now has to do his job - which was to hook the tractor up to the manure spreader. Which he could do maybe 60 % of the time. And today is not one of those days. The holes on the tongues don't quite match up. And he is supposed to then yank the tongue of the manure spreader over to line the two machines up. But the spreader is full, and even heavier than normal. And he is weak.

Just weak. As he always is.

And he can't do it and his dad is yelling at him because he has to get down off the tractor himself and do the work himself, all the work himself and he yanks the tongue over and it lines right up and he slips the pin in and he's yelling at Ike the whole time, the whole time, about how he has to do everything himself, all the time.

All the time.

And Ike stands off to the side. And he doesn't know what to do, or what to say, or where to look. So he looks up and he sees Akira, who is still smiling.

He is looking down at Ike and smiling.

He is smiling.

At him.

This year the high school is doing the musical BRIGADOON. In the fall. So that Mr. Grey could do a play in the spring. Even though Ike doesn't really know that show, he is nonetheless excited. He is nothing, after all, if not an actor. At least he thinks so - until he gets into the bandroom where the auditions were being held. And he has to sing his sixteen to thirty-two bars of "Almost Like Being in Love." There is no one else in the room except the band director, who could be related to Mr. Grey - at least in terms of his lack of cheerfulness.

And he's not smiling.

Of course. But still. . .

In that moment, Ike's throat closes up at the same moment that his sphincter opens wide. The sound coming from one orifice is tight and small and ugly, while the sound coming from the other orifice is. . .well, it's ugly too.

Now the band director is not only not smiling. He's also shaking his head. And when the cast list is posted on the bandroom door, he is cast as Andrew McLaren, the father of the heroine. A father again, who doesn't sing, after he played one of the "Papas" in FIDDLER ON THE ROOF last year. He went away from the door and cried a little bit before he went back and initialed his name.

Of course not enough boys tried out. There are never enough boys. And Akira wants to be in it. So. . . he is.

So now he's Scottish and Japanese.

And he's so excited. Even backstage he can't stand still. While Ike is off in a dark corner whispering his few lines to himself, Akira is back and forth and back and forth, in the dark backstage left. Then Ike sees his face open up as he no doubt remembers that he has to be on the other side of the stage. Akira dashes behind the curtain. Not dashes. Clop-clops. He's got the shoes on. And even when he's fast, he still walks the way he walks. Ike can hear the clop-clop sounds as they travel behind the curtain to stage right. Another cast member leans into Ike.

"Someone should probably tell Akira that he needs to be more quiet."

Ike can hear the laughter in the cast member's voice.

On opening night, Ike's parents take them both out to dinner.

"Isn't this exciting?" Ike's mom says to Akira. To Akira.

And then it's Saturday again. And once again it's time to empty the manure spreader. Which Ike pretty much filled on his own. So many pigs, so much shit. But scooping manure is one thing that Ike doesn't mind doing. Scoop, walk, drop. Scoop, walk, drop. There's nothing to it. And when he walks he thinks. And when he thinks, he dreams. And when he dreams, he makes up stories. Stories about old women who were witches. Witches who reached out with their sharp talons and kidnapped little children and made them do horrible things.

Make them do horrible things.

He told part of his story to his little sister once. She looked at him like it hurt her eyes to do so.

"That's just Hansel and Gretel. Just with no Gretel. No one will read that. You Dumb Bunny."

Dumb Bunny. Her insult name of the moment. She walked away, leaving "Dumb Bunny" ringing in Ike's ears. And he decided at that moment that there would be no more sharing of his thoughts. His dreams. His stories.

They weren't just anything.

But nonetheless. . .

He had filled the spreader while dreaming. And now it was time to empty it.

Akira was not with them today. Mom had taken him somewhere. Shopping to buy American clothes or some such thing. So Ike and his father were alone together today. And Dad was not on his best behavior. He would stare out as he was driving, but then frown and blink and look away for a second.

And when he backed the tractor up to the manure spreader, the tongues weren't even close. Ike rolled his eyes and pointed but his father frowned and nodded to where the tractor and the spreader couldn't possibly be connected. Ike jumped down and pulled on the tongue of the spreader, knowing full well he couldn't move it over enough to slip the pin in.

And that's when Ike's father started to yell. Lots of words, very loud, and so fast that Ike couldn't even understand most of them.

Though he did hear one word.

He heard one word loud and clear.

Lazy.

He heard lazy.

Ike bent down and renewed his efforts. His father could do it because he was strong. His older brother could do it because he was kinda strong. But he, Ike, couldn't do it, no matter how hard he tried. He looked up to tell his father there was no way he could do this, could he please come down and help him.

When something hit him on the head.

Hit him on the head hard.

And Ike had often heard that when people got hit so hard that they saw stars. He saw it on Warner Brothers cartoons, and may have even used it himself in one of his stories once. But until this moment he had always thought it was something reserved for cartoon land or his stories. But now there were flashes of light surrounded by a darkness so intense he thought he could get lost in it. He shook his head, the flashes of light lingering. He jerked his head up to look at his father and felt the throbbing.

And then he saw that part of the tractor was sticking out from behind the seat. He had lifted his head into it so hard that it knocked his cap off.

"What?" His father asked, fire burning in his eyes. Ike almost screamed back.

"I thought you hit me!"

"No." The word was almost spit out of his father's mouth. "But maybe I should have."

Maybe I should have.

Ike is in bed with his face turned to the wall. He heard Akira's voice in the darkness of the bedroom.

"Ike?" Akira says.

Ike holds his breath for a second before speaking.

"Yes?"

Ike hears the rustling of sheets. Akira has sat up in bed.

"Did I do something wrong?" Akira asked.

Ike held his breath again, but this time let the air out in a big sigh.

"No." His answer was blunt. He hoped that was enough.

It wasn't.

"Are you angry at me?" Akira continued.

Ike curled into himself, his knees touching his chest. He waited. He waited. He waited.

"No," he said finally.

Ike's mother sat across from him at the kitchen. She looked as if she were about to cry.

"Your father and I have been talking," she began. And paused and coughed. "We've been talking. And we're not sure that we'll be able to come see your shows anymore."

Ike thought he was going to vomit. He stuttered before he could speak.

"Wh. . .Why? Is it because of me and Dad?"

His mom swallowed. Hard. "You want us to pay for school and yet you won't help your father when he needs you to. So no more." She turned and left the room, the words trailing behind her.

"No more."

Ike sat for a long time after, looking at his hands.

He looked down at the piece of paper in his hands. It was folded so that he couldn't see the message written inside. Not that it mattered. He had it memorized before he wrote it down:

We were told we would only have Akira first semester. It is now almost halfway through second semester. Please find Akira another home for the rest of the school year.

When he walked into the office, Molly was resting her ample bosom on the counter. Her brow furrowed in intense concentration as she studied a folder resting on the counter in front of her. Just then, the phone on her desk rang, and she held up one finger as she turned to answer it. Ike waited but a second before stepping up to the counter. He put the folded paper on top of the folder and backed quickly out the door.

Once he was clear of the office, he turned and ran.

That was a Friday. On Monday Ike's parents were informed by the school that a new home had been found for Akira. He was gone by the end of the week. And once he was gone, no one spoke of him again. And on Saturday, Ike was once again in his rightful place, sitting on top of the wheel while his father drove the tractor. And when it was time to hook up the manure spreader, the tongues lined up and Ike slipped in the pin like he'd been doing it all his life. His father doesn't look at him as they ride. Rather, Ike studies his face as he stares out and away. He frowns and blinks, then shakes his head and stares again. Ike looks off in the distance and sees nothing. He has no idea what his father is looking at.

Until the next day.

It is Sunday and the family is at church. Ike looks up from his hymnal - he knows the words by heart - and he sees the gaze again. He'd never seen it here before. He followed his father's eyes, and this time he saw, at the front of the church, the large stained glass window of Jesus cradling a lamb in his arms. Ike looked back at his dad and saw the look he'd seen the day before.

He stared, frowned, blinked, stared.

Stared, frowned, blinked, stared.

Again.

And again.

And again.

SHOES ON THE LINE

EVERY DAY I WENT to school through this one neighborhood. The houses are all squat brick, usually painted one color with no accents. Dogs with saggy breasts run free and dart in front of your car. I drive real slow, because I don't want to run over anyone's pet. And it gives me time to look at where I am. So one day I'm driving slowly, but I want to go faster because I noticed it was 8:02, and I was already two minutes late, when something caught my eye. Up in the air, like a bird. So I look up and see a pair of tennis shoes hanging from the telephone wire. Their shoe strings were tied together so that the shoe was hanging on either side of the wire. Every day from that point on, I would look for the shoes when I drove by. Eventually a second pair of tennis shoes joined the first pair, and a little while after that yet a third pair joined the first two. And with each pair that hung there, the wire sagged closer and closer to the ground. I began to wonder if perhaps the wire would eventually break under all that weight. But there it was, day after day, bowed but unbroken, gathering more and more pairs of shoes. The shoes on the wire became a metaphor for me - I don't need to explain why. If you don't understand now, you will. At least I hope so.

Hope.

Now there's a good word.

THE JOKE

I'M NOT GAY. BUT $20.00 is $20.00.

Ike had heard before about the whole making eye contact from across a crowded room thing. But he thought it was basically bullshit. But now here Ike was, and there he was, across the room. And they were looking at each other. What was supposed to be next wasn't entirely clear - it wasn't like there was a manual or anything - except maybe close the distance between them. But as soon as Ike thought it, it was happening. He was heading across the room towards Ike, weaving his way between bored and horny and drunk couples and triples and singles talking to each other and themselves. And maintaining some crazy eye contact, and not bumping into a single soul on the way. Very impressive indeed.

And then he was standing right in front of Ike, who was tall now. But he was even taller, and he tilted his head down to keep the eye contact going.

"Hey," he said. Short. Sweet. No blinking.

"Hey back." Ike was trying so hard to sound smart and cool and sexy. And he wasn't so bad. First of all, he was 19. And young by itself had a certain degree of hotness to it. Blonde hair (though it was already thinning more than perhaps it should be). Porn star moustache. Cheekbones. Thin Body. Certainly worthy of a certain degree of looking. But he was taking it farther than maybe Ike could handle. He felt a little out of breath.

"Are you alright?" he smiled as he said this. Which was a change. His face was soft and round and every single other feature on his face - his eyes, his nostrils, even the skin on his cheeks, which was starting to flush from the effort - looked like it hurt to support that smile. His hair, wispy and pointing at an angle away from his head, looked like it was trying to escape.

But it was there, that smile. And he was working hard to keep it there. Ike appreciated the effort at least. He was breathing again. Ike broke eye contact and looked down as he tucked his shirt back into His pants. He looked back up.

"Okay. I'm okay," Ike said. And then looked down again. Because he had reached out and taken Ike's hand. The hand (his, not Ike's) was mushy, though the grip was firm. He held onto the hand and led Ike to a quiet corner. Or semi-quiet, since there was noise everywhere, and really, this was the only place that had two empty seats.

And they talked. Or rather, He talked and Ike listened. Or asked questions and then listened. Ike told him how he was born and raised on a farm, and how his father had wanted him to grow up to be either a farmer like him, or a minister. When it became obvious that wasn't going to happen, Dad walked around the house sighing. For weeks. And then wrote a check so that Ike could go to college to learn how to do something "more artistic."

His words, not His father's.

And that check was the whole amount. Though just a farmer, he made too much money for his son to get scholarships. So that's the one thing Ike felt bad about. That it was costing his family so much money for him to go there. So much.

Even as it was coming out of his mouth, Ike was surprising himself. That it was coming out of his mouth. Why was he saying it? Who was this stranger that he would open up and talk about something that was so deep inside him? But this stranger just nodded and smiled - still looking pained, but nonetheless - his hands bent at the wrists, angling dangerously close to Ike's legs. And when Ike paused, and swallowed, because if he didn't he was afraid his voice would waver, he leaned forward, still nodding, almost invading Ike's personal space.

"I can help with that," he said.

"You can?" Ike was taken aback. "How?"

"I work for the university."

"Oh. You mean as a dorm counselor or something?"

"No. I work in financial aid."

You could have knocked Ike over with the proverbial feather. But he had but a moment to process the information, because he kept going. People didn't know about it, but there were moneys available.

There were always moneys available. Scholarships and whatnot. You just had to know where to look. Some of them were small. But every little bit helps, right?

Why yes indeed. Every little bit does help. So when he suggested he knew of a small (the word he actually used was "tiny") scholarship that Ike would be eligible for, he was all about it. I mean, who couldn't use $300.00. Right?

Right.

And all you had to do was fill out a couple forms.

Which he would have tomorrow. If Ike could find a moment to swing by his dorm room. Because, of course, he was also a dorm counselor.

The forms, when Ike got them, were surprisingly basic.

Name

Age

Social

Address

Year in School

Major

And a place to sign at the bottom of the second page. That was it. Ike held it out to him.

"And now. . .what? I do what? Wait? Until. . .?"

"You wait until. . .now."

With one hand he took the forms and floated them over onto a nearby desk. With the other, he held a check out to Ike. He hesitated before taking it. When he finally did, he held it at arm's length to look at it. A check. With Ike's name on it. Made out to the amount of $300.00. And in the upper right hand corner was his name. And address. And phone number.

A personal check.

"Oh," Ike said. And looked up to see him standing right in front of him. Frighteningly close, as a matter of fact. Frighteningly close.

Ike made a sound, like a "Huh," even though he could have been clearing his throat. He put his hand up, fingers spread, and rested them on Ike's chest.

And shoved.

Not hard, but just hard enough to tilt Ike towards the floor. Except there was a bed, somehow there was a bed, and Ike landed on his back on a mattress that couldn't have been any harder if it tried. But there wasn't even a moment to sit up and get up, because he was on his knees in front of Ike, between his legs, his hands on Ike's crotch and fly and belt, unbuckling and unzipping and yanking down his pants and underwear in a move so quick and clean it felt practiced. He cupped Ike's penis, which moments before had almost been curled into itself like it was cold outside, and rubbed it once, twice, three times. He bent over, as if he was going to put his mouth on it. But he pulled his head up and looked Ike in the eye as he fiddled with his own belt buckle. Suddenly his hands were shaking. It was taking forever. Ike sat up, but he pushed him back down. "Fuck. Fuck. Fuck," he kept saying, almost to himself. Once his pants were down, he started stroking himself, hard, fast, like he was angry. Ike lifted his head to see what he was doing. Slowly, so as not to catch his attention and get shoved back onto the bed. But it didn't matter. He was looking down and working his arm. The object of his attentions was below the bed where Ike couldn't see. But he knew.

Finally he looked up. He looked sweaty. He pulled Ike down to the edge of the bed and lifted his legs up in the air. He slapped Ike's ass, once per cheek, and then scooted in between. His hand was on himself again and he grunted and shoved.

And grunted.

And shoved.

Until he took his hand off, thrust about a half dozen times, stopped and grunted again.

The whole time Ike lay on the bed and watched him. He felt so far removed from all of this, as if he were watching this happening on TV. Not on the major networks, of course, but rather on some porn channel. If such a thing existed in the late 1970s. Ike felt nothing. Was he supposed to be fucking him? He'd never done it before, but Ike knew how it worked. He'd seen pictures. He was supposed to be in his butt. And Ike felt nothing. Except wet. Wet and sticky between his legs and on his crotch. Wet and sticky.

He pulled out from between Ike's legs and reached over to a bedside table. He snatched a single tissue in his sweaty hand and held it out to him.

"You should probably clean yourself up," he said as he dropped the tissue onto Ike's stomach. In one swift move - no more shaking now - he snatched another tissue off the table and turned away from Ike to wipe off his junk. "And," he continued, talking to the wall but not to Ike, "I would cash that check sooner rather than later if I were you."

Oh yes. The check. Ike stood, again so slowly. The tissue on his belly drifted to the floor. As Ike adjusted his clothing, the stickiness gluing his underwear to his ass, He looked around for the aforementioned check. The tissue found it and was resting next to it. The check looked wrinkled, like he had been kneeling on it mere moments before. Ike bent over and picked it up gently, holding it with his thumb and forefinger. He was nowhere to be found. The bathroom door was closed, and Ike could hear water running. "Thank you," he said, louder perhaps than he needed to, to the closed door and the water. "Hmmm," the water said back. "And thanks," he added. "Hmmm," the closed door responded. Ike moved quietly across the room to the door, opened it to leave, and closed it behind him as if there was someone sleeping inside.

A little ways down the hallway was a trash can. Ike made a beeline to it, lifted the lid and threw up inside. Once. Twice. Three times, After wiping his mouth with His sleeve, wishing he'd picked up the tissue along with the check, he looked at the check crumpled in his hand.

And he looked back at the trash can, where his barf lay nestled amongst soda cans and cigarette butts.

And back at the check.

And back at his barf.

Then he shoved the crumpled check in his pocket and went to the closest bank. He couldn't sign the back of the check fast enough.

And that was his first time.

What did one gay sperm say to another? How do we find an egg in all this shit?

Lucy in the Sky With Diamonds. That's what he called her after maybe their third class together. She had a tendency to burst into class after it had already started, the door swinging open and clunking against the wall. Her hair was long and brown and totally ignored the clip on either side that tried, with limited success, to hold it away from her round, chubby face. The backpack was always open, and her hand was deep inside, digging through a flurry of papers - never a stack, always a flurry - that eventually made their way to the floor around her. At least some of them. Her name was Lucy, as she loudly declared while dumping her ample ass into the empty seat beside him, the seat that forever after, at least until the end of the semester, was hers.

Lucy.

Who became, in very short order, Lucy in the Sky With Diamonds.

By the time they were given their first acting assignment in class, to do a scene, it was all but obvious that they would be partners. From the stack of scripts the professor dropped into the center of the room like they were hot turds, they were drawn to the one with the longest title. OH DAD, POOR DAD, MAMA'S HUNG YOU IN THE CLOSET AND I'M FEELING SO SAD. Or it might have been that it was the first script they picked up, shoved aside by others, perhaps, who were daunted by the long title. He would play a nervous, nerdy virgin Mama's boy, and Lucy would play a slut who tried to seduce him. . .

"I don't have to act! I just have to be myself! Fuckin' A!" Lucy screamed so loudly the windows in the classroom shook.

. . .but ends up dead.

"I don't have to act! I can just lay there!" More screaming. More shaking.

They dived in with a vengeance, clutching their scripts so hard that their knuckles turned white, and making really intense eye contact and all the other shit that make actors actors. Or what they were told by the professor made actors actors. The time flew by, and before they knew it the class was over.

It felt like they had just gotten started.

"Let's keep going!" Lucy gestured to the sky that would soon become part of her nickname. "Why don't we go back to my dorm? We can keep running it there. And. . ." Her face lit up as she had the idea. "You can meet my man."

"Man? Your man? You mean you got a boyfriend?"

"Don't worry dude." She tossed her head. "If I wasn't with him, then I'd totally fuck you. So. . ." She shrugged. "Even so, I'm not saying a three-way is totally out of the question. So put that in your hat and smoke it. Okay?"

That certainly gave him pause. A three-way with Lucy and some anonymous boy toy.

On the way across the quad, they ran lines. For about five minutes. And then Lucy would go off on a tangent. About how much she hated school. How she could tell she was about to start her period, because her breasts were sensitive. Which was a good thing, since there was that one time without a condom. . .

But mainly she talked about him. How they met washing their clothes at the same time in the laundry room of the dorm. How she had to show him how to separate the white clothes from the clothes with color, and in exchange he gave her his digits.

"Digits?"

"Phone number! Jesus. . ."

How he had maybe not the biggest penis she ever saw ("Okay, I've really only seen two others, but this one was smack dab in the middle!") but how he really ("I mean, really REALLY") knew what to do with it.

Information he could have lived without, and will never unhear. But they were almost to her dorm, and maybe, just maybe, he would forget about it someday. Someday. Maybe when he was 97 years old.

He was still thinking about it, as a matter of fact, when Lucy rapped on a door, and said door opened.

And there he was.

And at that moment he had two thoughts, more or less at the same time:

Could we maybe perhaps possibly revisit that idea of a three-way? And,

So he knows what to do with his dick, eh? That is, all of a sudden, not too much information. It is, instead, just the right amount of information.

Fuck. . .

There were dimples in both cheeks and chin, and lots of smiling, and a sweater and jeans that fit just right in all the right places, and a handshake that was warm and firm and friendly.

Double fuck. . .

Speaking of firm. . .

He was a psychology major and a dancer, and his name was Max, which was the most perfect name ever.

"Nice to meet you," Max said. The handshake seemed to go on forever. "Lucy has told me so much about you."

"Oh? So much? Dare I ask. . .like what?"

"Oh. . .well. . .lots. You know. . .so much. I mean, isn't that what you say when you meet a friend of a friend?"

And instantly, he was charmed.

"Friend of a FRIEND!? Bitch, please!" Lucy smacked Max in his muscled arm. Again. It seemed to be a thing with them.

As did him coming to visit. He lived off-campus, and who wanted to walk all the way back there after class? So he would wander over to see Lucy and Max. They went out for pizza and then came back and watched whatever TV they could find and agreed on to watch. Max had a VCR that he said he worked five summers to buy.

"But that's what I use to watch my porn on," Max overshared.

More smacking of his arm. "Bitch. . . You don't need porn. You've got me!"

Indeed.

Oftentimes they would play games. Uno had come out a few years before, and they would play it for hours. Lucy was a beast when playing Uno, snatching cards up and slamming cards down like she was fighting the devil. It was exhausting. So Uno wasn't an everyday kind of thing. They would play other things. Sometimes, for instance, they play Truth or Dare.

Truth or Dare.

What could possibly go wrong?

For no matter who spun the beer bottle - emptied by all three in varying degrees, though he couldn't help but notice that Lucy drank more than her fair share - and no matter who the bottle pointed to when it stopped, the questions were always about sex. Always.

Are you still a virgin?

If not, how old were you when you first "did" it?

Did it hurt the first time? (This one was directed to Lucy, who answered "Fuck me!! Yes!!")

Have you ever had a dick in your mouth?

Have you ever eaten pussy? ("Fuck me!!! No!!!" Also from Lucy)

Until he spun the bottle, and it pointed at Max. Suddenly the air around him was thick and heavy. He opened his mouth and then closed it. Opened and closed it again. He knew the question he wanted to ask.

"SSo have you ever done a three-way before?" He finally said instead.

Max's eyes flickered in the direction of Lucy and then back and down.

"Uh. . .no. . .would be the answer to that."

"So. . ." He hesitated. This would be like dancing with the devil in the pale moonlight. "That means you've never. . ."

Lucy's wail almost loosened the fillings in his mouth. He and Max both turned to see her shaking her fists in the air.

"No!! That's not how this works!" She was almost channeling Linda Blair in THE EXORCIST. All that was missing was the head spinning. "One question! That's all you get! One question per spin!" She flung her hands up in the air and brought them back down into her lap, slapping her thighs as hard as she could. "Goddamn, I have to take a piss! You fuckin' people make my bladder hurt."

And then she was up and off, her hands slicing through the air, her skirt and long brown hair floating out and away from her as she went. He and Max watched her retreating figure until she was gone. Then Max turned back to him, though he was looking down at the floor. No intense eye contact from this one.

"So. . ." he said the one word long and drawn out, like it had three syllables. He appeared to be counting fibers in the carpet. "You had a second question?"

"I did." He rubbed his hands on his pants. The dance was about to begin. "So, you said you'd never had a three-way, right? That's what I heard you say?"

"That's what you heard. You're right about that." Now he was rubbing his palms together in his lap. He stopped and gazed for a long time at the one palm. He seemed to be telling his own fortune. "But that wasn't your second question, was it?

"No, it wasn't." He was tapping his foot now. He felt movement everywhere around him. "My second question was. . ." He cleared his throat. "So, if you've never had a three-way, does that mean then that you've never slept with a. . . another guy?"

"Ah. . ." Max nodded his head and continued to look at the carpet. "Ah. . ." he said again. The nodding continued. And suddenly , Max was looking up and at him. Right at him. Very intense eye contact now. Very intense. Evidently he had that effect on people.

"No. I haven't. Yet." The words came out of Max's mouth so fast that he almost didn't hear them. Almost.

"Yet?" He latched onto that one word and held onto it. "Yet? As in. . ."

"I've always wanted to." Max's eyes flickered but held. "I've always been curious."

"Well then. . ." He had felt earlier as if there was all this movement. Now everything seemed so very still. He opened his mouth to speak, but Max beat him to it.

"Listen. I'm gonna go." His gaze wavered again but held steady. "Let Lucy know when she gets back, okay?" He turned to go, but then paused and looked over his shoulder at him. "My room number is 115 by the way. Just in case. . .well. . .you know."

And then he was gone.

He sat in the common room by himself for a long time. What was taking Lucy so long? Was she taking a shit instead of just a piss? And why didn't he have a pen with him to write down the number?

115

115

115

115

He chanted it over and over to himself.

"You running lines?" His eyes must've been closed, because he opened them and there she was, standing right in front of him.

"Yes," he said, blinking. Wanted to make sure she was really there. "Why yes I am, as a matter of fact." He tilted his chin up to make sure he was looking her in the face. "How are you doing, by the way? How are your lines?"

"Oh. . .fuck. . ." She blew a raspberry. "'I'll open my mouth, and whatever comes out comes out. You know how I do."

"Yes I do. That's true." He sighed, slapped his hands on his legs and stood. "Listen, I'm feeling a little tired. I think I'm gonna head out. . ."

"Tired?? How old are you? Ninety-seven fucking years old?"

"Nope. Not until my next birthday anyway." He laughed, but even to him it sounded forced. Lucy looked at him like he'd just farted in her face.

"So I'll see you tomorrow in class?"

"Is the scene due tomorrow?"

No, not until next week. . .I think."

"Then I'll be there. I'll be in class."

She reached out and pulled him into a hug so tight that, for a second, he couldn't breathe. He felt, during the hug, her hand reach around to grab his ass and pull his crotch towards hers. And held on way longer than she needed to. He put his hands against her chest and pushed her away. She staggered and gasped.

"Well. . ." She clutched a boob in each hand. "If you wanted to touch my tits, all you had to do was ask!" She massaged them back into what apparently was their place. Then she leaned forward, offering them up to him again.

"I'm sorry. Were you finished?"

He waved her away. "Oh yea, quite through. Thank you. So. . .I'll see you tomorrow? In class? And maybe we could rehearse after?"

And maybe. . .?" She raised her eyebrows as she pointed at her newly relocated bosoms.

"Oh. . .well. . ." He continued waving. "I think we need to rehearse."

"So. . ." She continued pointing at herself. "A, B, or C? What grade would you give these?"

"Oh, I don't know. . ." He put his fingers to his forehead and pretended to think. "Uh, I think. . . a D minus, maybe?"

"Bitch!" She screamed, and flew at him, her open hands slapping towards his face. "You wouldn't know a great set of tits if they hit you over the head! They're an A minus at best! B plus at worst!"

"Okay, well let's hope we get an A minus or B plus on our scene when we do it in class." He began backing up and then pivoted away. Oh, to have such a good turn in his dance class.

"See you tomorrow, 'kay?"

Her voice, saying "'kay" back, and sounding supremely disappointed for some reason, faded into the distance as he picked up the pace and exited into the hallway, where he started chanting to himself.

     115
     115
     115
     115

Again and again and again, as he searched for a stairway going down. Which was at the end of the hall. He bolted down the steps, taking them two at a time. He was already breathless by the time he got to the bottom. He changed and counted as he walked.

     115

                             101

     115

                             103

     115

                             105

     115

                             107

     115

                             109

     115

111

115

113

115

115

115

There it was.

He stood in front of the door, in front of the numbers. He was no longer winded, but he couldn't seem to catch his breath.

Finally, he knocked.

The door opened just enough for Max to stick his head out. He smiled.

"You're here," he said simply, and opened the door wider to let him in. Max had changed his clothes in the short amount of time since he had seen him last. He was now wearing a pair of shorts and a tank top. Like he was going to work out.

Max closed the door and gestured to the desk and the chair that was already pulled out. "Wanna sit?" Max himself sat on the edge of the bed. Once he sat down, there was a surprising amount of distance between them. Though Max did lean forward as they talked.

"I'm so glad you came. I really am. You know that, don't you? I really am."

Max paused, nodded, pointed at him, and began again.

"Lucy told me about you. She talked about you a lot. She did. But I never. . .and now here you are."

"Yes. Here I am." As he sat in the chair, facing away from the desk, his left knee began to bounce. He'd seen others do this, many times before, but not him. Until now. It continued to bounce as they talked for a few minutes. How Max met Lucy (doing laundry). How Ike met Lucy (class). What Max thought of Lucy ("Very intense. But intense is good, right?") What he thought of Lucy ("Yeah. Intense. That's it. Intense describes her exactly.") And then there was a pause, a pause that filled the room.

"Can I show you something?" Max said finally. Without waiting for a response, Max walked around him to reach into a drawer and pull out a book. He was so close that he could smell his shampoo. Head and Shoulders maybe. So, dandruff - looking for a flaw. And then Max was in front of him, holding the book out to him.

So he took it.

It was kind of a how-to manual. For sex between two men. He flipped through the pages. There were lots of pictures of men in different positions. He'd never seen anything like that before - except for the one time it had happened to him. Max watched him intently the whole time, though he didn't know what to do. Look up and make eye contact? What then? The pause had returned, but this time it was a silence that draped itself across the furniture and windows and even into the air so that he found himself taking deep breaths.

Max finally spoke.

"The one thing that really stuck with me," he said with a shrug, "Well, besides the pictures, of course. . .somewhere it says, 'If you're curious about any of this, talk to a friend.'" Max nodded and Ike nodded with him. Max was the one to lock eyes with him.

"And you're my friend, I think," he said.

Afterwards, he lay nestled against Max. His face was against his neck. As he lay there, he knew that for the rest of his life, the smell of Head and Shoulders shampoo would give him an erection.

"You know," Max said,lifting his head up. His own head slid down onto the pillow. "In the morning you're going to regret this."

"What?" He lifted his head and looked at Max.

"Yeah. You will. You'll feel awkward and you won't be able to look me in the eye." Max leaned over and kissed him on the forehead. "But it will be okay. It really will. It'll be okay."

As it turned out, Max wasn't the one. The next day in class, he couldn't lift his head to look at Lucy, even though she invaded his personal space about once every twelve seconds. And if that wasn't enough, the professor asked them to do their scene. Which they did. And afterwards the professor told him in no uncertain terms that he should change his major, from theatre to anything else (doesn't matter what) as soon as humanly possible.

Oh, you're straight? Well, so is spaghetti, until it gets hot and wet.

He woke from a deep sleep to the sound of someone knocking on his door.

It was Lucy. He didn't even know she knew where he lived.

Her face was moist, and she was rubbing the back of her hand across her face, which made her cheeks pink. A tear would appear in the corner of each eye. She would dab at them, take her fingers down, and they would appear again. Like shiny, tiny little diamonds were coming out of her eyes.

Just in case you were wondering where the nickname came from. Besides the Elton John song.

"Lucy, what's. . ."

"FUUUUUUCKKKK!!!!!" The sound went on for an impossibly long time. Then she stepped into his room, slammed the door behind her and brought him into a massive, strangling bearhug. Her wet face was buried into his neck. Then came the sobs.

"He broke up with me! He fuck. . ." Sob. "ing. . " Sob. "broke. The. Fuck. Up with me!!!" He could feel her whole body shaking. "I mean, who in the fuck does that anyway! Who? I mean, tell me!"

Her body was shaking his body. It was like they were sharing a full body seizure. He lifted his face out of her mass of hair. He wanted to ask, even though he already knew. He wanted to ask so that he could hear the name.

"Who? Who broke up with. . ."

"Who?? What do you mean who? Max? That's who! You stupid fuck! Max broke up with me! You stupid. . ."

She stopped and pushed him away as hard as she could. Then she buried her face in her hands and shook her head. It looked like she was in slow motion.

He stood where he'd been shoved. He shrugged, even though she wasn't looking at him. Which, for him, was a good thing. Because he was smiling. Just a little bit. But a little bit was enough. So much enough, in fact, that he didn't know what to say. What does one say at a moment like this? So he shrugged again, and then a third time, before he spoke. Still, he stuttered before he could form a complete sentence.

"Is there. . .um. . . anything I can do. For you? Uh. . .what can I do?

Her body stopped moving at that point. She lifted her head slowly from her hands. Once again, slow motion. . .

Her eyes locked with his.

And then she crossed the distance between them, cupped his face in both hands, and put her mouth on his. His mouth was closed, but her tongue was like a fist that smacked itself through his lips. Once past the teeth, however, her tongue was like a fish, flopping around and slapping against every surface it could find - the roof, the inside of the cheeks, the other tongue. The tonsils even, perhaps?

He thought he was going to choke. There was no air getting in or out. He felt her take his hand, which was still hanging at his side, and put it on her right boob before wrapping herself around him again. Under the flimsy blouse there was no bra. And there was, of course, a nipple. He didn't know what to do with that. So, despite himself, his fingers decided to explore, moving across the nipple again and again.

And something rather surprising happened. He felt a vague stirring in his crotch. Lucy felt it as well. Softly moaning before this, she pulled away and looked at him. He gasped, taking in a huge mouthful of air.

"Fuck me," she said, very quietly for her. "Fuck me now." She pushed him on the bed (how had he gotten to the bed from the door, he wondered as he landed on his back), and then pulled her skirt up and her panties down in one quick motion. As she straddled him and reached down to open his fly, she whispered "Are you going to respect me in the morning?"

"I don't respect you now," he said without thinking.

"Oh, well then. . ."

And then he was in.

This went on for a while. If a month could be considered "a while." He would come over to her dorm room after class and they would fuck. If by fuck, you mean:

She would take off her clothes

Lay down on her back

He would take off his clothes

Climb on top of her

Move his pelvis back and forth for about five minutes

She would moan like she was being murdered

He would finish

Without moaning once

And go into her bathroom and clean himself off.

Thinking about Max the whole time.

Thinking about Max

Thinking about Max

Who he hadn't seen since he said he'd regret what they'd done in 115. Which he didn't, not really. He just hadn't really had a chance to show him otherwise. Things were just happening so fast around him. Sex with Max. Max breaking up with Lucy. Lucy having sex with him.

Jesus.

Who was he anyway?

But he kept coming back to this. Max breaking up with Lucy.

So Max must not have regretted what they did either.

And then, one day, he saw Max. He was walking across the quad to Lucy's dorm, and saw Max talking to a couple people. The sight stopped him. And in that moment, Max looked up. Like in some nauseatingly sweet romantic comedy. Max looked up and then walked over to where he was frozen.

And hugged him.

And then walked with him to Lucy's dorm room, where he, holding Max's hand, told her he was breaking up with her. If indeed "I'm going to stop having sex with you" meant the same thing as "I'm breaking up with you." And then they turned and walked away.

"I'm pregnant! I'm gonna have your baby, you piece of shit! What are you gonna do about that, huh? HUH?!"

She was not, as it turned out. The next week, in class, she sat as far away from him as she possibly could. As soon as she sat down, she screamed across the room at him, "I'm not pregnant, you fuckin' asshole! Cousin Flo just showed up. So aren't you one lucky motherfucker! Aren't you!" More of a statement than a question, really.

Why yes I am, he thought as he looked down at his desk.

Why yes I am.

How can you tell if a novel is homosexual?

He always gets his man in the end.

SINGING IN THE RAIN

YOU TOOK YOUR COAT off and stood in the rain. I bought you that coat, so I'm not sure whether that meant anything or not, you taking the coat off. Were you preserving a memory of me, or were you just saving an expensive coat from getting ruined. Or a third choice, which would have fit your tortured rebel personality the most – you wanted to suffer. The Byronic beauty exposing himself to the elements, dying for his love. Dying of a broken heart.

I was at the window looking down at you. The light was off in my room so I felt somehow protected by the dark, wrapped in silence, both vulnerable and safe. And yet I would touch my cheek to the glass and it was cold and all the heat went out of my body. All I could hear was the thunder of raindrops in my ears.

The cords in your neck stood out as you tilted your head back to see up into my window. I was afraid to move or even breathe. I thought the slightest suggestion would send you up the side of the house, smashing through to take me up and out into the rain with you, past the place where the horizon disappeared into the grey mist. Your white T-shirt was plastered to your torso and water ran down your elbows to the ground next to your bare feet. One arm reached across your stomach to hold the other arm, stiff from the cold. I could see you wet, in the shower, naked, rising from the swimming pool, the moonlight glistening on your skin. I could not endure that last memory. I turned away into the room.

But the memory continued. My bed was tousled. Warm from my body, imprinted with yours. Minutes before, the white sheets had wrapped us together as we had curved into each other. Now it was just there, a carcass without a soul. Something had thrown the sheets back and escaped from the room. Now it was ugly, but there had been something beautiful there once.

And then you sang. I turned back and looked out the window again because you opened your mouth and words came out that floated up through the rain. You sang. You sang words you couldn't speak. You sang words with meaning that I could only feel, not understand. And I knew, when you sang and broke my heart with your voice, that I would never know anyone to love like I loved you.

FIRST DANCE

EVEN THOUGH I WAS only an usher, I somehow ended up with the rest of the wedding party as they piled into the decorated cars to make the noisy ride to my sister's reception. In my car there was another usher, driving, and a groomsman up front. I sat in the back with Marilyn, one of the bridesmaids. So we followed the bride and the groom and three other cars through downtown Springfield, honking noisily as we went. The other usher and the groomsman talked about where the good bars in Springfield were. Every once in a while, they would try to include the back seat in the conversation, asking Marilyn if she ever went out, and quizzing me about where I was going to school. But mostly we were left to ourselves. Marilyn, who'd once had a crush on me when we still went to the same church, would ask me questions about theater. Was I doing anything now? How was school? That's the thing about weddings. They throw a bunch of strangers together, and we do the best we can to at least be polite. Most of the time, I just looked at my reflection in the window and watched other cars go by.

When we got to the reception hall, I was struck with the same thought that hit me that morning when I came to help decorate. It looked like a very odd place to hold a wedding reception. From the outside, it looked more like one of those fake storefronts in a Disney World western scene – a long wooden porch with an overhanging roof held up by beams. The inside wasn't much better, with wood stained plywood paneling covering the walls. Signs of businesses covered that. At least Janet and Kenneth did the best they could with the decorations that morning. Or rather, I should say, Kenneth's mother, a dour older woman who took it upon herself to supervise the affair. At one end there was an open space that would soon be a dance floor, with a bar to one side and a place for the DJ and the cake and the punch on the other. Just beyond the dance floor were enough tables to seat two hundred people. Floating in the middle of each table, above the pink and blue tablecloth and the tinsel running down the middle, were centerpieces of heart shaped helium balloons. Way at the other end, facing the other tables, was the table for the wedding party. Behind it was white latticework, also decorated in pink and blue.

Most of the two hundred were sitting down and eating when we peaked through the door. Beth, one of the other bridesmaids and my other sister, was at the buffet table filling her plate.

"Beth's in there! Isn't she supposed to be out here with us?"

"Beth's in there? Oh shit!"

Kenneth, not hearing the conversation, was telling the best man he was to announce the wedding party.

"Beth's inside! Should I go get her? Kenneth, should I. . ."

His head shot up for just a second. "Let's go!" And suddenly the door was open. The best man, who'd already put a Trojan Seed Corn Company hat on to accessorize his tux, opened his mouth and a homey southern accent poured out. "Ladies and gentlemen, let me present to you Mr. and Mrs. Kenneth Flower!"

Everyone in the hall applauded. Janet and Kenneth walked through latticework arches, paused for the crowd, and then looked around, not knowing quite what to do. As I came in a little ways behind them, I glanced over to the wedding party table and noticed that Beth was the only one sitting there. She was eating very slowly and she was not smiling. Out of the corner of my eye I saw the only other married bridesmaids at one of the tables talking to some friends. I steered to the left, to the buffet table. Eating was always my favorite part of any wedding.

My plate piled high with shaved ham, beans, potato chips, celery, carrots and dip, I navigated through the tables to where most of my immediate family sat. My mother, a heavy lady who nonetheless always found the best clothes for her size, sat in brilliant green and white lace. She looked tired. My dad looked like he carried some of the young handsome boy he once was in his black tuxedo. They were surrounded by three of their grandchildren. My youngest brother Tom was holding the hand of his very quiet girlfriend, protecting her from any number of unseen enemies. Beth's husband Doug sat across from them looking very uncomfortable in his new suit, and no doubt wearing boots for shoes. Beth had regaled me over the phone the week before about the trials and tribulations of buying Doug a new suit. But there was one thing he held firm on – the shoes of his choice. That was understandable, since he had an artificial hip.

By this time, everyone was at the wedding table, and Beth was no longer sitting alone. The groomsmen were dispatched from the table with bottles of champagne but weren't back yet before the best man, handsome with his dark hair and mustache, stood and raised his glass in a toast. He smiled, and his teeth shone a sparkling white. His charming southern twang once again wrapped around the words as he thanked everyone for joining Janet and Kenneth in their time of joy. He then turned to the couple and wished them both happiness and joy.

Kenneth stood up himself and once again thanked everyone for coming. He revealed their honeymoon destination – the Bahamas – and with a hand already wet from a wine glass, gestured towards the empty dance floor.

"We were supposed to have a DJ here at 7:30. And right now it's. . . (a pause as he looks down at his watch) 7:30. Hopefully she'll be here in a few minutes. So everyone, eat. Dance. Have a good time."

She did indeed arrive in a little while, and by 8:00 people were dancing to someone's antiquated idea of what the latest in country-western, pop and rock was. Or at least the Flower people were. Mrs. Flower, her face long since wrinkled into a perpetual frown, was up there hoofing it in her white cocktail dress. Kenneth's I'm-practicing-to-have-a-face-like-my-mother sister was up there, along with about two dozen of her closest relatives, dancing as only white people with no rhythm can. But then my family, Lutherans from way back, were never dancing, drinking, partying kind of people. By 8:30, one long row of tables occupied by relatives was vacated. The cake had been cut, the bouquet had been tossed, regards had been given. It was time to make what for many was a long trek back to the St. Louis area or the Milwaukee suburbs. Dad sat stiffly in his chair, looking more and more like John Gielgud. Mom made constant forays to the bar for diet Cokes, and nursed a couple pieces of wedding cake. She looked so so tired. The Flower family was having a blast. Janet and Kenneth were slow dancing in the middle of the room, ignoring the ever-changing tempos, her arms around his neck, her head upon his shoulder.

Someone came up behind me and put their arm in mine. I turned to see Beth, her face beaming. "Hi, little brother," she said, her words slurred slightly.

"Hi yourself." A little surprised at the physical contact. We were also not big huggers. "How are you feeling?"

"Just great!" She threw her head back and laughed. "At first, I wasn't very much in the mood. But then Don the best man said, 'You only have one sister and she only gets married once. If you're lucky. You should live it up a little!" She paused and tried to itch her nose but missed. "I suppose if I get so I can't stand up any more I should shtop, huh?" She threw her head back and laughed again. I looked closely at her. The way she said shtop made her sound like Elmer Fudd. But before I could say anything, she disengaged herself and ran over to where the best man was standing, dragging him out to the dance floor. They danced with their faces very close together and their pelvises touching. I looked over to where Doug was sitting by himself, cradling a beer in his lap. He was not smiling, his mouth totally disappeared into his substantial beard. After a moment he got up and limped over to the bar. He leaned against it, facing away from the dance floor.

A blonde blur flew past me, touching my legs as it went. I squinted at the dance floor to see my two year old niece Natalie stop and stare at the green glow stick in her hand. A star ball was going on the ceiling, and little white lights were going in circles around her.

"She's got a new toy," a voice said behind me. I turned to see Barb, my oldest brother's wife and Natalie's mother. Natalie was a last-minute miracle child. For years Pete and Barb had tried to conceive. Pete had not really been for having children anyway, but when Natalie arrived, his cynical truck driver's heart had somehow been pried open. Now he doted on her. He stood now, on the outskirts of the dance floor, watching her with a smile on his face.

"She's going to be tired tomorrow," I said. The first thing I always talked about to mothers, especially to mothers in my family, was about their children. It was an immediate and open line of communication, and with any luck would fill up the time for the next several minutes. Any mother could talk for a while about their children, and if they were my nieces and nephews, I didn't mind hearing about them.

"That'll be fine by me. Maybe then she'll sleep."

"She doesn't sleep very late?"

"Not when Pete's home. She's usually up before he is, peering over the edge of the bed, waiting for him to open his eyes. And if he some-how manages to get up first, he's up there talking to her. . .you know, he doesn't get to see her very much during the week, so he tries to make the most of it on the weekends."

I turned to look at Natalie again, and saw Beth and the best man dancing very close. Her arms were around Don's neck, very much like

Janet's were on Kenneth earlier. I looked around for Doug. He was still leaning on the bar with his back to the dance floor.

"Beth's not feeling any pain," I observed.

"She sure isn't. She's going to be feeling it in the morning though."

"Yeah," I agreed.

"You know, when I came in here, she was standing at the door, and I said 'Smile, Beth!' And she said, 'I hate it. I don't want to be here, I just want to be home. I hate it!'" Barb shook her head as she relayed the information to me.

I shook my head in response. "It doesn't look like she hates it now."

"No. It sure doesn't."

By this time the song had ended. She broke off from Don, somewhat reluctantly, and walked over to Doug at the bar. All I could see were their backs, but I could tell they were talking to each other. Doug's back stayed solid and unmoving. Beth kept turning to the side to try and look him in the face.

By 10:00, I'd talked to everyone I knew that was still there. My younger brother and his girlfriend had gone somewhere. My mother was now looking at her watch every five minutes, hoping for it to be over so we could go get Janet and Kenneth's dog and go home. She looked so very very tired that I was a little worried for her. I was talking to one nephew about science fiction, a subject I knew absolutely nothing about. My niece Casey came up to me, a spitting image of her mother, and it occurred to me that I hadn't seen Beth in a while.

"Where's your mother?"

"Don't know," she said, with the kind of nonchalance only a small child can muster.

And then I saw her. She came around the corner slowly, but still too fast, and she had to grab onto the wall for support. Her hair, in beautiful blonde curls earlier in the evening, was drooping badly by now. Her face was frozen in a mask of tight restraint. Any crack in the veneer at this point would be her undoing. She put one foot in front of the other very studiously, without noticing that they should really be side by side. She came over and sat down beside me. The descent took about ten minutes.

"Are you okay?"

She shook her head without saying a word.

"Too much champagne, right?"

That got a brief smile from her, before she froze her face back into a mask. She turned her whole body to look at me and nodded her head once again.

"Things spinning a little?"

That got her to smile again. I always had that effect on her. Once, when she cracked three ribs and punctured a lung in a car accident, I told her so many off-color jokes that she was laughing and screaming in pain at the same time. Now, I was threatening to make her throw up.

"Been sick yet?"

She didn't reply to that. Or move her head. But for the first time she spoke.

"I lost my corsage."

And then she stood up, very slowly, and walked in the direction of the bathroom.

For a while I looked after her, trying to remember if I had ever seen her like that before. She looked so unsteady and vulnerable.

And frightened. It was such a drastic change from how she had been before, from how I had ever seen her. She was the kind of sister who could and did give you a black eye if you snuck up on her from behind. She was the kind of sister who could run in the forest with the best of the guys. I wasn't supposed to see her like this.

Not sure what to do, I got up and went over to Janet, who was alone for one of the few minutes of the evening. If I didn't congratulate her now, I wouldn't have a chance later.

"Come on. Dance with me." I took her hand.

Reluctantly, she followed me out onto the dance floor. Vickie Sue Robinson's "Turn the Beat Around" was playing, and she was looking around for Kenneth.

"You happy?"

"Oh yes. Very." From the look on her face, I had every reason to believe her.

"I'm so happy for the both of you. I hope you'll be very happy." I listened to those words as they seemed to hang in the air. The clumsy ones, the badly chosen ones, seemed to stick around forever. She and Kenneth had been engaged for eleven months, and in all that time I tried to think of something poignant, something profound, some words of wisdom to pass onto her and make the moment special. More for me than for her, I suppose. But now I couldn't seem to control my thoughts, like I'd drunk too much champagne, not Beth. And that's what came out of my mouth. Why wasn't this the way I expected it to be?

"You know, Beth got sick."

"Really?" She registered genuine concern, and I was instantly sorry I said anything. "What happened?

I thought "What happened?" was sort of a strange response, but I said anyway "She had too much to drink is all."

"Oooohh. . ." She said the one word long and drawn out. "Listen, has she said anything to you about having problems in her marriage?"

I felt like I had fallen and landed hard on my back. "No. Why?"

"Well, I don't know. Doug's son Jess just said something to me. . ."

"What'd he say?"

"Well, he asked me if anything was going on because they seemed to act angry at each other. So then I asked her when we were getting ready for the wedding if anything was wrong, and she said Doug and she had been having problems for some time. And then she started to cry."

"She did?"

"Yeah. So then I didn't want to pursue it anymore. It was obvious she was really upset."

"Oh." Once again I couldn't control my thoughts. Except for one. Maybe she wasn't feeling pain of any kind. For a while the champagne took care of that. But eventually, as all good things do, it turned on her. Just when she needed a friend.

Janet had spotted Kenneth. She pulled her hand away from me and glided across the dance floor towards her husband. He smiled when he saw her, and wrapped his arms around her. She buried her face in the shoulder of his white tux. And suddenly I wanted it to be all over. I wanted the people to stop dancing, I wanted the music to stop, I wanted my family to be happy again. But I couldn't reach them all, they were too far away from me to pull in close to me where they would be safe. Some of them weren't even there anymore. There was no way I could save them now. I turned around and around, looking in all directions, looking for some hope or assurance, some thing that would make it all better again. I wanted to cry, but I knew the tears wouldn't wash away how I felt. It would only throw up a smoke screen. You're okay until the next time you hurt. And the hurt you can always count on.

And then I saw Natalie.

Her blonde hair glowed in the dark. She was dancing in circles, with little balls of light all around her. And she was smiling.

PRE-MORTUM

Walls gray like memory
No lights on
      No need to read (anymore)
Except Are You There God?
        Spine cracked on the bedside table
(I would get through that for her)
But shades are not pulled
        Determined sunshine does its job

She lies on her back
      Propped up with pillows
          Eyes closed
          Mouth open
Nightgown blue
      With flowers
Stubborn (few) curls frame her face
I sit beside her
      Listening to her breathe
It rattles
Morphine drip on the other side

        We are three to a bed.

Sister comes in
      Leans forward
        Looking
I study her hands
      Red
      Rough

Wedding ring tight as her marriage
She pushes blonde hair behind her ear
"It's time," she says
                    Voice going up like a question
She lifts the nightgown
                            Releases the tabs
Rolls the diaper down
Exposed nether hair is dark
                        And full
Unlike the head.

Sister on one side
                I on the other
We turn patient towards me
Her eyes fly open wide
                        Pupils, brown irises swing back and forth
Then she sees me
                And while Sister washes and powders behind
Mother looks at me

                Searches my face
                                    And her own face relaxes.

I whisper to her
                Using my calm voice
And as I look in her eyes
                    I am reminded
Of olden days
When doctors would look into dead people's eyes
To see if final images were recorded there
It was never proven
                But that day I know. . .

Because I see myself in her.

THE JOKE PART DEUX

THERE ARE THREE STAGES to relationships.

The kitchen sink stage.

The bedroom stage.

And the hallway stage.

In the kitchen sink stage, it's new, you're horny, and so you fuck everywhere. The toilet, the bathtub, the kitchen sink. Wherever the mood strikes you.

In the bedroom stage, you've both gone to bed, you're not sleepy yet, and you think, all I have to do is roll over and make it happen. So you do.

And in the hallway stage, you pass each other in the hallway, look at each other, and go "Fuck you."

BLOCK THE SUN

IKE HAD SEEN HIM at the gym before. Once. A whole row of machines that were practically empty and he had walked right up to the one Ike was on, the abdominal crunch, as if this were the very machine he had to use at this very moment in his life. They had made eye contact, and Ike pushed harder, thinking that maybe he would tell him he was doing it wrong. But he just leaned back against the glass wall, not even looking Ike's way. As he waited he idly scratched the inside of his thigh, the scratching gradually turning into a gentle stroking. This made Ike look away, embarrassed at the aggressive intimacy of the action, and finished his set looking at the floor. But when Ike got up to leave, wiping his forehead with a towel, he snuck another glance his way. His smile at that moment was totally disarming.

That had been months ago, and he had been stored in that small cache of memories Ike called upon when he needed to reassure himself he was desired, attractive. He didn't visit there very often, because they were mostly tiny moments he had wished were much more, and they had the power to uplift and depress at the same time. So it was a rainy-day-only kind of place, where Ike stored these memories, and he kept a tight lid on it at other times. But here Ike was, on the exact same machine, coming up from the eighth crunch of his second set, and there he was again. Just coming in the door, so he was quite a ways away, but Ike saw him instantly. Ike completed the set with his face up, even on the downward motion, bad alignment for the spine to be sure, surprised he even recognized him.

Was it Ike's imagination, or did The man seem to be looking around as he entered? Don't read anything into that, he told himself as he hit rep twelve. Gyms are known as much as social centers as places to improve your physique. Ike, who years ago had returned to the same bar at the same restaurant for weeks after a bartender made one personal implicating remark to him. He had often quietly scolded himself for holding onto these little pieces of contact. It made him seem like a desperate man, and certainly no one was that silly. If he had found someone who loved him enough to marry him and stay married to him for four years, then there should be nothing desperate about him.

He went straight to the locker rooms, apparently not seeing Ike, got off the machine, wiping his face with his towel. He knew that as soon as he was done, he would look at his reflection in the mirrors lining the wall behind the machines he always used. His reflection always puzzled him. In front of a mirror he felt like a Picasso cubist painting, nose too large, both eyes on the same side of the head, mouth facing both sideways and forward. Even today he spent time twisting his features, sucking in his cheeks, pouting his lips, squinting his eyes, smoothing out his forehead. But his face was uncooperative putty, always returning to its original shape after being manipulated. His nose had a bump in it from being broken when he was six years old. His eyes were sky blue and set deep into his face, which he could some-times use to make himself alluring. He could also pretend the lines beginning to form at the corners of his eyes were laugh lines, though he knew differently. Long ago he had taken to wearing his hair in a 90s version of Mia Farrow in "Rosemary's Baby" – he referred to it as low maintenance. And even though his ears were just a little too large for such a hairstyle, he usually turned the liability into some sort of an asset. Besides, his husband said his short hair and large ears made him look like a pixie. That was his idea of a compliment.

Ike normally didn't wear much jewelry, especially not at the gym. After a panic several months before when it had slipped off during a workout and hadn't been found until the next day, even his wedding ring stayed in his locker during his workout. Conservative grey shorts and a dark blue T-shirt that didn't make his stomach look too big or his legs too skinny was his workout outfit of choice. Nothing too alluring, granted. But then, he was a married man.

Ike sighed as he moved onto the next machine, another abdominal machine where he lay down with his feet resting bent on a higher pad (not unlike being in the stirrups at the doctor's office when certain private parts were being examined), gripped a bar for each hand, and pulled his chest up to his knees. And suddenly he was beside Ike doing his crunches. He had appeared so quickly, just a glimpse of him out of the corner of his eye, that it startled Ike, and he had to stop between reps to take a deep breath. He seemed to be looking at the floor, deeply involved in his exercise, so Ike continued with renewed vigor. Maybe he had just better finish up what he was doing quickly and move onto the next machine. Or skip a few and move farther down, away from the other guy. He probably didn't even remember him.

But when Ike was finished and lying there catching his breath, he snuck another glance. He was looking right at Ike, with that disarming smile that reminded him of a movie star.

"Hi. How are you today?" Hardly original, but certainly friendly. And there was that smile, which made up for everything.

"Good." Ike also tried to smile, which probably came out more like a grimace since he was getting off the machine. "And you?"

The smile stayed, though he sighed and shook his head. Oh great, Ike thought, I get one of the two people on the planet (the other being his mother-in-law) who actually thought a truthful answer was expected of that question. "Okay."

Not bad, he thought. A decent compromise. Ike was writing in his workout notebook, which was probably a futile gesture, since he saw no change whatsoever in the past several months. But it was like recording mileage for his car – it was proof that things were happening, a record of living.

"You keeping a journal?" he asked. There was a joking, slightly teasing quality to his voice that made Ike look up. He was still smiling his movie star smile, his brown eyes seeking contact with Ike's. This was the first time Ike'd really gotten a look at him up close. He had a long face and a narrow nose, and his cheeks creased with the smile. He wore his red-brown hair short (thinning on top, which he found irretrievably sexy – none of that wrap-three-strands-around-the-head stuff), and a close-clipped beard. He had nice shoulders, at least in the sleeveless T-shirt he wore, and his legs looked muscular.

"No, just a log. Of my progress." Ike almost stumbled on the word "progress," since if he'd look at it he'd see he'd been doing the exact same weight for the past three months.

The eyebrows arched, but his eyes stayed on Ike's face. "Does it help?"

"I don't know whether it actually helps or not, but it makes me feel like I'm actually doing something instead of just wasting my time. It's a record of. . ." Ike stopped, at a loss to explain himself further, thinking maybe it sounded foolish. "It's a record."

"Maybe I need one of those." The smile briefly vanished as he suddenly became all business. He stuck out his hand. "My name's Joe, by the way."

Ike hesitated for a second as he reached out to shake his hand. "Joe? Ike. Spelled I-K-E."

Joe contemplated it for a second. "Cool." He nodded his head in approval, and the movie-star smile returned.

A moment of silence followed, and Ike was suddenly eager to keep the conversation going. "So is this your regular workout time?" Ugh, a weak attempt. But Joe didn't seem to mind. He shrugged his shoulders as he contemplated the answer. "No, I can't say that it is. It usually depends on when I can fit it into my schedule."

"I. . ." Ike said, and then stopped. He was going to say, I know, the last time I saw you it was in the late afternoon, but that carried implications with it that he wasn't ready to approach.

"What?"

"Nothing. I. . ."

"Is this your regular workout time?"

"Well, it is now. I'm a teacher and I'm off for the summer. . ."

"Oh really? You're a teacher too?"

"You mean you're a teacher? Where do you teach?"

And Joe named a university nearby. He was a professor, which didn't really compare to a high school English teacher. Ike almost regretted that he had tried to keep the conversation going – he wasn't sure he wanted to continue in this line of questioning. "So what do you teach?"

And Joe told him. Chemical engineering or some such thing. He asked Ike the same thing and it sounded so pedestrian – composition, senior English. Six classes altogether. "Busy schedule," Joe said, and then there was another pause. Ike began to wonder how far along he was in his routine. Was this where they part and finish what they were there for, occasionally smiling and saying hello to each other as they passed each other in the gym? Would Ike come back each time and look for Joe and not see him? Ike could just see it – Joe's car door slamming shut just as Ike pulled in, Ike flinging his bag over his shoulder, not knowing that Joe had just shifted into reverse and was pulling out of the parking lot. Another single precious moment that Ike would store in the place with the tight lid, and only open when he was feeling really ugly or sentimental or in need of being desired? A lid to open when he and his husband were having sex and the lid had to be open for him to even breathe?

Stop it, Ike scolded himself. You sound like such a desperate, pitiful man. And you're not. You're young, you're hot (well, if not hot, you at least "have style"), you're a professional – even if the people you deal with every day were teenagers whose hormones were as much out of control as yours were right now. Time to just stop thinking like this right now, finish his work out and get out of here. Maybe Joe would never come back. . .

"You want to get together sometime?"

The question startled Ike. It was as if he had said the words himself, but the tone and timbre of the voice were Joe's. Ike looked at him to make sure he had indeed spoken. Joe looked at him expectantly, his eyes searching his.

"Yes." The answer came more quickly than Ike had expected. "Yes, I would like that." Another pause, oh so brief, but one he couldn't stand. "What are you doing this afternoon?" Ike was a steam engine now, gathering speed, moving along a track that may or may not have many more stops before it came to the end of his destination. He closed his notebook, rather surprised that the cover had a giraffe on it. He turned it over and then looked down at the blank back cover.

"Not a thing," Joe responded. The words were starting to hang in the air, carrying other words that went unspoken. Ike looked up, hoping to read the unspoken words written somewhere in front of him.

"Would you like to grab lunch somewhere?" "Grab" lunch. Ike wasn't sure where that had come from, but at least it sounded better than the begging that went with "Would you like to have lunch with me?"

"Absolutely." Joe had his business face on again. They had been two people in a conference and had come together on an equitable agree-ment. "Where would you like to go? What kind of food do you like?"

"Oh geez, I don't know." And then Ike added, even though he was sure it made him sound indecisive, "anything would be fine with me."

"How about. . ." And then Joe named his favorite restaurant, and Ike was agreeing without even thinking twice. The steam engine was moving quite fast now, and he wasn't sure he was any longer in control of it. He tried to pull back a little bit on the brakes.

"Well, how much longer do you have. . .?", hoping that would give Ike time to think, to judge the wisdom of going to a restaurant he went to many times with a man he had just met. Who was not his husband. But he turned his wrist to look at his watch, and that single gesture was like reaching up to take his hand off the brake, slide it off without any struggle whatsoever.

"Oh, I'm finished. I was kind of messing around today anyway. Too distracted."

Too distracted. Ike thought about that as they went their separate ways to the locker rooms to get their bags. His hands shook so that he missed the first number of his locker combination. Too distracted. That could mean anything. Gyms, this gym, was notorious for being a meat market. But Ike preferred to think that Joe was talking about him, and he looked at himself in the mirror on his way out. His ears were not too large. His complexion was perfect. His ass was not too large. His stomach was just the right size.

Once in the parking lot, however, the steam engine slowed just a bit.

"Where are you parked?"

"Right here." They stopped in front of a red Geo Prizm.

"Should we take both cars?"

"Where do you live?" The question actually made perfect sense, because the proximity of the restaurant to the homes could be a deciding factor. But coming out of Ike's mouth, it had a sensual quality, almost too intimate and personal to be discussing so soon.

Joe didn't miss a beat. "By the university," which more or less decided that he should drive. That and the fact that Ike found himself within seconds of hopping into the cabin of a Ford Bronco was once again speeding the engine up to the point where his mind was racing. Ike felt hot, and hoped that it at least looked like he'd had a good workout.

"Sorry for the mess." Joe climbed behind the wheel, pitching his gym bag behind the seat casually. Ike looked around – people said that all the time. Years ago it was dates hoping to impress – his husband, while still a boyfriend, may have even said it a time or two. Nowadays it only came when he was at someone else's house. He hadn't heard it in this context from a man in years.

Ike looked down at the floor of the truck. Change was scattered all over, a smashed piggy bank. Without the piggy pieces. "You certainly do have a whole hell of a lot of change." Ike had spread his legs to look down at the floor, and he didn't know where the "hell" came from. What if cursing offended him? He was becoming someone he didn't even recognize anymore.

Joe guided the truck onto the street running alongside the gym, and then turned left. As they passed strip malls and doctors' offices and grocery stores and nightclubs, Ike let him do most of the talking. Or at least maneuvered it in that direction by asking all the questions and listening very closely to the answers. He had become a very good listener being married to Max for the past four years. Anything a person said could be the impetus for another question, though that was a skill that, once learned, he had practiced very little in conversations with his husband. But there were questions he didn't want asked of him, so he kept the attention focused on Joe as he drove down the street. Joe was an intelligent man, had his doctorate in chemical engineering in fact, and could speak quite candidly and eloquently on anything Ike asked. Joe told him how he hated where they lived, how the developers were ruining the environment here, how you had to drive so far to get anywhere. Joe had visited New York City six times last year, and he wanted to live there. He liked the fact that in the space of one block you could get groceries, pick up flowers, drop off your laundry, and stop by for a quick drink. He liked that sense of neighborhood. He also thought that where they currently lived was a cultural wasteland (Ike agreed with him there, perhaps a little too vehemently), that it couldn't seem to support an orchestra, ballet company or professional theater group, but could sell out tractor pulls and World Wrestling Federation matches.

"And besides, I've been having a really bad time of it lately," Joe said, almost offhandedly, his eyes still on the road.

"Oh?" Ike wasn't sure he wanted to hear where this was leading, but at least it would keep the questions from coming his direction.

"Yeah. I was recently divorced from my wife."

"Oh?" Ike paused, about to apologize before remembering the situation had nothing to do with him. "How long were you married?"

"Nine years." Joe's eyes remained on the road. Nine years seemed like a long time to Ike. It was longer than he had ever held a job, longer than he had known his husband. He couldn't keep the surprise out of his voice when he asked, "Nine years? What could possibly go wrong with a marriage that it would end after nine years?"

Joe waited a second, carefully choosing his words. "It wasn't a 'what-happened' so much as it was a gradual process. . ."

"Just drifting apart kind of stuff?"

"Well, not so much that as the fact that our sexual appetites became incompatible. Mine never waned – as a matter of fact it probably got even stronger. The same, I'm sorry to say, could not be said for my wife. And I'm not very good at leading a double life, seeing someone else and lying about it. So I just stuck with it for a while, a long while, but I just couldn't do it anymore." A long pause where it felt like Joe was holding his breath. "I don't know. It's been very difficult. But it certainly wasn't from lack of loving her." He took his eyes from the road briefly to look at Ike. "I guess that's not a very good reason, is it?"

Ike shrugged his shoulders, feeling the same way he felt when he didn't know what to say to someone mourning the death of a loved one. "I don't know whether there's any such thing as a good or a bad reason for doing something. You just know that you aren't happy. . ."

"And you make some changes," Joe added.

"And you make some changes."

They had arrived at the restaurant, a fairly new place well-known for its endless salad bar. It seemed a fitting place to go after they had both worked out. Ike very badly needed to change the subject, so as he climbed out of the truck he asked, "Now you're a what kind of engineer?" This time he sounded dumb, but at least it led away from the discussion about relationships.

"A Chemical engineer."

Which means what? I have no idea what engineers do."

So he explained it to Ike as they went down the mile-long salad bar with their plates. When Ike was dating, he would always eat less than usual, so that his boyfriend thought he was watching his caloric intake. He watched Joe's plate as they went down the line and he talked, choosing ingredients similar to Joe's and taking smaller portions. And he listened, because he really did want to know what Joe did and how he went about it. Everything was fodder for questions later. Any kinds of questions. Like asking, "Are you seeing anyone?"

As they walked back to Joe's truck after lunch, Ike found himself walking closer to him, almost so he could feel the hair on his arms touch his skin. Joe sighed again. "I guess it's time to take you back to your car."

"I guess so." But the engine was racing at full throttle by this time, and Ike had no desire to make it stop. "Do you find," he asked, "that there are a lot of good looking people who work out at that gym? I mean, really good looking people."

"Oh yes. And it sure was busy today."

"You know, I have this theory," Joe announced as he climbed back into his truck.

"Yeah? What's that?"

"That most people – not all, mind you, but a great portion – work out like they make love."

Ike grimaced at the notion. "There's so much grunting."

"Well, I don't mean the grunting so much, but the whole aggressive nature of the thing. The approach I guess."

Those words were in the cabin of the truck and they couldn't get out. Unless they were pushed out by other words. Ike responded slowly. "Are you. . .aggressive. . .when you make love?"

"Would you like to find out?" Joe spoke before Ike even knew it. Who was this strange man in the cab of this truck talking this way to a man he had just met? He felt very hot now. As if reading his mind, Joe reached over and turned on the air conditioning. He adjusted the vents so that the cool air blew on Ike's face.

"Yes, I would," Ike answered very quietly.

Joe had already turned the truck in the direction of the gym, and Ike was charmed by the rather complex maneuvers (turning left, pulling into a parking lot, backing up, and heading east on the same street) it took to get pointed towards Joe's house. And he was charmed by the apology (once again) for the condition of his apartment, since he had just moved in over a month ago, and by Joe's over-inquisitive desire to find the right music to put on the CD player. Joe had a cat named Oscar (Ike would've pegged him for a dog man), and as he sat to remove his shoes, Ike crouched on the floor to pet the cat, who immediately arched his back to meet his gentle hand. His hand was shaking, so to hide it he scratched Oscar behind the ears.

"Hey," Joe said. Ike looked up and Joe was sitting on a black leather chair in his sleeveless T-shirt and tight gray workout shorts. He sat with his legs wide open, and it looked like he already had an erection. Joe was looking straight into Ike's eyes. All he had to do was lean over. Ike kissed Joe on the top of the head first. And then suddenly their mouths were together, wet and demanding, Joe's lips sucking viciously on Ike's tongue as it probed his mouth. He reached underneath his arms, pulling Ike to him. Ike straddled his lap and Joe reached around and cupped one hand around the right cheek of his buttocks and pushed his pelvis into his groin. Joe was hard already, Ike could feel it, and he reached down past the waistline of Joe's shorts and grasped him firmly in one hand. They were still kissing, and a groan escaped from Ike's lips and filled his mouth with air.

They broke apart, gasping for breath. "Here," Joe said, "Let's go in here." He pointed to the bedroom as he disappeared into the bathroom. Ike went in, and immediately liked the fact that the bed hadn't been made yet from the night before. He took off his clothes and lay on his stomach on the bed, breathing deeply, feeling the engine about to derail. Ike closed his eyes, trying to hear the steady rhythm of the train on the tracks. He heard Joe come out of the bathroom, and before he knew it Joe was stretching his naked body over his, covering it completely, wrapping around it like a cocoon. Joe's fingers moved across his skin, so lightly they were barely touching, and Ike could feel his skin grow, blossom with highly acute sensations under his touch. Then Joe got off of him and turned him over. At first the air hitting his skin felt cool after the warmth of his body, but then Joe was down between his legs and it didn't matter. Ike's cock was in his mouth. It was all feeling. Joe's fingers, gently yet insistently holding his legs apart and at the same time framing the hair around his dick like a V.

Joe's tongue, deep and then at the head, again and again and again, touching places that needed to be touched, badly. Ike's face, buried in the pillow, smelling like a combination of Joe and his laundry soap. Joe's hands as they stroked his head and followed the outlines of his ears.

For a second Joe was away from him, and there was no bodily contact at all. Ike opened his eyes and saw him looking down at himself, rolling a condom onto his erect penis. "Be gentle," Ike said, even as he was wondering why he said it, and Joe looked at him with that movie-star smile. "Don't worry," he said.

And then Joe lifted Ike's legs into the air and slid into him, no forcing at all, his body ready to accept him. Joe was all over him again, kissing his hair, his mouth, his neck, his chest. Briefly Ike wondered if he would know better than to give him a hickey, and equally briefly he wondered if adults even gave each other hickies. And then he forgot all about it, and all of his senses went down to where Joe's penis slowly pulled itself almost all the way out to the tip and then insistently drove itself all the way back in.

Ike had no idea how long they went on like this, though if he could've willed it, time would've paused for as long as he wanted. He could tell Joe was about to come because his breathing was getting quicker and shorter as he kissed Ike's throat. Joe lifted his body, dripping with sweat, and thrust his pelvis into Ike one final hard time. The muscles of his buttocks were flexed with the force of the thrust, and his whole body froze for a second before quivering with the effort. His mouth moved silently for a moment, then exhaled air so loudly it sounded almost like a groan. Ike could feel him, down below, emptying himself into him.

He lowered himself slowly onto Ike, kissing him every place his lips could reach, before rolling onto the bed next to him. Ike had not come, but that was all right. The touching had been enough. He listened to Joe breathing heavily, and tried to match his shaky breathing to his own, so that they inhaled and exhaled at the same time. His hand reached out and grasped Ike's, entwining their fingers together. Joe swallowed loudly and finally asked Ike, "Do you want a glass of water or something?" and even though he said "That would be nice," Joe lay there for minutes longer, holding Ike's hand. Ike didn't really want him to break the connection anyway. Finally, however, he did, and their sweaty palms pulled apart as Joe rose to go to the kitchen.

Ike rolled over on his side, facing the nightstand and the wall. There was a pile of snapshots on the nightstand next to a lamp. Though he knew they could possibly be private, he felt reckless and happy, and he picked up the pile. At the same time he shouted into the kitchen, "Who are the pictures of?"

Joe walked back in with two glasses of ice water at that moment and Ike asked again, "Who are the pictures of?" He felt daring and flirtatious. Joe smiled that smile, set the two glasses down within arm's reach on the nightstand, and sprawled on his stomach, taking the pictures from Ike as he did so. Ike lay beside Joe and he went through the pictures slowly, so as not to bother him. There were pictures of Oscar, of Joe receiving his doctorate, of his ex-wife (who Ike didn't think was all that pretty), and the house they used to share. Then they came to a recent picture of Joe. Ike could tell it was in New York, because he recognized Times Square in the background. There was another person in the picture, and Joe had his arm around her. It was not his ex-wife.

"Who's that?" Ike asked, trying hard to make it sound only like casual interest. He flashed that smile. "That's my New York connection."

"Your what?" Ike knew he was being obviously obtuse, but he needed to hear the words.

"I met someone in New York. About a month ago. This is her." And then as Ike stared at the picture, too stunned to speak, Joe talked about the woman in the picture. Her name was Michaela. She was a massage therapist.

They had met at a gym.

She was younger than him, but had been sick a while back and had had a hysterectomy, so she could have no children. Having no children from his first marriage, being a father was pretty important to Joe. But Michaela (or "Mickey" as he called her) was very special to him, and he felt like it was something they could work out. And Ike listened to Joe, listened to him as he had listened to him all the other times this afternoon. Ike listened to every word.

By the time Joe'd dropped Ike back off at his car, he had approximately an hour to get back to the house and start preparing dinner before Max came home from work. Joe gave Ike his business card with his work phone number on it (the worst days to reach him there were Mondays and Wednesdays), and he wrote his home number on the back. Then there was an awkward second when he held the pen in Ike's direction, started to take it back, and then extended it again. "Want to give me yours?" He had never asked if Ike was married. Telling himself he shouldn't, Ike found a piece of paper on the floor of Joe's vehicle, in amongst the change collection, wrote it down and handed it to him.

"Since you're off for the summer, maybe we could get together again and do something, something social," he said. "That would be nice," Ike nodded, remembering the glass of water back at Joe's apartment that he never drank.

"Or we could always have a repeat performance of today." Joe looked at Ike. He was looking back, searching his face. The movie-star smile wasn't there. Ike waved and Joe drove away slowly. He stood and watched until the truck pulled out of the parking lot before he got into his car. When he closed the car door, the lid closed too, and the contents inside made room for another memory.

When he got home, he was eagerly greeted at the door by Maisie, his pet greyhound, who instantly began a sniffing inventory of Ike's clothing, trying to figure out where a cat smell had invaded her territory. He dropped his keys and the mail on the dining room table and walked slowly into the kitchen. He didn't have a clue what he was going to make for dinner. Ike paused in the doorway, and looked back at the opposite wall where a wedding picture of him and Max was hung. That was four years ago, and of course they were both smiling. That picture reminded Ike of a book he had read in high school, where the

English teacher went on and on about how the weathered sign of an eye doctor who had gone out of business was symbolic of a god who had been there but had now gone and left his children to fend for themselves. "The Great Gatsby," he thought it was. In high school they thought the symbolism was cool, but in college they had laughed at it as being something too pretentious and obvious.

Lately, however, he had been thinking about that book, usually every time he looked at the wedding picture on the wall. After all was said and done, it was just a picture.

Ike walked through the kitchen onto the back porch and then outside. One of the reasons they had rented this house in the first place was because there was a pool in the backyard. As Ike stared at it, the late afternoon sun glimmered on the water, water he used to dive into every day. But more and more it had become something of a bother – it took too much time to put suntan lotion on his fair skin, and the mosquitos were so bad around the pool – so he hardly used it anymore. The sun reflecting off it was very bright. Ike thought of a thing he used to do as a little boy, where he would hold his hand out at arm's length. If he closed one eye, he could block out whatever he didn't want to see. Ike held his hand at arm's length now, seeing how much of the pool he could block out. He tried one eye and then the other, because sometimes that helped. But no matter what he did, he couldn't block out the whole view of the pool. It was just too big and his hand was too small.

He tilted his head back and held his hand in front of the sun. The white ball itself was hidden, but the glow on either side turned the edges of his thumb and little finger a brilliant red-orange. He opened his fingers wide, letting the sun come through, lighting up all his fingers like fire. It was then that he noticed he hadn't put his wedding ring back on. The glare from the sun made his eyes water, and he felt a tear run down his cheek. And a mosquito danced among his fingers, looking for a place to alight and draw blood.

MAX AND THE TEDDY BEAR

EVERYTHING REMINDS ME OF something else. I will be one of those old guys who people will be afraid to say anything in front of for fear it will cause an avalanche of aimless reminiscences. So what I remember is this: How shiny and straight the hard oak boards in my dining room floor were. At a Christmas party at my house, I had met an older man who was just a boy when he helped lay the floor in the house in 1925. Lay the floor – a strange phrase that gave me pause and made me feel like a pervert. I imagined this man, much younger, the sweat on his neck beading up, the dirt running into the back of his shirt on a hot summer day as he meticulously cut the boards so they were all the same size. His tongue sticking out with the effort of lining up all the boards exactly straight, his face down to the ground checking for preciseness. No doubt it wasn't done that way, even back then, but it made me feel good to think that someone put so much work into something I now owned. The summer after I moved in, I had urethane put on all the hardwood floors in the house. Now, even if I hadn't cleaned for weeks, I could still see my reflection looking up at me.

How weird and sleepy Corey's voice sounded when he spoke to me over the phone. Corey tended to go on and on whenever he called, and I had already started to count how many boards there were from the entrance to the dining room table when I caught the tone of his voice. It had the sound to it that would prompt people to say, "Have you got a cold?" The kind of sound that would make my mother do a double take and immediately bring a Kleenex over, hold it in front of my nose and say, "Come on now, blow!" Which made me, not real strong yet on the concept of blowing, breathe in instead.

And of course, I remember Corey saying, "Max's dead." His voice had the same snot-filled, he'd-just-been-crying sound to it, except this time with a quiet little choking noise on the end of it.

I remember the pen as I wrote down the particulars on Max's visitation. The pen was rough, had obviously been chewed on, and my first impulse was usually to throw it away. It had no doubt come from school, where one of my students had left it discarded on the floor of my classroom. Or worse yet, had given back after borrowing and unconsciously mutilating. About to run out of ink, it wrote in a pale black line, and I knew I would use that as an excuse to throw it away later. Unless, of course I remembered what I wrote with it. Pens, too, are allowed to have a history.

Max and I had a little bit of a history together. A little bit. Like six years worth. We were friends and then we were more than friends and then I cheated on him and then we broke up. That was our history in a nutshell. Not much, I suppose, but it was something. And it was ours. Max was studying to become a child psychologist, though I don't think he ever got there. I would often imagine that the same voice he used to tell me he loved me would be used to talk to comfort a troubled child. And then he would use his long fingers to stroke the child's forehead, speaking in low tones, chasing away the monsters, until the child's forehead relaxed and he closed his eyes. But as I said, he never got there, so it really just amounted to me imagining.

Corey was Max's friend after he and I broke up. Friend. That's the word they always used, even though I knew it was more than that. I always knew. I don't think it happened right away after, but eventually he was just there. Actually, we ended up going to see a movie together once. It was an accident, as events like that often are. A friend and I went to see something called "Pennies From Heaven," one of those Steve Martin movies that was supposed to be better than it was. So I went with my friend, and he went with Corey, and we all four just happened to be in the same theater at the same time for the same movie – one of those "it's a small world" things. Afterwards we went to dinner, and I can honestly say it was one of the best days of my life. It was just one of those nice relaxing dinners where you don't have to worry about preparing the food or how you're going to pay for it, and can simply enjoy each other's company. We're all allowed a certain, perhaps infinite, number of those. I guess what makes that one stick out in my mind was that it never happened again. Corey, as always, went on and on, and I tried, as I usually did, to get Max to smile. It was a challenge, but that day it happened at least seven or eight times. After that, I reached out to him from time to time. He would be polite, but brief each time. From the sound of his voice, there was no smiling going on anymore.

After all, I was the one who cheated on him.

The day of his visitation I don't remember what I wore, though I'm sure a tie was involved. I do remember debating on whether or not I should wear cologne to something like a visitation. There was something about my cologne, no matter how "manly" it smelled, that somehow added a strangely sensuous lightness to any situation. I think that's what finally convinced me to wear it. It was Photo by Lagerfeld.

I thought the funeral home was just down the street, an intentionally grey building with a strange Swiss-chalet looking steep roof. Many times I had driven past and seen the stone cat, turned green by the weather, clinging to the roof tiles. I remember thinking what an odd thing that was to have for any house, but particularly on a funeral home. That night I soon knew it was also not the right place – the funeral home's unlit windows and empty parking lot were already beginning to blend into the gathering dark. The cat, however, seemed to glow, as if lit from within. When I lived briefly in New York City I would have to walk across Central Park every day to work at the Institute of Fine Arts. Every time I made sure I left the park at the same place, where the statues of Hans Christian Anderson and Alice in Wonderland reflected into a pond. If I walked past those two statues every day and touched each one as I went by, I knew the rest of the day would somehow be okay. Somehow, that stone cat on the roof of the funeral home had become like Alice in Wonderland for me.

Though with Alice I always knew where I was going. This time I had to go back home and look in the phone book to find where the Statler Bros. Funeral Home was – not a good way to add to an experience I was already dreading. When I finally got my bearings and headed down the road almost exactly the same distance in the opposite direction and got to the funeral home, the visitation only had half an hour to go. A blonde man in an ill-fitting suit was in the parking lot directing traffic, which I thought was odd since the lot had only about a dozen cars in it. And he gestured so generally that I wasn't even sure I'd pulled into the right space. Except that it didn't seem to matter, given that as soon as he gestured he turned away, appearing pre-occupied, as if his sole job at the funeral home was to direct traffic, and he had long ago tired of such menial tasks and longed to work with the dead bodies – the goal of any aspiring mortician.

The inside of the funeral home was, as I had expected, unusually quiet. Corey had arrived ahead of me, and he stood apart from the other people there, his hands crossed in front of his crotch, as if protecting his genitals from death. This was a Corey I had not seen before, since he usually immersed himself in any crowd of people, whether he knew them or not, and started talking. A smile flickered across his face and disappeared as I walked over. "This feels so weird," I whispered in his ear. He smiled briefly and said nothing. I looked around, trying to think of something else to say. There was an aisle down the middle of the room, which looked like a church sanctuary, with pews on either side. There were a few people sitting on either side in the pews, but most of the family and friends were standing in the back in clusters, talking in whispers.

Unexpectedly, Corey began whispering in my ear, telling me what little he knew about Max's death. Unknown to most, including myself, Max had been taking medication for depression. The Friday before, he had checked into a hotel on the beach. He was found the next morning by a hotel maid. As I took this all in, my mind finally acknowledged what I had refused to see until now.

The open coffin was at the other end of the room. Just as I saw it, Corey whispered in my ear. "Would you come with me? I want to pay my respects, but I don't want to go up there alone."

I went, albeit reluctantly. One thing I can't remember is the last time I had seen a dead person. I watched my feet until I got up to the front – my black shoes were a little worn, and the carpet was a garish red, as if it was supposed to remind mourners of Christmas and somehow ease their suffering. I'm sure a study of color's effect on mood had been done as a doctoral dissertation somewhere, though I also read once that the holidays were the most depressing time of the year for a lot of people, so I wasn't sure the color scheme was working.

I stood to the side while Corey went up to the coffin. He was, after all, Max's "friend" now. He stood there for several seconds, his head bowed down. His back was to me, so I couldn't see if his lips were moving or not. Then suddenly his head snapped up, like he was a dog who'd just gotten an impatient yank on his collar, and turned and walked away. He stopped and stared fixedly at the floral arrangements. There were four good ones on that side, mostly traditional, with white and pink and yellow flowers. One had a generous sampling of orange tiger lilies.

I don't know what the other thing was that was on that side. It looked like a Carmel ice cream cake, except that it was obviously made out of some kind of orange and brown foliage. The odd thing about it was that it was in the shape of a teddy bear. The bear had a smile of white carnations. One eye was winking. Dwarfing the bear was an enormous background of what looked like palm fronds. The green background was unnaturally large, and it was only by looking hard that I could see where letters used to be – an "H" and an "A," then a little farther down a "B," an "I" and an "R." I was surprised that such a thing could have been delivered to a funeral home in the first place, let alone put out, even without its inappropriate message.

I looked down. What caught my attention first was the fact that Max had hair. He had always shaved his head, but now there was a fringe of medium-length red hair around the sides. It had been combed so that it was off the ears. He also didn't have his glasses on, wire-rimmed granny glasses that I never saw him without in the last years I knew him. As if to compensate for the glasses not being there, as if he were afraid he would get a headache if he tried to see without them, his eyes were tightly closed – almost too tightly since there were wrinkles at the corners. His lips looked pursed, like he was trying to blow a bubble. The pancake makeup on his forehead was beginning to flake like the pie crusts my mother used to make.

I looked around for Corey. He'd left the flowers and was in the back of the room talking to a man I didn't know. My feet as I walked towards them felt strange, my mind premeditating every footstep before it happened. I was almost beside them before Corey acknowledged me.

"This is Max's brother Matthew." He certainly looked like Max. His glasses were a more conservative tortoise shell, but the lenses were also round. He was also balding, but what brown hair he had was clipped close to his head. His lips were not quite so full. Like with his brother, I wanted to see him smile.

"Max has hair," was the first observation out of my mouth.

"Yeah. He'd started growing it back lately. I don't know why." We were shaking hands as we talked, and I remember thinking that it was odd that I didn't know Max had a brother. Just like I didn't know that Max had red hair. I wondered what else I didn't know about him. His favorite food, his favorite color – I couldn't think of what they were. Now that it was too late, now that his eyes were sewn shut, I couldn't remember what color they were. I thought of asking his brother, but when I opened my mouth, no words came out. I wanted to say I was sorry, I wanted to say I didn't know Max was hurting. But somehow words didn't seem like enough, and as I stood there, I felt like one of the fish my brother caught when he forced me to go along with him in an attempt at male bonding in our childhood. He'd fling the fish onto the dock, and I stood over it watching in horror as its mouth opened and closed in a silent gasping. Then I ran screaming down the dock – now I felt trapped, unable to get away.

And then Matthew spoke. "I couldn't get my brother to understand. . ." he said and then stopped, shaking his head. I looked at him for a long time, feeling the words he spoke suspended in the air, knowing that if they could only find the other words that would make them into a complete sentence then I would hear them and know. I listened for a long time, though all I could hear was the hum of the air conditioner in the room. But suddenly my feet were moving again, and not out the door but down the aisle towards the coffin. It felt almost as if I was running, like I was breathing hard and couldn't stop. I looked down at Max again, looked for a long time, for a twitch or a sigh, anything that would tell me he was still alive. When nothing happened, I spoke.

"I'm sorry." I was surprised at the sound of my own voice cracking, like I was still an adolescent and my voice was changing. "I'm so very sorry." I searched the flaking pancake and rouge on his cheeks for an answer. I looked up and the first thing I saw was the flower teddy bear. He was frozen forever in that bizarre wink. But now he seemed to be winking at me. I looked back down at Max.

"What? Is this supposed to be some sort of symbolism or something?" I smiled as I said this.

And then I felt like maybe I was free to go.

LITTLE PINK PILL

HE ONLY WANTED TO feel alive.

Jan was going to be here in half an hour, and the evening ahead promised to be very alive. But right now Ike wanted just a little pick-me-up. Just a little something to make him feel more present. More "there." There was a little plastic baggy in his hand before he even knew how it got there. Six little pills. Pink. They were usually engraved with something. These had Es on them. Jan had introduced him to these six months ago. One of these babies, and. . .half hour, hour later, you felt. . . Well, Ike could never describe the feeling. At least not yet. In his limited experience. But eventually he would describe it as like leaving your body, and looking back at where you used to be, and where part of you still is. And being so goddamn happy about it.

So one of those, and then he waited. Outside in the rain for Jan. He pulled up, and he looked out the window, Ike could see him smiling. It could be that Jan has wanted to fuck Ike ever since they've known each other. And Jan was nothing if not eternally hopeful. Or, Ike thought, he probably already did a little pink pill himself, and was already outside his body looking back.

"Get your ass in here," Jan called out, louder than he needed to be. So yeah, he was high. Ike went around to the passenger side and Jan added, also too loudly, "You wanna do a little somethin' somethin'?"

"You mean, like. . ." So maybe he wasn't?

"Of course, of course! So how' bout it? Before we get started?"

And then he had a little vial in his hand, screwed off the lid and was tapping a little white powder onto the side of his other fist. Then he bent over and it was gone. He threw his head back and shook it from side to side, his mouth open. He made a low groaning sound.

"See?" Jan said, his head still tilted back. "That's how it's done! Easy as can be!" He laughed as he dropped his chin to his chest and looked at Ike. "You gotta try it!"

And so there was more white powder and Ike took it up his nose. He sniffed, sniffed again, and felt shit in the back of his throat. He coughed. Coughed again. Jan laughed. Ike looked at where he heard the laughter. Something was already happening. He was already stepping outside of himself. He was already starting to turn and look back.

Ike watched Jan as he drove. Jan had gone through a period where he had found religion. Really found it. Speaking in tongues and shit. And then, just as suddenly as he'd found religion, he lost it. And found other things instead. Jan had opened all kinds of doors for Ike once he'd come back into his life. Lots of doors that Ike didn't want to see behind. Like fucking teenage boys.

So Ike had heard.

And Jan had hinted at it, though he never came right out and said it.

And even darker stuff.

Like films.

They arrived at the bar and it was very busy parking lot full of cars people everywhere no room practically to squeeze past anyone to get to the bar because of course they had to have a drink at least one drink though come to think of it maybe five would be even better finally they got their drinks vodka and cranberry for Ike rum and coke for Jan and clutched them as they waded back into the crowd Jan wanted to be near the dance floor and the music though the music was loud and everywhere so anywhere was close to the music Ike held tightly onto his drink it almost felt like the hand holding it wasn't his anymore Jan swayed back and forth to the music he wasn't really on the beat but it didn't really matter he was probably dancing to the music inside his head he would point out a shirtless hot man then another one as if Ike had never seen a shirtless hot man before and he smiled Jan always smiled he turned and his face lit up even more than it already was Ike turned to where Jan was looking and at first he saw so much that he saw nothing and then someone emerged from the crowd and Jan went over and hugged him he took him by the arm and led him back in Ike's direction he was saying something but because of the loud thump of the music Ike could only see him moving his mouth hey Ike this is Jan said though Ike doesn't hear the name it sounds like gibberish the man with gibberish for a name raised his hand but to wave not to shake and said hey then he and Jan turned away and talked to each other low Ike can't even read lips he couldn't see lips only backs and loud music with an insistent beat a beat that wouldn't stop and the sounds of people trying hard to be happy the two finished talking and Jan put the gibberish for a name man on the back the man turned around and waved at Ike before disappearing into the crowd Jan took his time coming back over to Ike he's smiling always smiling that Jan he gets very close to Ike leaned in and whispered into his ear he's murdered someone Jan said Ike pulled away so that he could see Jan's face Jan nodded yeah two actually how do you know that because he told me Jan reached and took Ike's hand come on he said let's do some more this evening is just getting started.

So more white powder and another pink pill

Mouths

        So many mouths

                So much kissing

His lips hurt

        Can't find

                What's his name

The person he came with

        What's his name

                Where is he

Where is

        Where

                Fuck you

Fuck you

        There

                Fuck

Fuck

        Fuck you because

                Because

Because mouths

        Kissing mouths

                Kissing

The wrong mouths

        Mouths he kissed

                Fuck you

Again

And gone

                          Gibberish man

Murder man

There

                          Suddenly there

A drink

Holding out a drink

                          Here

For you

Holding out

                          Something

Something in drink

Pink

                          It's pink

Where

Where

                          Bed

In bed

His bed

                          Murder Man

His bed

Fucking

                          Fucking

His bed

His hands

                          Hands around neck

Choking

Choking

                          Choke. . .

Ike woke up. The sun was out but he had no idea what time it was. Or where he was. On the floor. He could feel the carpet on his cheek. He sat up and immediately it was too much. He bent over and threw up in his lap. He had a pounding headache.

He looked down at his lap for a long time.

The vomit was pink.

He had only wanted to feel alive.
But now he only felt bad.
Really really bad.

BRANCHES

YOU LEAN AGAINST THE door for a second and breathe deeply. The wall of the bar is moving in a small circle but slows down as you stand still. One more breath, inhale, exhale, and the wall stops altogether. You study the hand in front of you as it supports your weight against the door. Branches of blue veins lead up to the spaces between your fingers. When you were young, you would stare at the veins, trying to see the blood pulsing through them. You stare at the veins now, but there is no movement - not among the branches, not the wall.

You see the doctor's face from earlier in the day - round, soft, more kindly than anyone in his profession has any right to be. Even his glasses were oval, encircling his moist blue eyes. His hand rested on your knee and you looked down at it. The nails looked chewed. His fingers patted your leg. "It's all right to cry," he said and you lifted your eyes to meet his. It looked as if he had put his own philosophy into action. Then he took his hand off your knee and turned to write in a chart. Your chart. You looked back down where a moment before an attempt at comfort had occurred.

The wall of the bar begins to move again. You close your eyes and try to see the circles. Inhale. Exhale. You open your eyes again and your hand is still there, holding up the wall. You concentrate on the veins winding up to the fingers. Inhale. Exhale. The circling slows and stops and you listen to yourself breathe. Your chest is moving up and down. You've been panting. The heavy breathing in your chest also makes your shoulders go up and down, which leads to muscles in your arms which leads all the way down to the wrist and the hand leaning against the door. The branches of blue veins. The end of the road.

You put all of your weight against the hand, and the door swings open. You take two steps and you are standing in the snow. You see your breath in clouds in front of your face and the cold flushes your cheeks. You watch the white of your breathing appear and disappear into the black sky. The door of the bar slams behind you, and it reminds you of the sound of wood breaking. You turn to look and you see the OPEN sign in the bar window go out. You hear the door lock click. You turn back around and smell the winter night. There is no sound. You close your eyes again and feel the cold on your lips, across your eyebrows, into your nostrils. You take a step forward and the snow crunches beneath your feet.

You see the doctor's face again. "It's all right to cry," he says. Your eyes fly open so quickly that the circular movement begins again. The panting has returned and you look around you. There is a clicking sound to your right and you turn in that direction. There is a person standing several feet away, huddling on the other side of a bus stop sign. He is trying to light a cigarette, and his hands are cupped in front of his mouth holding the lighter. You stare after him. The doctor's voice echoes in your ears.

You hear your footsteps as you cross the distance to the bus stop. He doesn't look up as the lighter finally starts and you see the bright orange ash on the end of the cigarette. "Hey," you call out and he turns in your direction. He is young and looks a little like your doctor. He doesn't wear glasses, however, and has more hair - a lock of it has fallen down over his forehead. His eyes are also blue. He looks at you, but his face registers nothing as he stuffs the lighter into his pocket with one hand as he holds onto the cigarette with the other. He takes a long drag and says nothing. "Do you know what time it is?" you ask. He looks up and behind you at the bar and then back at you. His mouth turns down on one side and his nostrils flare. He takes the cigarette out of his mouth and pauses a second before exhaling smoke into the air between the two of you. He makes a sound deep in his throat, shakes his head, and starts to turn away.

You feel the doctor's hand on your leg. Before you know it, you reach out and touch him on the crotch. He reacts as if he has been shocked by electricity. He jumps back and his arms reach out in front of his body. "What the fuck?" His voice reverberates on the empty street. You step in his direction and reach out again. His right arm swings in front of yours, and the cigarette in his hand flies into the snow. He staggers backward and once again you come in close enough to reach out and touch between his legs. "Fuckin' stop it!" he growls, and you see his face is bright red as he steps away from you into the light of a street lamp.

You feel his fist make contact with your nose though you never really saw him swing. You hear a low cracking in your face and suddenly your nose is soft and you feel something warm and wet on your lips. He hits you again and again in the face, and your mouth tastes like blood as a tooth comes loose and slides into your throat. You choke and fall over onto your knees to the ground. The snow you see is speckled with red. He kicks you in the side, and you can feel his boot connect with the hardness of your ribs. There is a snapping and you are lying face down, your nostrils filled with snow. You see nothing anymore, just feel your side as the boot makes contact with jagged edges and soft tissue. The whole time he is screaming a single word at you, repeating it over and over again. After a while it doesn't even sound like a word anymore.

He stops kicking you. You can hear him panting. The sound seems to come from a great distance. His hands are on your coat, and he turns you over roughly. His face is blurry, but you hear him very clearly as he calls you the word one more time, over-enunciating it so that it has a sharpness to it. You hear him spit before the phlegm lands on your face in a big, wet glob. You want to laugh, but there is pain cutting through your face, and teeth are loose in your mouth. Then he is gone. You hear his footsteps in the snow as he runs down the street. It is quiet again. You listen to yourself breathe - it is slow and gurgling. You try to lift your arm to wipe your face, but it feels impossibly heavy.

You close your eyes tight and then open them as wide as you can. There are no stars in the sky, and the only light is from the street lamp. All you can see above you are the black branches of a tree. You stare up at the branches, and you see them move in a breeze that also cools your wet face. You see the doctor from earlier today, for just a few seconds. "It's all right to. . ." he starts, but then he is gone. And it starts to snow, very gently at first. Large, lazy flakes float down and land on your face, until you can see no more.

PULP

I REALLY HATE HOSPITALS.

I mean, I really hate hospitals. First of all, there's the smell. What's with the smell in hospitals anyway? Is there really such a thing as too clean? I think there is. The lack of smell can be the worst smell, to tell you the truth. I mean, I was never very good at school - finishing high school was a struggle, and I dropped out of junior college - but it seems to me that the absence of something means there's going to be space for something else to fill that absence. And in hospitals, the possibilities are endless.

Vomit.

Pee.

Blood (yes, blood has a smell. Leave me alone.).

Antiseptic.

Bleach.

I could go on and on.

There's no vanilla. There's no chocolate. There's not even any coffee. I mean, I know it's not a bakery or a restaurant, but come on.

Second of all. . .

Sorry, there is no second of all.

No, wait. There is. Second of all, no one ever goes to a hospital to have a good time. I know that things can turn out okay after going to the hospital. But that's not the starting point. The starting point is pain and suffering.

And death. Death is everywhere in the hospital. And no amount of disinfectant or bleach or lack of smell can make death go away.

So there.

And third of all. . .

Wait, no. There isn't a third thing. For real this time. There's just the two things. Smells and death. That's all. That's it. But that's enough. Smells and death. Smells and death are why I hate hospitals.

And yet, here I am. At a hospital. But I'm here because I have to be. Because I need to be. I'm here because of my brother. My brother, who evidently listed me as his contact. Who evidently was beaten to a pulp in a bar fight.

In a bar fight. Which doesn't seem anything like the brother I grew up with. The brother I grew up with would've avoided a fight at any cost. Would've run from a fight if given half a chance. But we haven't talked in years, so who knows what's happened between then and now. Years. So imagine my surprise when the hospital called me to let me know where he was. Me. Not either of his sisters. Not his younger brother. Especially not Dad. Me.

Me.

Concussion. Broken nose. Broken ribs. Punctured lung. Sounded bad to me, even though the woman on the other end of the line sounded oddly calm about the whole thing. Well, they've probably done this a lot before. I mean, a lot. I would hate to have to tell people that a relative was broken, even if they may have done the breaking to themselves. So you have to tap it down. I mean, it's not their relative. It's mine, in this case. And all those broken bones and punctures and concussions sound pretty serious to me.

So here I am.

At a hospital.

Which I hate.

Speaking of which, I can't help but notice that the elevator smells like someone threw up in it. And then sprayed Lysol. Two smells on top of each other. It's all I can do to keep my gag reflex in check. Then the elevator doors open, and suddenly I'm flooded with light. I hate so much light. But at least some of the smell steps out of the elevator before I do. I put my sunglasses back on, like some jerkwad celebrity on an awards show and walk straight to the desk where a young woman in a nurse's uniform is shuffling papers around like she's playing cards.

Can you tell me please what room Ike. . .

Ike? You mean, like the president?

She sounds tired. Calm but tired.

Yeah well yeah. Actually it's Isaac, which isn't like the president. But yeah. Ike. Like the president.

I hate explaining that to people.

She waved down the hall and then returned to playing cards. I mean, shuffling papers. And I'm on my own, since she didn't tell me exactly where Ike is. So I walk down the hall, looking in all the doors.

Until I find him.

And he looks horrible.

His eyes were underlined in bruise. Tape, or a bandage, or both, covered most of his nose. Lots of swelling, and he looks very pale. One arm was draped across his belly, and his hand appeared to be holding his side. He was hooked up to machines, of course, and the beep of his heart filled the room.

I stood just inside the room, not knowing what to do. I wanted to leave. But I was the one who was called. I was the one. But now that I was here, I wasn't sure what to do next. He looked like he was asleep. And besides, smell and death was everywhere in this room. It stood between me and the figure in the bed. And I hated smell and death. As I said before. I lifted one foot and then put it back down. Shifted my weight from one foot to the other.

As if on cue, Ike's eyes fluttered open. He had wanted to be an actor at one point - I don't know whatever happened to that - so he would know a cue when he heard one I suppose. His eyes flickered around the room before landing on me.

Hey, he said. He smiled. Somewhat. It was leaning to one side, the smile. At least he still had some of his teeth.

Hey.

Big pause.

Brother.

What are you doing here? The smile faltered as the other side of his mouth took its turn to jog upward.

They called me.

They did?

That's right.

Who's they? Who called?

Well. . .the hospital I guess. The hospital called me.

Did they? Well good. . .For one brief second one side of his mouth joined the other one to lift upwards in a smile. Then it slid back down.

. . .I'm glad they did. Then his attempt at a smile disappeared alto-gether. His hand hugged his side, the fingers spread out. The room was quiet. I could smell nothing in the room. Which made me nervous.

So. . .I began.

What happened to you?

There was that half smile again. His eyes were closed. At least I thought so. The skin in his sockets was so dark that I wasn't entirely sure.

Oh this. He gestured with his free hand toward his face.

This. . .he paused, as if he was trying to remember. This is me pissing someone else off is what this is. Brief moment of a full smile. His eyes were still closed.

Ah. . .I didn't know what to say to that. I mean, what do you say while looking at a face that looks like ground beef? Because of that, more silence.

Oh. So that's what that is, I said finally. I'm glad you told me. Because otherwise I'm not sure I would've known.

Not the best response, I know. But smell and death. So. . .

More silence. His eyes were still closed, so he could have been asleep for all I knew. But then the hand gripping his side waved out away from his body, in the general direction of a chair by his bed. If his eyes had been open, he would have been looking at the ceiling.

While don't you stay awhile? Sit down and take a load off?

Ah. . .once again, I didn't know what to say. Staying meant I had to step into the smell and death, even more than I already had. And I hated smell and death. As I've said before.

Come on.

The hand waved again for a second before it went back to hold his side.

They called you. The hospital. They called you.

So I stepped forward. One step. And then another. And before I knew it. I was in front of the chair and my legs were bending and I was sitting. Though my back still wasn't against the back of the chair.

So why?

He turned his head and opened his eyes. I think. I mean, how hard would you have to hit someone to cause that kind of bruising?

Why what?

I pointed at his face. Especially at the dark circles where his eyes were supposed to be.

What do you mean why what? Why this. Why did you piss him off? And why did he hit you. Repeatedly.

Oh. . . He turned onto his back again and tilted his chin up to the ceiling. That. . .Big pause. Heavy sigh. Well, that is a story for another day.

Well. . .I looked around the room and shrugged. Why not now? Today seems like a good day. Today. . .I mean, why not today?

He remained focused on the ceiling. Oh, he said That's where we are, are we?

I don't know Ike. You tell me. I mean, they called me. Like you said. They. Called. Me.

I hit each word for emphasis. He rubbed his side but didn't look at me.

Why yes. I did say that, didn't I? He made a sound like a grunt. Did they tell you? While they were talking to you on the phone, did they tell you?

Tell me what? That you were beaten to a pulp? Of course they did. That's why I'm here. They told me you were beaten up. And I came. I mean, give me some credit.

He turned to me on that. He was smiling again. Both sides of the mouth this time.

Oh I am. I am giving you some credit. Some. . .credit. . .

It was like he was winding down.

But not that. The other thing. Did they tell you about the other thing?

Other thing? What other thing?

The smile disappeared in a flash.

I'm sick. His voice cracked. I'm sick. Did they tell you that?

All the smell and all the death pulled into my lungs in one moment. I found myself looking for words.

Wha. . .What do you mean you're sick?

I mean I'm sick. The crack had gone from his voice. I have cancer. . .

I tried. I tried to get it away from me. I tried to get it off of me. I tried to get it out of me. Before he said it. But it was too late.

. . .and I am dying.

There.

There it was.

Out of his mouth and out into the air. Where it found me so that I could hear it. And I didn't know what to do with it. I coughed. I coughed again. It was stuck in my throat and I couldn't get it out. I coughed again. Ike joined me, which felt odd at that moment.

So, he said after the cough, if you have any questions, now would be the time.

I coughed yet again. I wanted to ask. Really I did. But I couldn't say the word.

So this. . .this. . .

Cancer.

Yeah. That. What. . .uh. . .what kind are we talking about here?

Really? That's where we're starting? Huh. He looked up at the ceiling again, and then back at me. I guess I should've guessed that one. Well, to answer your question. Colon. Stage four. Not that it matters. He swallowed. What matters is that it's dying. Active dying. He swallowed again. Hard this time. Which means. . .your heart stops. And your lungs stop. And your brain stops. And. . .and. . .

And he stopped. He stopped.

And buried his head in his hands.

And cried.

No, not cried. Sobbed.

Sobbed until he couldn't breathe.

Sobbed until he had to hold his side.

And still he cried, his whole body involved in the process.

And I watched.

I watched the whole thing.

I watched because I didn't know what else to do. I mean, I suppose I should've probably gone over to his bed and given him a hug. A big old fat brother bearhug. But, I mean, I hadn't seen him in a while. So I wasn't sure we were in hug mode at this time.

Plus, he was the smell now. He was the death. And as I may have said before at some point, I hate both those things.

So I waited. I just waited.

And finally he was done. He took one long, long gasp. And he was finished.

So, he said. He was taking long deep breaths, holding both his sides with both his hands. Maybe I said it wrong. Maybe. What I meant to say, I think, was I wanted to talk. I just wanted to talk. To someone. To you.

Another deep breath. He sighed it out.

Because you're the one they called.

He wiped his face before turning to me. If I looked really hard, I could finally see his eyes. The whites were very red.

I got stories, man, he said. I mean, I've been to hell. And I want to tell it to someone while I still can. Beth is busy with a divorce and Janet is busy making babies. Little brother is doing whatever with whoever. And Dad. . . He paused. Well, Dad is being Dad. So you're the one. The one who gets to hear. Because you're the one they called.

Wait a minute. At some point I had relaxed back into the chair, but now I sat up. I've been to hell. Isn't that a little. . .I don't know, a little. . .

For the first time Since I'd arrived, he chuckled. With half a mouthful of teeth, which would've otherwise sounded kinda weird. And I would've hated it. No, this was a good chuckle. Or at least a decent one.

Melodramatic? Is that the word you're looking for? Yes, but no. I've actually been there. To hell. I've seen it. So let me tell you about it. Please. That and my other stories. So they're with you when I no longer am. So that they're somewhere. When I'm nowhere. Please. Please.

So I sat back. And I listened. And I heard about him. And there was smell. And there was death. And I really hated it.

AFTER AND BEFORE

Your shoes clunk against the side of the car as the hands pull you through the door. Arms wrap around you and pull you in close once you're inside. Another arm reaches around from the front seat and cranks the window up. And then it is very dark inside the car. So dark that you can't see anything. Anything at all.

The person holding you has skinny arms. You can feel them through your clothes and their clothes. But they are also very strong. You are all tangled up in a blanket. You try to pull your arms out and reach for something. The skinny arms reach out and pull them back.

"Go! Go, Dolores, go!" An old crackly voice screamed to the front seat of the car. The voice sounded a little like Grandma, though you never heard Grandma scream. Ever. "Go, I tell you!" The screaming Grandma voice said again, and you feel the car jerk to the side and then forward. The tires make a sound like more screaming. The car is going very, very fast.

And you start to cry.

And not just cry. But cry hard. Your sound fills the inside of the car. And a skinny hand, fingers like sticks of wood, slaps over your mouth. Slaps hard to stop the hard crying.

"Be quiet, you!" The screaming Grandma voice says. Screaming. "Be quiet, or I'll give you something to cry about!"

You can't possibly imagine what that might be. So you keep crying. You want to be back with Grandma. This isn't Grandma. This is some woman who smells like after you went to the bathroom number two. Or like that time when your older sister, who's only eight, helped Mommy cook supper, and then you spent half the night in the bathroom using it for another reason besides to go number two. This not-Grandma person smells bad.

The skinny stick fingers go over your mouth again, but your mouth is open and you bite down on one of the fingers. A high pitched sound comes from the not-Grandma who smells like throw up.

"The rag! Ma! Use the rag, Ma!" The voice, very loud, comes from the front seat. And then, there is a cloth over your whole face. It smells bad. There have been so many bad smells to. . .

When you wake, you are still in the back seat of the car. It's going very fast. You are wrapped up in a blanket so that you can't move your arms or your legs. But your head is uncovered and you can see. You look up to see who belongs to the skinny arms that are still around you.

It's Mrs. Strube.

As soon as you look up at her, she tightens her grip on you.

"You gonna behave yourself now?" Her voice is high and cracked as she speaks. She shakes you. "You better. You better behave. Or I'll use the rag on you again!"

Someone in the front of the car screams.

"He awake MA? Is he awake?" The car swerves with the words.

"Dolores! For heck's sake, watch what you're doin' for heck's sake! Before you get us all killed! Geez. . .you're gonna make me swear if you're not careful." The car moved back and was staying in its lane while she was talking. It was still going very, very fast. You have begun to cry again, but softly this time. You didn't want Mrs. Strube screaming at you too. She does start screaming again, but to the front seat again.

"And Dolores! Watch where you're goin' for heck's sake! You're gonna miss our turn-off. It's comin' up! Right here! Right here!!"

You feel the car swerve again, and so hard and so fast that for a moment you forget to cry. You freeze, and Mrs. Strube makes a sound like a cawing bird as the car hits bumps and more bumps. It wasn't slowing down hardly at all.

And then the car stops.

You fly forward, away from Mrs. Strube and bumping into the front seat. And then she is on top of you, making weird sounds. She is very heavy, and it is suddenly very dark in the back of the car.

"Geez, Dolores! Geez! For heck's sake! What are you trying to do? Kill me? For heck's sake!"

The car door flies open and suddenly there is so much light everywhere. Except for under Mrs. Strube, where you are. But, she is crawling off of you and out of the car, a mass of darkness pulling away.

And in the doorway stands the nurse, the woman with the moustache who was pushing Mrs. Strube in the wheelchair.

And there is something about the way she looks at you, but suddenly you are very afraid.

"Hiya there, little boy. You're my little boy now." And she reaches into the car and drags you out. You are moving your arms and legs with all your might but it doesn't matter. If Mrs. Strube was strong with her skinny stick arms, the nurse - Dolores? Did you hear Mrs. Strube call the nurse Dolores at some point? - was much stronger. She has a grip that hurts on both your arms, and you're kicking with your new shoes, kicking into the grass and the dirt. But she is holding you out away from herself and you can't reach her. You look over at Mrs. Strube, who is leaning on the car. You look back at the nurse, who is looking at you in a way you can't take.

And the crying comes up and out of you again.

"Oh no, you don't" Her arm swings up and slaps you across the face. It surprises you so much that the crying stops. And then the hurting begins, spreading across your face like fire. You sniffle, you can feel the crying coming back, but you don't want her to hit you again. Dolores pulls you so close that her nose is almost touching yours.

"Now you listen to me." You can feel her breath on your face. "I'm your mama now. And you're my little boy. And you. . ."

She shakes you.

". . .you are going to do as I say. And behave yourself. You hear me?"

She shakes you again. Harder.

"You hear me?"

She shakes you so, so hard. So hard it feels like your teeth are rattling in your mouth.

"Nod your head if you hear me. Nod. Your. Head."

And you try real hard to. You try. But it's like it hurts too much to do it. It hurts. And you start to cry again. Your mouth is open, you're crying so hard.

And she hits you across the face again. If your teeth weren't loose before, they most certainly are now. And it shocks you into silence. She continues to shake you.

"What did I tell you?"

You sniffle but do not speak.

"Huh? What. Did. I. Tell. You??"

The shaking almost hurts worse than the slap. You hear Mrs. Strube's voice, off to one side, where she is still leaning against the car.

"Dolores? Honey. Maybe you should just. . ."

Dolores lets go of you with one hand and points at Mrs. Strube. "Ma! No! Stop! This is my baby now!"

She lifts you up and cradles you against her sweaty body. You push against her, but it's no use. She leaves Mrs. Strube gripping the rear bumper of the car and runs up the steps and into the house with you. You're still pushing.

She is holding you so close, and the inside of the house is so dark, that you can't see anything. It smells bad, worse than the sweaty smell of Dolores. You are choking on the smell. Dolores' steps are very loud as she crosses the room. You hear a doorknob turn and a door creak as it opens.

"You stay in here now. Hear me?" And she pulls you away from her and shoves you to the floor of a space that's even darker than the rest of the house. A closet. Dolores is a shadow big as a giant in the doorway. She starts to close the door, but then leans in so far that her face is almost in front of you.

"I'll be back in a minute. And while I'm gone, you be quiet in here. Ya hear me? Be quiet!"

The door slams shut. You can feel the air on your face. You thought the house was dark. This closet is so dark you can't see your hand when you hold it up in front of you. And it smells like the rest of the house. You start choking again. You try to cover your nose, but then you throw up into your hand and onto your jumpsuit and the floor. Your breakfast. And now the closet smells even worse than it did before.

With throw up dripping from your fingers, you listen to the sounds on the other side of the door. You still feel sick, but you also want to know what is going on. She has turned on a light, and a strip of that light runs across the floor at the bottom of the door. You listen closely. At first you hear nothing. You reach up and try the doorknob. It turns but the door does not open. You push against it with all your weight, but you are only six years old. It is locked. You put your ear to the door and you hear the wheelchair rolling up onto the porch and into the house. Dolores and Mrs. Strube are talking but you don't understand anything they're saying. The sound gets closer and then farther away. Then you hear Dolores' heavy footsteps as she comes back in your direction. The steps are so heavy that the floorboards creak, even inside the closet.

The door flies open. There is more light in the house now, so you can't see much of Dolores as she stands in the doorway. To you, she is just a giant dark monster that casts a shadow over you as you sit on the floor.

"You gonna be quiet now?" the giant dark monster asked. You don't answer. You have started to shiver. "Okay, well it's time for lunch sweetie. Come on, I'll take you into Grandma. You two can eat together."

She bends over to pick you up, and it's only after she's holding you close that she notices and smells. Her head pulls back away from you. Her face looks funny.

"What the. . . Did you just barf? What the. . ." She holds you out and away. She looks at you and shakes you, then looks down at her nurse's uniform.

"Look! You got it all over yourself! And you got it all over me! Well, that's it! No lunch for you mister!"

Her grip tightens around you so that you can hardly breathe. She pushes the door closed with her body and made thump thump sounds as she hurried you out of the room.

Once in the bathroom, she once again pushes the door closed with her body, and practically drops you onto the floor next to the tub. She turns on the water and then her hands are all over you, finding the buttons to take off the jumpsuit. If you move or start to say anything, she punches you with her fist.

And everything comes off. Your blue jumpsuit with the elephant on the front. Your shirt. Your shoes. Your socks. Your underpants. Everything.

And then she lifts you up and puts you in the tub. Where she then holds your head underwater.

Right away you struggle. But you're only six, and she is so much older and bigger and stronger than you. You can't open your mouth to scream, because then water would get in. And besides, there is no one else around to hear the scream. Except maybe Mrs. Strube.

You can't breathe.

You can't breathe.

You can't. . .

And then she lets go, and you sit up in the water, gasping. Your eyes are closed, but you hear her voice in your ear.

"You see? This is what I can do to you."

You're wiping water from your face. Your whole body is shivering even though the water is very hot.

"So behave."

And she reaches up, pulls down a washcloth, rolls a bar of soap around in it and rubs it all over you. Even though you just wiped off your face, it is now covered in soap and your eyes sting. You're trying to wipe it away when she grabs your arms and rubs the washcloth from your hand to your shoulder and then into your armpit. Same with the other arm.

And then she slides the washcloth down your chest and belly and into the water.

And she is washing you down below, rubbing you in a place. In a place where no one touches you. No one except you when you stand up to pee. Or when you sit down to pee. Nobody but you. But now she is washing you down there.

And she keeps washing you down there.

She keeps washing.

Eventually she takes you out of the hot water and dries you off, and puts your jumpsuit covered in dry throw up back on you. And then you are back at the closet.

"Back in you go," she says as she opens the door. "No lunch for you until you learn to behave yourself."

She slams the door in your face, and once again you are in darkness. Except for this sliver of light from under the door. You look up and see that the door doesn't go all the way to the top of the doorway. That light is also spilling into the closet and makes a sliver of light behind you. You hear Mrs. Strube and Dolores talking somewhere in the house but you can't really understand them, so you're not listening anyway. You're focused on the sliver of light from the top of the door. Behind it, in the dark, you hear shuffling. It stops and then starts again. And then fingers inch forward into the sliver of light.

There's someone else in the closet.

Eventually Dolores did come and let you out of the closet, you and this other little boy. Sitting across from him, with Mrs. Strube sitting between you at the head of the table, you look at him, and it's almost like looking in a mirror. He's small like you. Sitting across from him, you can look him directly in the eye. He's got blonde hair and blue eyes like you. But his blonde hair is going every which way on his head. The white parts of his eyes are red. And he's dirty. His shorts and shirt are dirty. His arms and legs and bare feet are dirty. His face is dirty, like someone rubbed mud on it. And he doesn't look up. Instead, he's staring at the top of the table. Or at his hands - one hand is picking at the nails of the other.

"What's your name?" You whisper across the table.

"No talking to each other! Shut up!" Mrs. Strube screams across the table. The other little boy keeps looking at his hands, one picking at the other. "Dolores told you not to talk to each other!"

Just then Dolores walks up, a bowl in each hand. Steam is coming off the bowl as she drops it with a clunk in front of you. You look down.

It's oatmeal.

You hate oatmeal. Mommy has tried to feed you oatmeal at least three times, and you couldn't do it. You hate the way it feels in your mouth. You hate the taste. And one time you burned your tongue, it was so hot. You hate everything about oatmeal. And now you're looking down at something you hate almost more than anything else.

Dolores has dropped the other hot bowl in front of the dirty boy. "Eat up!" She shouts, like she's talking to the whole house. "It's good for what ails you. But be careful. It's hot. . ." And she laughs, a sound that reminds you of someone chewing crackers with their mouth open.

You continue to look down into the bowl. You are hungry. You haven't eaten since breakfast, and you have no idea how long ago that was. So you don't know what to do. You reach for the spoon sticking out of the oatmeal and leaning against the side of the bowl. And then you put your hand down. Again you lift your hand, and again you put it down. Across from you, the dirty boy reaches for the spoon in his oatmeal and brings it to his mouth. He purses his lips and blows on the spoon. He then puts it in his mouth and chews, again very slowly. There is oatmeal on his mouth. You look down again and watch the steam rising up out of your bowl.

"What?" Dolores shouts to the house, but also to you. "Something wrong with your food? You need to eat it right now buster!"

You reach again for the spoon. It almost hurts to hold it. You take a little tiny bit onto your spoon and bring it to your mouth and blow on it like you saw the dirty boy do. Your hand is shaking as you put it to your mouth.

It tastes like nothing. There is no sugar or water in it, so to you it tastes like you have throw up in your mouth. Except that it's not throw up yet if it hasn't been thrown up. So you spit it back into the bowl.

Dolores screams. "WHAT. ARE. YOU. DOING?!?" You don't look up at her. Instead you stare at the dirty boy who continues to chew very slowly before he dips his spoon back into his bowl. She continues. "I worked really hard on that you little piece of crap! And you are going to eat it, or I'm going to make you eat it!" And she walks up to you and slaps your spoon out of your hand. It clatters across the floor. You turn to watch it, but she grabs your head and jerks it back around. She grips your head with one hand and reaches into your bowl of oatmeal with the other hand.

And she shoves this handful of oatmeal into your face. And rubs it in.

"Open your mouth. Open it! And eat that oatmeal because I made it for you!"

And she continues to move her hand. And the oatmeal is everywhere. It's in your nose and in your mouth. So much oatmeal in your mouth. And you can't breathe and you start to choke, and the oatmeal comes out of your mouth and between her fingers. She gasps and pulls her hand away and looks at the oatmeal stuck to it before she reaches over and pulls you up out of your chair by your collar. "You come with me" sounds like a growl when she says it. Dragging you behind her, she walks around Mrs. Strube to the other side of the table where she takes hold of the dirty boy by the back of his shirt. He drops his spoon as she pulls him away from the table. She drags you both away from Mrs. Strube, who does not turn to watch.

Dolores takes you to a door a little ways away from the room with the table. She lets go and you both sink to the floor as she opens the door so fast that you can feel wind. She points.

"Look," she whispers for the first time as she looks where she is pointing. "Look at that.'

You see the dirty boy lift his head and look, so you do too. You follow her arm pointing.

It isn't another closet. It was darker than the closet and there were steps going down.

It is a basement.

Dolores continues to point. "You see that?" She is still whispering. "You see that? That is the bad place. And if you're not careful, that's where you're going to end up."

And we're back in the closet. For a long time you don't talk to each other. But finally you ask him again what his name is. David, he tells you. He has no idea how long he's been here. He's been in the dark closet so much that he couldn't tell. Besides, no one had told him what the big hand on a clock and the little hand on a clock did. He was just six like you.

"That lady?"

"Which one?"

"The big one."

Yeah. . . "

She's scary."

Yeah. She is."

She's mad. . ."

"Yeah."

". . .all the time."

"She scares me."

"I know."

And you start to cry. Again. But softly, so that Dolores or Mrs. Strube couldn't hear you. And he sits in the dark, with the sliver of light going across his face, and watches you.

You don't know how long you're in the closet. There is no little hand or big hand on a clock to watch go around. There is only dark. Sometimes you hear heavy footsteps and the roll of the wheelchair across the floor in the house. Also sometimes there are voices. Words you mostly don't understand. The words "never find us" make it to your ears. So does "not our house." But mostly it's just sound.

Finally the door flings open, and you close your eyes against all the light that comes in. Even with all of Dolores standing in the doorway, big and scary like a monster. She stares down at you.

"Well, let's try this again," she shouts before reaching in to pull you both into the light. She puts you back at the table, back in the same place. And Mrs. Strube is where she was before, as if she had never left. Dolores shoves a bowl back in front of both of you again. You are scared to look down. Please, not oatmeal again. But it smells different this time, so you do look down. There are noodles floating with what looks like little pieces of chicken. It smells so good. You look over at David, whose eyes are wide as he looks down into his own bowl. He grabs his spoon and so do you. You can't get the spoon into the soup and the soup to your mouth soon enough. As good as it smells, it tastes even better. David is shoveling the soup into his mouth so fast that you almost don't see the spoon. Little bits of chicken and noodles stick to his face.

And then you hear the crunch.

David has just slid the spoon out of his mouth and is chewing and then there is a crunch. He pauses and looks at you before he reaches inside. He moves his fingers around for a few seconds before he slowly pulls them out. He is holding onto something. It's hard and curved and maybe white. And you know it. You've seen it before when Mommy came at you with the clippers and took hold of your hand and went at it with the clippers and this flew into the air.

It's a fingernail.

And in the same second that you knew what it was, in that same second, you feel something in your own mouth. But it isn't hard, this thing in your mouth. It feels like a snake baby against your cheek. You reach in and pull it out.

And pull.

And pull.

And pull.

It's not a baby snake. It's hair. Long hair. Dark, like it came from a head of black hair.

You gag. You've barely eaten any of the soup, but you can already feel it coming back up. Across from you, David starts to cry.

"Woa. . .Wo wo wo. . .Stop it right now. Stop it!!!" Dolores is screaming now. "I worked very hard on that! And I was trying to be nice. . ."

And her fist hits your face.

You feel your nose go mushy under her fist. The chair with you in it falls backwards. You hit the floor hard. You see what looks like stars in front of you. Your face feels wet, especially your nose and your mouth. You put your hand up to touch the wet and then look at it. Wet and red all over your fingers. And then the pain starts. Your whole head.

"And you," you hear Dolores shout. David's crying turns to screaming. His chair falls over too but he's not in it. There is a lot of movement you hear as Dolores carries him away from the table.

"Dolores, honey," Mrs. Strube starts. "Maybe you should just. . ."

David's screams go higher and stop her. You turn over onto your tummy and push yourself away from the chair. Blood drips from your nose onto the floor. You hear struggles a little ways away. And David screams. You turn over and sit up and blood drips onto the elephant on your jumpsuit. You see more of what looks like stars. David is screaming. You scoot on your butt around the table and Mrs. Strube, who tries to reach for you but can't quite. Every scoot hurts, but you keep going. And David is screaming. You get around the table. There is blood on your face and on your hands and on the floor. In front of you, but so far to scoot, so so far, Dolores is standing in front of the open door to the basement. To the dark. To the bad place. And David is screaming and fighting her. He is swinging at her face and kicking at her body. And screaming. And Dolores is saying "You you you" over and over and over, breathing deeply in between each one.

And David is screaming.

And you will never know if she dropped him on purpose or if he struggled so much that he got away on his own. But suddenly he is no longer in her arms. And you hear a crack, like something breaking. It sounds so far away, and yet so close.

You never see David again.

You have no idea how long you've been in the closet, in the dark, this time. You've cried almost without stopping. You knock on the door and say you're hungry. You hear nothing, and no one comes to feed you. You fall asleep with your arms and legs tucked into your tummy. You wake up and have to go number two. You knock and call out to them. You hear nothing and no one comes to let you out. You fall asleep. When you wake up, you've gone number two in your underpants. You cry and you call out, but you hear nothing. No one comes to get you. And you cry.

A loud sound wakes you up. It sounds like someone shouting. And then nothing. You hit the door again and again and again. And you call out. You call out. You call out. You finally hear footsteps.

And then the door opens.

A man in a uniform is standing in front of you, in the light. He bends down and holds out his hand.

"Come here," he says. He wiggles his fingers. "It's okay. You're okay. You're safe now."

And you go to him, and he picks you up and carries you through the house and out onto the porch. There are people and cars everywhere. And light. There is so much sun that you haven't seen in so long that you shade your eyes with your hand and squint. You can't see anyone's face.

"Ike! Sweetie! I'm here! Mommy's here baby!"

And you turn. It's Mommy and Daddy. Mommy is crying and Daddy

looks like he's sick. Mommy is holding out her arms.
    And you run.
    But they're so far away.
    They're so far away.
    They're so far away.
    They're so far. . .
    They're so. . .

    They're here.

COME OVER

IKE IS SITTING ON a bench in a park. He is lifting his face up to feel the sunshine.

It's so warm.

And so still.

He is trying so hard to linger with the warmth and the stillness. The park was just a block from his brother's house, and ever since he got out of the hospital he would try and make the one block walk. When it was sunny. And it was sunny today. It wasn't always sunny like today. And it wasn't always easy to make it to the park even if it was sunny. Every day it got a little less easy. Some days it was actually hard.

Just. . .hard.

He hadn't been out of the hospital very long. Staying with his brother. Soon he would be going back. Hard to say when exactly. Lots of bad days lately. But not today. Today, for some reason, was quiet. Very little pain today. His doctors told him that there would be a time, right before the end, when he would feel fine.

He would feel healthy.

And coherent.

And sane.

But he thought that would be right before the very end. So he didn't know what this was. But he would take it.

This was sunshine.

And this was stillness.

And he would take it.

He gazed out over the park in front of him. His gaze felt lazy, as did the turning of his head. There was a sidewalk a few feet in front of the bench where he sat. Moms and the occasional Dad pushed strollers past. A couple of nuns also. Ike briefly wondered if it was too late to ask them to hear his confession, even though priests usually did that. Also, he wasn't Catholic. He wasn't much of anything, not anymore..

College students were tossing a frisbee. A family was on a blanket having a picnic. Off at the other end of the park was a playground with swings and a jungle gym and a teeter totter, and delighted squeals carried through the air over to him.

There was so much going on.

Maybe too much.

Maybe he should not have come to the park. Maybe he should go back to his brother's house.

But he wanted the sun. And the warmth. That's all he wanted in that moment. So he closed his eyes and focused on the warm on his face.

That's all he wanted in this moment.

That's all he wanted.

That's all. . .

And then he heard a voice. A high-pitched breathy child's voice. And the voice was singing.

The itsy-bitsy spider

Went up the water spout

Down came the rain and washed the spider out

Out came the sun and dried up all the rain

And the itsy-bitsy spider climbed up the spout again.

Someone knew their words. Ike opened his eyes and turned in the direction of the singing. A small child was on the sidewalk almost directly in front of him. He was doing the hand motions to the song as he sang. He would take a few steps and then stop, totally focused on the song and his hands. A few more steps and then he stopped again. When he got to the part about the spider crawling up, the boy's arms went way over his head. The light caught his blonde hair and made it glow. He was wearing a blue jumpsuit.

And he was alone.

Ike watched him until the boy had almost passed him. Then he called out.

Hey.

The child stopped, his hands in midair. He looked around.

Hey, Ike called again. Over here.

The boy turned and saw Ike. He looked at his hands and then back at Ike. He waved the child over.

Come on. Come over here sweetie.

The boy looked back down at his hands.

It's okay, Ike said. It's okay to come over. The child looked back up at Ike with almost impossibly wide eyes and then strolled over to him and Ike saw the elephant on his jumpsuit for the first time. He patted the bench next to him, and the boy, without any hesitation, hopped up and nestled next to him. Without quite knowing why, Ike put his arm around the child.

As soon as he was snuggled against Ike, the boy continued Itsy-Bitsy Spider and doing the hand motions. This time, however, he was whispering the words to himself. He did the hand movements close to his body. Ike watched him for quite a while before he spoke.

So. . .are you lost?

No. The child stopped singing, though his fingers continued to move.

You're not?

No I'm not. The boy stared at his hands as they went through the motions. I know where I am. I'm here. He reached down and touched the bench before bringing the hand up to be a spider again.

Ike smiled. Well, you're right about that. So what about your parents? Where are they?

I don't know. The child continued to watch his hands.

Then I guess they're the ones that are lost, right?

I guess. Right.

Ike took the boy's chin and turned his face towards him. The child's hands stopped being a spider and came to rest in his lap.

Well, don't you worry. . .

The boy's eyes.

You're safe. . .

So big.

You'll be safe. . .

Those eyes would see so much. So much.

You

Will

Ike needed to say it for the boy. And for himself.

Be

Safe.

SPECIAL THANKS ACKNOWLEDGEMENTS

After a book of stories, please allow me one more. It was the height of the Pandemic, and I, like many others, was isolating. I took to pulling out stories that I had written over the course of a very long life. It soon became apparent to me that perhaps quite a number of them were about the same person. So I began putting them into some kind of order and shaping them into a manuscript. And then my hard drive crashed. And I thought I had been saving, but I wasn't. Needless to say, I was devastated. I went to a local company, which couldn't help me. But they did refer me to a national company, who could, at considerable cost, retrieve the stories off of my hard drive. I told the man at the local company that, if those stories ever saw the light of day, that I would thank him in the acknowledgements/special thanks. Of course, the name of both the company and the man have been lost to the sands of time. Still, I want to mention him - and keep my promise.

I have thanked her before, but I really can't thank that beautiful angel Amy Cianci at St. Petersburg Press enough. "You know you wrote something weird, right?" and "Well, I love it" will resonate in my mind forever. And to David Warner, who looks at my work with a cool and kind eye - bless you, my child.

My siblings - John, Laurie, Deanna, Tim - are in these pages. We had this incredibly interesting, endlessly storied childhood together. It's possibly a little bit of a miracle that we didn't kill each other (out of sheer love, of course). So thanks for that especially. I may be remiss in telling my friends how much they mean to me - I'm trying to get better at that. I am blessed with a good number of pals, so it might be a bit much to name them all here - though I do especially want to mention Bruce and Ike (yes, I used his name for the protagonist), who both do way more for me

than any friend should. And Tessa - thank you so much for helping me name other characters (especially one - she knows which one).
Zoe. And those who came before. Ruby. Sonny.
At some point, this wonderful, beautiful man named Bill chose to love me. It has made all the difference, and I am (for a writer) at a loss for words. This is, as is everything, for you.

ABOUT THE AUTHOR

KEVEN RENKEN is an American writer of literary, fantasy and LGBTQ fiction. His first novel, WELCOME TO THE DAY (2019), was a finalist for five independent book awards. His second novel, GRAPHIC: THE NOVEL (2022) won the Bookfest Award in the category of contemporary fantasy fiction. Originally from Illinois, he now lives in Tampa, Florida with his husband Bill.